BURGLARS
AND
BLUESTOCKINGS

JULIE BERRY

sourcebooks
young readers

Published by Sourcebooks Young Readers, an imprint of Sourcebooks
P.O. Box 4410, Naperville, Illinois 60567–4410
(630) 961-3900
sourcebooks.com

Source of Production: Versa Press, East Peoria, Illinois, USA
Date of Production: December 2022
Run Number: 5027918

Printed and bound in the United States of America.
VP 10 9 8 7 6 5 4 3 2 1

For Gabriel, Frederick, and Abigail Salisbury,

that magical trio.

CHAPTER

1

I liked the world better when magic was my little secret.

When I first found Mermeros, the djinni, in a sardine tin in a rubbish pail, for one shining moment I had him all to myself. A djinni of my very own! Me, a schoolgirl, of no particular family, no special pedigree, no notable fortune. Just a bank clerk's youngest daughter, finding all that power—power I might use any which way I liked, with nobody's permission required.

Imagine it. All those wishes! Three massive wishes containing infinite possibilities. Just think what I might do: Sail the seven seas. Circle the globe in an aeronaut's balloon. Sled the Alps. Tour Mayan temples, photograph Mount Fuji, watch the sun set over New Zealand, or hear my echo call back to me from far rim of the American Grand Canyon. (Does it do that? Only one way to find out.) And then, back home, before my trunks were even unpacked, form a cricket league for girls—for girls!—all over the British Isles and lead my own team to a championship. After that, perhaps, when I was grown-up, good and ready, I'd settle down to a cozy little cottage somewhere, with several dogs, a pony or two, rooms full of books, and all the toasted, buttered muffins I can eat.

Was that so much to ask?

Evidently it was.

The shining moment didn't last. No sooner had I met Mermeros—that sour-tempered old fish of a djinni—when he first came spiraling odorously out of his sardine tin, than others caught sight of him, too, and before you could say "Bob's your uncle," they wanted him for themselves. That rascal orphan, Tommy—who has since become one of my best chums, but who made my life a galloping ruckus until we decided to stop being rivals for Mermeros—he got in on the action, trying to nab the sardine tin. A nasty girl from my boarding school saw Mermeros, too.

The ruthless tactics of her greedy tycoon of a father to steal my wish-granting djinni made Tommy's antics look like a Sunday school picnic. Yet he was nothing compared to the fiend who followed after him—a so-called "professor" specializing in magic—the rubbish kind, not what's real. This repellent person actually *kidnapped* Tommy's newly adoptive father to get his hands on Mermeros. Treated him shamefully. Tied him to a chair for days! It took police, friends, relatives, and a pair of flying carpetbags to put a stop to his foul plot and bring Tommy's dad, Mr. Poindexter, safely home, Mermeros and sardine tin and all.

Just to be firm on this point, I did say "flying carpetbags." And here's the dreadful bit: *everyone* saw them. Everyone involved in our little escapade, at any rate, and goodness knows how many other Londoners besides. They were eyewitnesses to magic. There was no more hiding the truth. The secret was out. Pandora's box had opened. The djinni, as the saying goes, was well and truly out of the bottle. Or in this case, the tin.

If my adventures had taught me nothing else, they'd taught me this: where magic went, danger followed.

And there I was, the eye of the storm, the yolk of the egg, the nucleus of the cell.

Magic, Mermeros, and me, Maeve Merritt. A recipe for mayhem.

In the days since we'd brought Mr. Poindexter and Tommy safely home from that kidnapping fiend, "Professor" Fustian, there'd been a great deal of talk—private talk—of magic and Mermeros, and what to do about him, at the Bromleys' home in Grosvenor Square.

I should pause to explain. My best friend, Alice Bromley, whose parents had died when she was young, lived with her grandparents, Mr. and Mrs. Bromley. I'd lived with the Bromley family ever since

Alice and I left Miss Salamanca's School for Upright Young Ladies. We'd been roommates there at the time when I first discovered Mermeros. Alice had left when her grandparents no longer found the school suitable.

I left when the school no longer found *me* suitable.

I was expelled. Evicted. Chucked out on my ear. I despised the place, so I didn't terribly mind, but still, one has one's pride. Just when I thought I was doomed to another grim boarding school or, worse, a life of dreariness at home with my mother and sisters, Mr. and Mrs. Bromley invited me to live at their elegant London townhome as Alice's companion and classmate in the private schooling arrangement they were establishing for her under the tutelage of Mr. Abernathy, a scholar gentleman from Oxford. I jumped at the chance, and Mr. Abernathy, that chipper Scotsman, began the dubious task of molding our young minds. Alice lapped him and his lectures up like a cat's dish of cream. As for me, my mind was fairly moldy already. Nevertheless, I liked him just fine, and I think he liked me, too, when we weren't off chasing after djinnis. But now he, too, had become a believer.

I rather wished he hadn't.

At the conclusion of our most recent adventures, just days ago, one very significant thing happened that had nothing to do with magic. My eldest sister, Polydora, became engaged to be married to Constable Matthew Hopewood, her beau.

That very night that we'd all returned safely home, Constable Hopewood asked for our dad's permission, just prior to at a celebratory dinner Alice's grandparents hosted for us all at their Grosvenor Square townhome.

Asking for a father's permission to marry his daughter is all very right and proper, I suppose, but a bit silly if you ask me. Polydora is old enough and sensible enough to make her own decisions on that score, though one could easily argue that where her infatuation with that blond-whiskered policeman was concerned, she had entirely lost her head. Still, Matthew was a solid individual, very much the right sort, and even I would've given my consent if anyone had asked me, not that anyone did. I like to think I'd had a sizable hand in bringing this union about, not that I'm the romantic type—far from it! But Polydora is my favorite sister, and her happiness is my own. Most days.

So there we were, making merry with the lovebirds, raising toasts and cracking jokes, with a great deal of backslapping of Matthew Hopewood, and general twittering at Polydora, and goggling over her new ring. My sister Evangeline was in raptures because now she, recently married herself, could boss Polydora to her heart's content about how to plan her wedding, and our other sister, Deborah, sulked in a snit of jealousy because Polydora occupied everyone's attention for once, which served Deborah right. Evangeline insisted on asking our parents what they would give the newlyweds as a wedding present. How on earth should they know yet? What with the general festivity of the occasion, and the parade of treats the Bromleys' serving staff kept bringing out from the kitchen, magical matters hardly crossed my mind that night, which was a bit of a welcome change for once.

Then the night drew to a close. My family took their leave, blushing bride-to-be and all, and those of us remaining began to shift our way upstairs in the direction of settling down to bed. I went to the kitchen in search of mugs of warm milk and, if I could secure them, some of Mrs. Tupp's famous coconut cakes. Mrs. Tupp, the Bromleys' cook, knew how fond I was of them. I was successful on both counts and left the kitchen clutching two warm mugs by their handles in one hand (one for me, one for Alice) and a plate of cakes in the other.

Mr. Poindexter, still quite exhausted from his recent ordeal, called to me from the first landing of the stairs. I trotted over to where he stood in the doorway of his room, clad in pajamas, a housecoat, and slippers. He had missed the party, being too weary from his recent injuries and ill-treatment. He leaned against the doorjamb as though standing on his own was more effort than he could muster. It pained me to see him looking so spent.

"Yes, Mr. Poindexter?"

He glanced from side to side to see if anyone was close by. This piqued my curiosity to no end. He pulled a key from his housecoat pocket and locked his bedroom door.

"Maeve," he said in a low voice, "I've made up my mind. Having a djinni is much, much too dangerous."

The tips of my fingers fizzed.

"I understand," I said quickly. "I'll take Mermeros back."

He let out a laugh. "Very funny."

I hadn't been joking.

"I was wrong to think I could keep such a powerful secret guarded," he went on. "It was arrogant of me. And look what happened. It put Tom in terrible danger. That business with the tower! That horrible ruffian! If something bad had happened to me, Tom would have gone, bang, right back into the orphanage, and from there to one of those abominable labor mills." He shuddered. "I can't bear to think of it."

Plenty of people had no choice but to think of orphanages and poverty and miserable drudgery in northern factories, thought I, which was perhaps hypocritical of me, as I stood on a Persian rug in an elegant mansion, holding a porcelain plate of coconut cakes.

Poor Mr. Poindexter rubbed a hand over his jaw. It was still bruised from the rough handling he'd received as recently as that very morning.

"I've made up my mind," he repeated. "I'm getting rid of Mermeros."

A chill fell over me. Get rid of Mermeros? My rascally djinni? *Formerly* my rascally djinni, but he would always be my rascally djinni. We were bonded, you might say. Attached at the gills, that crotchety old fish and I.

"But, Mr. Poindexter," I protested.

He raised a finger to his lips to remind me to speak softly.

Fine. "If you, er, get rid of him, someone else will find him," I whispered. "Maybe someone terrible. Someone who will use his power to...I don't know, rob the world blind, or start a war."

Mr. Poindexter frowned and nodded. Feeling encouraged, I plowed onward.

"A djinni isn't something you just leave lying around," I said. "That's too much power. Much too much power, all in one sardine-tin-sized package."

"You're right," said Mr. Poindexter. "I don't plan to drop him in a rubbish can or chuck him into the sea, if that's what you mean. I need to put him somewhere where no one will ever find him."

I'd found Mermeros in a rubbish tin myself, back when all this business started. Then again, Mermeros himself had told me that it had been some three hundred years since he last served another mortal human. Obviously there weren't sardine tins then. So I really doubt someone just chucked him in a bin with yesterday's trash. Some deeper magic was at play. Something that shifted his home container around to suit the era.

"I'm not sure it works that way," I told Mr. Poindexter. "I don't think burying the tin in the darkest mine shaft, or in a coffin, or whatnot, will necessarily contain him. Remember, he's not just a tin of fish."

"If he were," muttered Tommy's father, "life would be much easier."

"But then you'd never have met Tommy," I pointed out. "Or any of us."

He looked away.

"The simplest way," I said, not that I wanted to help this project along, "would be to cast your third wish. Then he'd be gone from your life forever."

He shook his head grimly. "I've considered that," he said. "Wish for a toasted cheese sandwich—what harm could that do?—and then be done with it all. But that's no different from leaving him on the washroom counter at Victoria Station. Who knows where he'll go next?" He sighed. "No, I think it's best to find a way to retire Mermeros for good."

"But Mermeros is a *person*," I protested. "Well, not a person, but a being. He has a mind. A soul. Or something. You can't just abandon him. Leave him all alone forever."

Mr. Poindexter sighed. "He won't starve, Maeve, if that's what you mean," he said. "He's thousands of years old. He's magical. He won't *die*."

"But he's practically family!"

Effie, an upstairs parlormaid, passed by us on the stairs and cast a curious glance our way.

Mr. Poindexter waited for her to be out of earshot, then rested a hand on my shoulder. "We must be more cautious about this," he whispered. "We mustn't allow the servants to overhear any of this talk of magic."

I willed myself to keep still.

"I have to think first about what's best for Tommy," said Mr. Poindexter. "That's what being a parent means."

I couldn't give up yet. "You said you were saving Mermeros for Tom," I told him. "That's what you told me."

"There's been a change of plans," said Mr. Poindexter flatly. "I need to save Tom *from* Mermeros."

I fumed silently, trying to think of what to say.

"Maeve," Mr. Poindexter said, more gently, "Tom has a bright future. He shouldn't spend his time dreaming of fanciful, magical wishes. He's at an age where he should be thinking of his interests. His education. His ambitions. His hopes." He rested a hand on my shoulder. "He doesn't need a djinni and magical wishes to live a full and happy life."

I took a deep breath. This was horrible. The thought of willfully, deliberately getting rid of something—someone—as monumental as Mermeros and his magic made my mind quiver in protest. Throw away all those wishes? Unthinkable! Outrageous.

But then I saw the concern in Mr. Poindexter's eyes, one of them blackened and bruised, a nasty shade of purple tinged with yellow. All of it, a direct result of him possessing Mermeros.

Siegfried Poindexter would give up the world for Tom. He was a good man, and good people, I've come to realize, are hard to find.

But still: Mermeros!

Then again: Tom.

I sighed. "If you've made up your mind," I said, "why are you telling me?"

He cinched the sash of his housecoat a bit tighter around his waist. "I may need your help," he said. "I haven't yet figured out how to solve the Mermeros problem, nor when to do it, nor where. Nor how, when the time is right, to break it to Tom." He met my eyes sorrowfully. "I thought that if you understood the reason why, you'd be better able to help him when the time comes."

My own heart was breaking, but I didn't have the heart to refuse him. He was right. At least, he believed he was. And Mermeros was his now. So what good were my objections?

"I'll help any way I can," I told him.

Mr. Poindexter smiled with relief, but also a tinge of sadness. "I know you will, Maeve," he said. "I know I can trust you."

He held out a hand, and we shook on it, then he retreated to his room. The bolt of his door lock clicked shut behind him. I took my coconut cakes and milk up to bed with me, so troubled in my thoughts that I actually forgot to eat them, which, in my case, is saying something.

CHAPTER

2

The next morning, Mr. Abernathy attempted to resume our studies in the schoolroom, and Tom, who was staying with us until his father felt well enough to return home, was obliged to join in. The magical events of the last few days—flying carpetbags!—had clearly dominated scholarly Mr. Abernathy's every waking thought, however, and our tutor was not his usual self. Whereas ordinarily he deplored any lack of focus, now he would interrupt himself to ask us questions about how I found Mermeros and how we discovered that those shabby old carpetbags could fly. Alice and Tom were happy to answer his questions, but I found it troubling. Had magic fever struck our rational-minded Oxford scholar, too? Was no one safe from it?

Finally, there came an interlude when he seemed, at least for the moment, occupied with reviewing Alice's Latin composition with her. Tom and I sat in a window seat overlooking the park, ostensibly reading from a Latin grammar, but actually watching a pair of old men play chess in the park below. If I was bad at Latin, Tom was worse. They'd certainly never taught him much of even the Queen's English at that Mission Industrial School and Home for Working Boys, never mind the classical languages of the past, though they could stay buried in the past as far as I was concerned. I had other things on my mind.

So, evidently, did Tom.

"Maeve," Tom whispered, "I need to talk to you."

"Talk, then," I told him. "What's the matter?"

He dropped his voice lower still. "I think," he said, "my dad is planning to do something about Mermeros."

Oh, *no*. Tom already knew. Now they both were trusting me with their secrets. How could I walk that tightrope?

Mr. Abernathy glanced our way, and for a moment we buried our noses in our grammar books. After a moment's pause, I dared reply.

"What do you mean, something *about* Mermeros?" I asked Tom.

He glanced over to see if Mr. Abernathy was listening. "I think..." he said, "I think he plans to get rid of him."

I gulped.

"What makes you think that?" Pretending innocence. Stalling for time. Practically lying to my own chum. This was dreadful.

"He talks about Mermeros," whispered Tom, "and about magic,

"Think about how many orphanages there are," he said. "In London alone. Or all of Great Britain. Or all the world. How many orphans there are."

It was a sobering thought. "I can't begin to guess."

"What if," he said, "wishing could find them all homes?"

I sat up straight. "You can't be serious," I said. "I don't think even Mermeros's power can go that far."

He'd clearly thought of that. "Even if it could only help *one* other lad or girl find a proper family," Tom said, "it would be worth it. And I'll bet old Mermeros could do one or two better than that." His gaze my way was penetrating. "You'll help me, won't you, Maeve?"

I hesitated.

"Master Thomas," inquired Mr. Abernathy, who had somehow materialized before us. "Miss Maeve. How are your conjugations coming along?"

I tried to think of a not-too-guilty, not-too-dishonest way to reply. Tom spoiled it by dissolving into laughter.

"I thought as much," said our Scottish tutor. "Master Thomas, come with me, and let's see what you've learned thus far in your studies at that school of yours."

I watched Tom follow Mr. Abernathy back to his desk. I surely wouldn't have said so when I first met him, but that lad was all right. A thoroughly good egg. I would use my wishes entirely on selfish things, if I could somehow buy a second crack at them. I knew I would. And yet, here, Tom wanted wishes to help other orphans.

And Mr. Poindexter was determined not to let it happen.

Tom was right. Even though things had gotten much better for him of late, since his adoption, he had still spent his life facing horrors and hardships, losses and loneliness, watching other kids enjoy freedom and fun when all that was left for him was waiting, waiting.

I had to help him make those wishes. I owed him that much.

And I'd promised Mr. Poindexter I'd help him prevent any future wishes from happening.

Mr. Poindexter trusted me.

Tom trusted me.

Oh dear.

CHAPTER 3

That was Monday. Come Tuesday afternoon, we were all seated in the drawing room, having tea and sandwiches after the day's studies were done—me, Alice, Mr. and Mrs. Bromley, Mr. Abernathy, Tommy, and his dad, Mr. Poindexter. The latter two had been here two days now, but Mrs. Bromley wouldn't dream of letting Mr. Poindexter go home, she insisted, until he'd been seen to by a doctor and had received a few days of good feeding and rest. The doctor had come and gone, but Mrs. Bromley wasn't done playing nursemaid.

Mr. Abernathy was first to break the silence after Mrs. Bromley had finished pouring the tea.

"I can't stop thinking about it all," said Mr. Abernathy. "To think, I've seen a human fly! On a magic *carpetbag*!"

Mrs. Bromley frowned, and Mr. Poindexter shifted uncomfortably in his seat.

Mr. Abernathy didn't notice. "All this business of magic makes me want to revisit the tales of magic and fairy folk from my native Edinburgh," he continued. "What truth might lie folded in between the fairy tales? What aspects of the old myths are actually real?"

I glanced at Tom. He and his dad were avoiding each other's gaze.

As for me, I thought Mr. Abernathy's plan was a topper of an idea. Upstairs in my room, locked inside a diary to which I held the only key, was a tiny scrap of a magical map. It was a map of the world, showing the location of its hidden magical objects. A souvenir, you might say, of our recent troubles. My bit of map was of the eastern Scottish coast. By gum or by golly, I'd get there one day to find those magical treasures. Preferably, one day very soon. Perhaps, if Mr. Abernathy wanted to go researching Scottish magic, we could all go. A summer field trip. A learning holiday. With a quick nip over to the seashore. Where others dug for seashells, I would dig for buried magic.

Mr. Poindexter interrupted my thoughts. He had, it seemed, still been brooding over Mr. Abernathy's magical musings. "Magic is deadly," he said. "Such power ought never to have been discovered."

Tom stifled a squawk of protest.

"Real or otherwise," continued Mr. Poindexter, "true or false, humanity is better off without it."

Mr. Abernathy shifted in his seat. "Oh, come now, Siegfried," he cried. "Where is your curiosity? Your sense of adventure? Mankind was made to learn, to explore, to discover the secrets of nature." He took a sip of tea. "Nature, as it turns out, is bigger than we thought. That's all."

Mr. Poindexter muttered to himself and took a morose bite of a cold chicken sandwich.

Mr. Abernathy was undeterred. "I think I shall embark on my folkloric quest," he said. "When I'm next in Scotland, I'll undertake my research. I'll start at the Advocates Library. They're sure to have any number of texts."

"But what would rereading them actually tell you?" inquired Alice's grandfather, Mr. Bromley. "You can read storybooks all you like, but how would you separate fact from fiction?"

"The Tuatha Dé Danann," mused Mr. Abernathy. "Kelpies. Camelot."

Mrs. Bromley, that gentle soul, had sat for some time fidgeting in her seat. Finally she set down her teacup and saucer like a judge's gavel.

"*I* think," she said, "we've had quite enough talk of djinnis. And carpetbags."

Mr. Poindexter nodded emphatically, but Alice and I blinked at each other. This outburst was so unlike Alice's grandmother that we were both taken aback.

"If the servants heard us, they'd start looking for positions elsewhere," Mrs. Bromley continued. "This unearthly business of magic should be left in the past. Pray, let us speak no more of it."

I took a sip of tea to hide my face behind my teacup.

I could understand Mrs. Bromley's frustration. If anyone had told me magic was real—before I'd seen it for myself—I'd have said they were gibbering.

But wishing magic away wouldn't make it so.

"My apologies, ma'am," Mr. Abernathy murmured.

Mr. Poindexter stirred his lemonade. "Keeping it quiet around the servants is very wise."

Mrs. Bromley plowed onward, determined to change the subject. "It's time to think about these bright young ladies' futures," she said. "Isn't it, Mr. Abernathy?"

Mr. Abernathy dabbed at the corners of his mouth with a linen napkin. "What did you have in mind, ma'am?"

"Why, their educations, of course," replied Mrs. Bromley. "Preparing for university."

I nearly dropped my cup. *University*?

"But, Grandmama," said Alice, "that's so far off in the future."

Mr. Bromley chimed in. "It's still a few years away, I grant you," he said, "but it's not too soon to start thinking about where you might enroll, and to start preparing for the entrance examinations."

Mr. Poindexter nudged Tom with his elbow. "You listen up, my lad," he said. "A little more effort at your own studies wouldn't hurt any, either."

Tom shrugged. Summer was almost here, and school was probably the last thing on his mind.

Mr. Linzey, the Bromleys' butler, appeared silently, as if he had shimmered into being.

"A visitor for you, sir, madam," he said in his grave, buttling voice. "Mr. Bromley's cousin, Mr. Wilberforce."

"Here?" Mrs. Bromley's voice squeaked. "That is to say, what a lovely surprise."

Mr. Bromley's mouth twitched. "Do show him in, would you, Linzey?"

I poked the rest of my sandwich into my mouth, very curious to meet this relative Mrs. Bromley would rather avoid.

Mr. Linzey soon returned. The large man following him swept into the drawing room like a hurricane. A backdraft of air stirred the curtains.

"Mr. Eugene Wilberforce," murmured Mr. Linzey.

The man himself interrupted him. "Theodore," he boomed at Alice's grandfather. "Adelaide." He kissed Mrs. Bromley's reluctant hand. "Don't tell me you were having tea!"

"We always do at this time of day, dear Eugene," she said. "Would you care to join us?"

"Don't mind if I do," said "dear" Eugene. "Just to be sociable."

While Mr. Bromley made the round of introductions, I watched this newcomer curiously. He was probably in his forties, with thick mutton-chop whiskers and an oily face. Everything about him—his nose, his hands, his eyebrows, his teeth—seemed large and looming. He settled into an easy chair and proceeded to remove a cigar from his pocket and light it with a phosphorus match that he struck against the mantelpiece.

Alice nearly gasped. Cigars, indoors, in mixed company? It simply wasn't done.

"Well now, Eugene," said the ever-hospitable Mr. Bromley, "what brings you to town?"

"Business," said Mr. Wilberforce mysteriously. "Various meetings." He cast a significant look at his cousin, Alice's grandfather. "Some of us must use our wits and our toil to make our way in the world. Not all of us can relax in the luxury of a button empire."

Now Alice's eyes bulged. She didn't like to even think an unkind thought about anyone, but this man's shocking rudeness knew no bounds. Yes, Mr. Bromley had made his fortune in button manufac-turing, but to speak so brazenly about it was absolutely insulting.

"Are your meetings tomorrow?" inquired Mrs. Bromley, perhaps not realizing how hopeful she sounded.

This thought was waved away by a hand clutching a ham and pickle sandwich. "In a fortnight," he said between bites. "I thought, there's no better time to visit the metropolis than in the cool of springtime and see good old Theodore and Adelaide."

A fortnight? He planned to stay *two whole weeks.* As for the cool of springtime, spring had nearly given way to summer, and the heat, endured underneath all required layers of underclothes, was enough to make a camel wilt.

Mrs. Bromley fortified herself with a sip of tea. "You'll be staying at your club, I presume?"

Mr. Eugene Wilberforce pursed his lips. "Rather not," he said. "Too expensive there. And the service ain't what it ought to be. I'm staying here."

Never mind camels; the whole room wilted then. All but Mr. Wilberforce himself, who sat puffing on his cigar, even though Mrs. Bromley had begun coughing delicately. He didn't care. The clouds of foul-smelling smoke he puffed out rivaled those of a Manchester factory.

Mrs. Bromley rang the little brass bell on the stand beside her. In short order, Mrs. Harding, the housekeeper, entered the room.

"Would you be so kind," Mrs. Bromley asked her, "as to arrange for a bedroom to be prepared for Mr. Wilberforce? Mr. Bromley's cousin?" She gestured toward him without a hint of reluctance. Ever the hostess. "He'll be making an extended stay."

"Certainly, ma'am." Mrs. Harding made her departure, a picture of propriety, but I could tell from the stiffness in her spine that she knew what we were in for.

Mr. Wilberforce continued addressing the room with all the humility of Henry the Eighth, on the eve of a wife's beheading (take your pick).

"You there, sir," he said to Tommy's father. "What's your name and occupation?"

Mr. Poindexter gulped. "I beg your pardon. Were you addressing me?"

Cousin Eugene made no attempt to soften his manner. "More likely you than that skinny carrot-top of a lad, wouldn't you say?"

Mr. Poindexter suppressed a smile. "Siegfried Poindexter, at your service," he said. "I keep a shop here in town. Curios, artifacts, antiquities. That sort of thing."

"Rubbish," declared Cousin Wilberforce. "No point to it. Who'd waste their money on such rot? Fools, that's who. Where's your shop?"

Tom's eyes narrowed and his hands curled into fists. Not that he would sock Mr. Bromley's cousin—never—but I didn't blame him for wanting to.

Mr. Poindexter nodded genially. "Mantlebury Way." He seemed amused. "Do stop by if you're in the neighborhood."

Eugene Wilberforce thrust out his lower lip and surveyed the room. It seemed as though he was searching out his next victim.

"Don't let me disturb you," he told us. "Carry right along with your normal business while I'm here."

Silence fell. I'll wager we were all considering the prospect of two weeks with Cousin Eugene and wishing fervently for some "normal business" to take us elsewhere.

Mr. Poindexter was the first to break the silence. "I declare, I'm feeling fit as a fiddle," he announced. "You're a marvelous physician, Mrs. Bromley. Your cure has worked its magic. I think Tom and I will take our leave. We've intruded on your hospitality long enough. In the morning, we can make our way home."

Mrs. Bromley's face fell, but she corrected it with a bright smile. "We hate to see you go."

Too right, she did. We all hated it. There went the fun. I knew Mr. Poindexter wasn't feeling fit as a fiddle, by any stretch of the imagination, but I couldn't blame him for wanting to get away.

"Mrs. Bromley, Mr. Bromley," said Mr. Abernathy. "I've been meaning to ask you if now wouldn't be a good time for me to visit my aged mother in Edinburgh and, er, pursue my research there. That is, if you could excuse me from the young ladies' classroom for a time."

"So soon?" Mrs. Bromley gulped, then nodded. "Certainly," she said. "Please give your mother my very best."

I took a bite of petits fours. They were all leaving us. Fleeing to escape two weeks of Eugene Wilberforce at breakfast, lunch, tea, dinner, and supper. Not that I blamed them. Our merry house party was dwindling, leaving us with no one to make conversation with but this unpleasant Cousin Eugene.

"Here," demanded that, er, gentleman, jabbing his cigar in Mr. Abernathy's direction. "Who are you, again? Where're you from? What's your story?"

Mr. Abernathy's eyes glinted, but he chose to remain amused rather than annoyed. "Hamish Abernathy."

"That's right. You're the Scottish chap. Tutor to these little girls here."

We were solidly thirteen, rounding the corner on fourteen, thank you kindly.

The "Scottish chap," who was a spry sixty years of age, nodded. "I have that great pleasure, yes."

Cousin Eugene scowled. "What's the matter? Can't you find a post teaching lads?"

It was Mr. Abernathy's turn to be stunned. "I could not be more pleased with my pupils than I am."

That might be stretching the truth in my case.

"But then, what do you teach them?" pressed Mr. Wilberforce. "Watercolors and dancing?"

Tom snorted into his lemonade. Mr. Poindexter had to cough to keep himself from laughing.

"Certainly not," replied Mr. Abernathy. "We study Greek, Latin, mathematics, science, philosophy, composition, literature, rhetoric, and history. A complete curriculum."

And geography, I thought.

Mr. Abernathy met my gaze and smiled. "And geography," he added. "Miss Maeve's favorite."

"With supplemental instruction," added Mrs. Bromley, "from tutors in art and music."

For a moment, Cousin Eugene Wilberforce seemed at a loss for words. "But...but whatever *for*?" he demanded. "Why, by Jove, would you waste the time and the expense teaching all that to little girls? What will they ever *do* with it?"

Mr. Bromley came to his wife's aid. "Surely, Eugene," he said placatingly, "the merits of education hardly need defending."

"But they're little *wenches*," Cousin Eugene protested, as if we weren't there, as if we weren't staring straight at him. "It isn't healthy. It isn't natural. Their bodies aren't made for learning." He thumped a hand across his stout middle as if to say, *Mine is*. "The stress of examinations will rob them of their youth. They'll develop nervous strain."

It was touching, the concern he suddenly felt for our health.

"Tosh," declared Mr. Bromley. Strong language, from him. "Look at the roses in their cheeks. They're a picture of health. Learning hasn't done them a particle of harm."

"Now, *this* lad," Mr. Wilberforce went on, pointing to Tom, "will take his education and put it to good use for the empire in some manly endeavor. Will Greek and Latin make these little chits of girls into more contented wives someday? Will it teach them better how to raise children or pour the tea? I should think not."

"*Non scholae, sed vitae discimus.*" Mr. Abernathy shaved off a thin slice from his pear. "Isn't that right, Miss Alice?"

"How's that?" demanded Mr. Wilberforce.

Alice nodded. "*Cuilibet fatuo placet sua calva.*"

One might almost think it was an incantation, that Alice had cast a hex over the men in the room. Mr. Abernathy gulped on his bite of pear. Mr. Bromley was seized with a fit of coughing. Mr. Poindexter had to look away, ostensibly to scratch the back of his scalp, but I saw the laugh struggling to escape. Only Mrs. Bromley, Tom, and I were left to gaze at each other in bewilderment. Us, and a red-faced, fuming Cousin Eugene.

I really ought to pay more attention to Latin.

"The fact," sputtered Eugene Wilberforce, "that she can ape some phrases you've trained her on proves nothing." He waved toward an ornamental (and birdless) birdcage in one corner. "Even a parrot can do that."

"Now, I *say*," broke in Mr. Bromley, in a tone more severe than

I'd ever heard him use. "Are you insinuating that our beloved grand-daughter is a mere parrot?"

Cousin Eugene realized his mistake. "Not at all, not at all," he said. "God knows, I'll wager, some girls can be downright clever." He swallowed a deviled egg in one gulp. (None of his large teeth were involved in the transaction.) "But all the same, I maintain that this new craze for teaching girls the same as boys and trotting them off to universities if you can't find husbands for them, will lead to no good. Women who won't marry! Wives who won't know their place!"

"Are you married?" I inquired.

Dear Cousin Eugene turned and regarded me as if he'd just discovered a maggot in his lettuce salad. "And what business is that of yours?"

"Approximately as much," I told him, "as my education is any business of yours."

Now I'd done it. Insulted Mr. Bromley's own relation, right to his face.

Cousin Eugene's face turned lobster red. He pointed a hammy finger at me. "You see?" he sputtered. "Such impertinence as this is exactly my point!"

Mr. Bromley's eyes twinkled at me. "But she does have a point, Eugene, don't you think?" said he. "Maeve, my cousin has thus far remained a bachelor."

"By *choice*," the bachelor thundered. As if he had bravely fended off the droves of females clamoring for his hand.

"Naturally," agreed his older cousin.

Mrs. Bromley rose and began collecting teatime cups and saucers from us.

"Dear Eugene," she said sweetly, "I must say, your timing is unfortunate. I wish you'd written so I might have altered my plans. As it happens, the girls and I are leaving on a trip tomorrow."

Alice's head popped up like a Jack-in-the-box.

It was the first we'd heard of it. From the look on his face, it was the first Alice's grandfather had heard of it, too.

"I've had a letter," Mrs. Bromley went on, "from my dear friend Elizabeth. At Cambridge. She's invited me to come for a visit and has specifically asked me to bring the girls."

"Then that's no trouble," said Mr. Wilberforce. "A visit can easily be postponed. Plenty of summer left for all the croquet and tea parties you could wish."

Mrs. Bromley shook her head apologetically. "My friend Elizabeth," she said, "is the mistress at Girton College, at Cambridge University. For *women*." She rested a hand on my shoulder and the other on Alice's. "I am one of the school's patronesses, and we have important fundraising business to discuss." I had never heard this before. "Also, I want these young ladies to see what a women's

With that, she bustled off. Alice and I mounted the stairs.

"Alice," I said, "what was Mr. Abernathy saying? *Non scholae* something? That part means school or studies. I think."

Alice paused. "It means, 'We do not study for school, but for life.'"

I thought back on the conversation. "That's the right stuff," I said. "Learning for its own sake. It ought to have put Mr. Wilberforce in his place. If he'd known what it meant."

We reached our room, and I sat down upon my bed. I waited to see if she'd confess without me prodding her. Apparently not.

"*Alice*," I said, "come now. What did you reply back to Mr. Abernathy?"

Her face turned violet pink. "Oh, nothing."

I vowed I would spend more time with Virgil, going forward.

"We both know it wasn't nothing," I told her.

She tried to protest, then gave in.

"*Cuilibet fatuo placet sua calva*," she said. "It means 'Every fool is pleased with his own folly.'"

You could've pried me off the floor. Cousin Eugene Wilberforce was a fool pleased with his folly if ever there was one. And here was Alice, demonstrating a most excellent use for her Latin instruction. Zinging a bully verbally for the first time in her life.

Alice tried not to grin, failing grandly.

I poked her in the ribs. "What if he'd known enough Latin to understand you?"

She gave up the struggle. "The risk was worth it."

"Alice Bromley," I told her, "I'm proud to know you."

The next morning saw the household up early and on the move. Alice and I came down in our housecoats to breakfast to find a row of trunks and traveling bags lined up in the foyer, and Tom and Mr. Poindexter about to leave. Among the luggage I saw the two carpetbags—*magic* carpetbags—that had given us such thrilling adventures and had helped us save Mr. Poindexter from his horrible captors. It tugged at my heart to see them go away.

At a moment when no one else was watching, I squatted down beside them and gave them each a pat. They do have personalities, strange as that may seem. I think of them as a pair of mischievous puppies. I wondered how they felt, mighty and magical though they both were, to be carrying Tom's pajamas and socks.

"See you soon, friends," I whispered to them. "We're off to Cambridge, but we'll be back, and we'll find a way to have more adventures."

The bags wriggled happily, and I laughed. I rose to see Tom

watching me with a grin, and Mr. Poindexter, standing behind him, watching also and looking worried. Mrs. Bromley appeared and explained to us that Mrs. Harding, the housekeeper, had insisted upon coming along on our journey to assist Mrs. Bromley with her luggage, clothing, and general care. Rose, Mrs. Bromley's own maid, would be given some time off, along with Flora and Betsy.

I wasn't fooled. Our housekeeper, and the rest of the upstairs staff, had orchestrated this switch, all wanting to get away from Mr. Wilberforce as much as we did.

Alice and I entered the breakfast room, and I begin filling a plate with eggs, mushrooms, and toast, but no sooner had we sat down to eat then Cousin Eugene came huffing in with his trousers pulled up over his nightshirt and his hair askew. He barged through Mr. bernathy's quiet perusal over coffee of the *Daily Telegraph* to ask why he needed to leave so soon, and where his mother lived, a whether or not her health could withstand the strain of a visiting son. Mr. Abernathy's genteel manners were tested to their limit, but he m aged to answer Cousin Eugene's questions without laughing at hin aight to his face.

W the time came to bid farewell down at the street to Tom a r. Poindexter as they entered their hailed cab, Cousin Eugen upted Mr. Poindexter's thanks to his hosts by asking him wh sold Egyptian art at his shop or not, and what train stop was nearest to it. He issued orders to Steven and Michael, the footmen, about how bags should be carried and stowed, and made himself a general plague to the entire household. He was so loud and conspicuous that even the old chess players across the street, getting an early start on the day, paused setting up their board to wonder at him.

I watched him, half laughing, half amazed by his boorishness, until a moment's fleeting expression showed me, I thought, the truth: he was sorry we were all leaving. He must be lonely and had probably looked forward to company.

The cabbie drove Tom and his dad away. We waved them off until they were out of sight. Then Mrs. Bromley and Mrs. Harding shooed us back upstairs to finish dressing. Effie helped us with our braids, and Mrs. Harding popped in several times with reminders about parasols, hats, handkerchiefs, and gloves.

Finally we came downstairs, reasonably presentable. Cook handed us each a tin of her homemade biscuits to fortify us for the journey, and we hugged her goodbye. Mr. Bromley sent Steven to ask the driver to ready the carriage, which would take everyone to the train station—Mrs. Bromley, Mrs. Harding, Alice, and me, bound for Cambridge, and Mr. Abernathy, bound for Edinburgh. When all the luggage was secured on top, and Cousin Eugene had driven Steven and Michael to distraction, we climbed into the spacious carriage, leaving Mr. Wilberforce standing alone on the front steps, waving us off, looking rather forlorn, still in his trousers, nightshirt, and slippers.

City traffic is a horror on even the best of days, and this wasn't the best of days. Lanes and thoroughfares were choked with carriages, cabs, omnibuses, and even that new rarity—horseless automobiles. I found them fascinating, but they certainly belched out a great deal of noise and smoke. Come to think of it, they reminded one of Cousin Eugene. Mr. Bromley's driver, Benson, maneuvered his way through the press of vehicles and eventually deposited us at Liverpool Street Station. Out at the curb, Mr. Bromley waved down a porter to load our luggage onto a tottering cart and take it inside for stowage on our respective trains. Then Alice's grandfather helped us each descend from the carriage for one last hug—even Mrs. Harding, though Mr. Abernathy only got a firm handshake—and a fond embrace for Mrs. Bromley.

I found a few shiny guineas clinking in my jacket pocket after I'd stepped away from my farewell. The dear man had nimble fingers. He could've been a London street thief if, I supposed, he'd been raised very differently. I thought once again, as I often did, how lucky I was to live with the Bromleys, to dwell in the warmth of their family circle, instead of wasting away at some stifling, dreadful school, or, worse, sitting at home with my mother and Deborah, watching the weekly shopping circulars in great anxiety to discover when milliners might hold sales on hats.

The porter returned with our luggage claim tickets, and Mr. Bromley reluctantly took his leave. We hurried inside and said goodbye to Mr. Abernathy, whose train was leaving sooner than ours. He tried to extract from us a promise to keep working on our Greek and Latin while we were apart. Alice agreed, but I only laughed.

We found our train platform, then took seats near a lunch counter and ordered slices of quail and venison pie. We finished just in time for the conductor's call and found our way onto the train. The Great Eastern Railway would carry us to Cambridge.

Normally there's nothing I like better than travel. To watch the world slide by past train windows is a glorious thing. But this time, I couldn't focus on scenery, or even on the novel I'd brought along—*Jane Eyre* by Charlotte Brontë. (I'd enjoyed *Wuthering Heights* by Emily Brontë so much that I thought I'd give her sister Charlotte a try.) My thoughts swung between Mr. Poindexter and Tom, and back again.

Alice and her grandmother talked eagerly the whole way to Cambridge about Alice and me going to university someday. Mrs. Bromley had never had the opportunity, she explained, to attend university. In her day, it "just wasn't done." It was only beginning to be done in our day, and certainly the Eugene Wilberforces of the world felt it should never happen so long as the earth shall stand, but it was at least possible now in 1897. Some city colleges had even recently begun granting actual degrees to women. Not our grand old universities at Oxford and Cambridge, of course. But even there women could take classes and sit for exams. And that was the main thing.

"It's the *learning*, girls," Mrs. Bromley declared on the train ride. "The chance to stimulate and develop the minds the good Lord gave you, and not idle them away on frivolous things. That's the real prize. A trained mind ready to face whatever the world may bring."

Rousing stuff, I suppose. Alice hung on her every word. (Mrs. Harding sat knitting with tight lips and eyebrows raised. I supposed she was torn between never wishing to disagree with her beloved Mrs. Bromley and finding all this talk of girls going to college highly questionable.)

As for me, I didn't know what to think. I wasn't the scholar Alice was. Yet I would need an education far more than she would if I wanted to be a free woman as an adult, without needing to marry. Alice would be wealthy, but I'd have to make my own way, and I wanted a husband as much as I wanted smallpox. But my mother would have fits at the thought of me becoming a scandalous "bluestocking" girl, off chasing higher learning (and, people assumed, chasing college boys—hardly!). My father probably wouldn't love the thought of paying the tuition and board.

My father is the right sort all around, and no complaints, but the

Merritt family isn't made of money. Dad wouldn't ever be so putrid about it as a Eugene Wilberforce, but when considering the expense, all to educate a daughter, he might well wonder, as did Mr. W, what was the point?

I was lucky to study now under Mr. Abernathy. Lucky the Bromleys had invited me to live and learn with Alice. Lucky to receive an education on par with any boy's in the whole of the British Isles. But when it all ended, then what would become of me? What, in fact, would I do with it? It galled me to repeat Cousin Eugene's question. If Alice really was intent on attending a university, she and Mr. Abernathy would put their heads together and make a study plan, and before I could blink, she'd be taking top scores in all the entrance exams. That was Alice.

It surely wasn't me.

I watched Alice talk excitedly with her grandmother, and it hit me, right in the ribs: our jolly little arrangement at Grosvenor Square would someday come to an end. No more Mr. Abernathy leading us on educational field trips all over London. No more festive little evening parties with Mr. and Mrs. Bromley, with parlor games and party crackers popping and bright rainbows of boiled sweets. No more late-night gossiping and trading novels with Alice in our shared room. It would all come to a stop. Not today, not tomorrow, but on a day that would soon come chugging round the bend.

Our train did the same, pulling into Cambridge Station with a hiss of steam and brakes, and I tried to banish glum thoughts from my mind. It wouldn't do, having me mope all about Girton College when Mrs. Bromley was so excited to show it to us, even if I surely wouldn't go there. Alice almost certainly would.

When all the luggage was deposited upon the platform, our bags were nowhere to be found. There must have been some mix-up at Liverpool Street Station, with our bags ending up on another train altogether. Mrs. Bromley greeted this inconvenience calmly and began making arrangements with the stationmaster for the luggage to be delivered to Girton College once it was located. This led to forms being filled out and all sorts of questions being asked. A distraught Mrs. Harding stood wringing her kerchief between her gloved hands and muttering about incompetent porters. Her bag had contained a cameo brooch given to her by a beloved aunt. Not worth much in money, but much in sentiment, apparently.

While this drama unfolded, Alice and I found ourselves seated upon a bench watching travelers come and go, and trains pull in and out of the station. Near where the station met the road toward town, a few stalls were set up for a bit of a local market, selling edibles and knickknacks. I watched the sellers hawk their wares to passersby until I couldn't bear to wait any longer. I rose from the bench and tapped gently upon Mrs. Bromley's arm.

"Yes, Maeve?" she asked me distractedly.

"Do you mind," I asked her, "if Alice and I go look at those market stalls?"

She nodded. "Stay together," she told me. "Stay where I can see you both."

"Come on, Alice," I told my friend. "Let's go browsing."

Friendly vendors greeted us, many of them older men and women dressed in rustic farm clothing. The tables they spread before us were a jumble of things one might find in any little market. Shining jars of crab apple jelly and damson jam, and home-labeled bottles of dark elderberry cordial. A pile of felted wool caps. A pail of eels. Wrapped paper packages of butter and pungent local cheese. Homemade Savoy biscuits. Slabs of honeysuckle-scented homemade soap.

Alice paused to admire a stall selling delicately sewn doll clothes. We were far too old for dolls, but Alice will probably still think dolls are precious when she's eighty-two. (The ones Aunt Vera had given me, long ago, I'd used for target practice with a slingshot I won from a village lad in a game of hopscotch. The dolls didn't last. I have quite a shot.)

While Alice went into raptures over the lace on a doll's pinafore, I found a table of rag-and-bone shop items, hovered over by an older woman with a crinkly smile.

"Hallo, duckie," she said.

I would've "halloed" her back, but Alice would've been horrified. "Good day, ma'am," I told her, and began poking through her wares.

These items weren't adorable or delicious, but they each had a story. I wondered about the people who had used them, and the lives they'd lived in the houses where these items were once new. Slightly dented kitchen implements, old cast-iron tools, a few bits of mismatched chinaware, a chipped comb-and-brush set of yellowed ivory. Frayed table linens. A kettle that was probably used during the Napoleonic Wars. *Who bought you*, I asked the items inwardly, *Were you a gift? A find? An apology?*

A pair of tarnished silver handmirrors caught my eye. I picked them up and examined them. They made a matched set, with a filagree pattern of fine engraving along the back and handles, only worn away in a few spots. A bit of silver polish, I thought, would restore their shine. I held them up to the light to compare the mirrors. The glass was unbroken, and its silvering was intact, not cloudy or wavery.

"Feeling vain, are we?" Alice teased, joining me. "Mirror, mirror on the wall...?"

I laughed. "On the *stall*..."

We stood side by side, examining the mirrors, tilting them this way and that, watching our faces crowd the image. The disorienting feeling reminded me of sitting before my mother's boudoir with its three angled mirrors, wondering what was a reflection and what was real.

"I like these," I told Alice.

She was surprised. "You *do*?" She picked up a gruesome-looking farm tool sporting a long, jagged, rusty blade. "I would have thought *this* was more to your liking."

I grinned at her joke. "I wonder why there are two of them?"

Alice took the mirrors from me and held one before her and one off to one side. "To see the back of your head, silly."

"Why would anyone want to see the back of their head?"

She groaned. "People often do," she said, "when they care what their hair looks like."

"Foolish waste of time, if you ask me," I said. "If you're so concerned about your hair, wear a hat."

I probably shouldn't provoke Alice as much as I do, but it's too much fun. I like to think I keep her life from ever sinking into dull boredom.

"Two pretty girls deserve two pretty mirrors," crooned the smiling older woman.

I had no need for mirrors, yet I heard myself asking the woman what they cost. The price would take a large bite out of Mr. Bromley's gift. It made sense; they were silver. I should put them back, and yet, I couldn't.

"I wonder," I said aloud, "if Polydora would like these as a wedding present?"

"Lovely," cried Alice. "Mrs. Harding could clean them. They'll wrap up beautifully."

Mrs. Harding crossed the pavement to where we stood.

"Your grandmother is ready, Miss Alice," she said. "They've promised to bring us the missing bags when they turn up."

"Excellent," Alice told her. "Well, Maeve? Are you buying them?"

I hesitated. Now or never. Part with the mirrors, or part with my money?

"I'll take them." I reached for my little coin purse. The elderly woman wrapped the mirrors in brown paper and string, and I tucked them under my arm, then hurried to follow Alice, her grandmother, and Mrs. Harding into a hired carriage. Here was Polly, only just barely engaged, and here was I, likely the first in the family to obtain a wedding gift. Fancy that.

Half an hour later, we stood with growling stomachs before the stately grounds of Girton College, in the village of Girton, some two miles north and west of Cambridge itself. It was here that the first college for women studying at Cambridge University had been built.

The day was sunny and hot, and the air, this far from London, was remarkably clear, the sky a bright bottle-blue. Heat shimmered above the freshly mown school gardens.

The main building loomed up before us in modern brick splendor at the end of a stretch of grassy lawn. Towers pointed into the heavens. Violin music of several different levels of ability wafted from various dormitory rooms, open to the fresh air.

A footman greeted us and inquired about our bags, but we had to send him away empty-handed. Mrs. Harding went indoors to see to the arranging of Mrs. Bromley's room and to meet the other domestics, while a tall, stately woman approached us along a gravel path. Mrs. Bromley greeted her warmly, then beckoned us to her.

"Girls," she said, "this is my dear friend, Miss Elizabeth Welsh, Mistress of Girton College. Elizabeth, this is my granddaughter, Alice, and her friend and classmate, Miss Maeve Merritt."

Miss Welsh shook hands with us both. "Welcome to Girton."

She wore a long, dark dress with a ruffled front and a silver brooch. She moved calmly but with energy, and her eyes seemed to miss nothing. Her hair, only lightly gray, was neatly arranged in a bun at the nape of her neck.

She embraced Mrs. Bromley. "I was worried that you had missed your train," she said.

"Our luggage was lost," Mrs. Bromley explained. "Routed onto the wrong train, I'm sure."

"How distressing," murmured the Girton mistress. "I hope they'll sort it all out quickly. In the meantime, we can loan you anything you need to be comfortable."

Mrs. Bromley pressed her hands between her own. "Thank you, dear Elizabeth."

Miss Welsh turned her gaze toward Alice and me.

"How old are you?" She seemed to truly want to know.

"Nearly fourteen," I told her.

"A splendid age," Miss Welsh declared. "You could sit your

entrance exams in a few years." She smiled. "We'll have you here in no time."

Mrs. Bromley beamed. "Won't that be exciting, girls?"

Alice clearly thought so. As for me, my heart felt as heavy as our missing trunks. Alice would come here, and I would not.

"Tell me, Miss Alice," said Miss Welsh, "what would you wish to do with the blessing of advanced education?"

Alice's eyes shone. "I–I think I should like, one day, to open a school." She glanced at me. My mouth must've been hanging open. "But not a typical one. Not like Miss Salamanca's, where we went before. A nicer one. Where boys and girls can learn together, and where we aren't so nitpicked to death. Girls especially."

Her grandmother's eyes bulged slightly at the suggestion of coeducational learning, but she blinked it away quickly.

Alice, who hadn't noticed, gestured toward the door of the Girton College building, where long-skirted girls and women came and went, clutching books and papers to their chests. "I feel I should want an education so that I would know how to select the best teachers and, oh, attract and enroll the students, and administer the funds, and the...building, and the staff, and that sort of thing."

Miss Welsh beamed. Mrs. Bromley dabbed at the corners of her eyes with a handkerchief.

Alice? Found a school? It sounded so...grown-up. And stuffy.

Where was the adventure in ordering chalk, ink, and paper, and cold mutton for luncheon, week in and week out? I wanted to see the world, and she wanted to *run a school*?

Then again, one day Alice would be a grown-up woman, and a wealthy one. She already had a solid plan, which was far more than I could say.

"That is a worthy ambition," Miss Welsh said gravely. "Most admirable, and most inspiring. You are quite right. It does take a great deal of management to run a proper school. You're wise to prepare yourself early." She turned to me. "What about you, Miss Merritt? What would an education allow you to do?"

Alice had had a perfect answer at the ready, and I had nothing.

"Eat, I suppose," I told her. "Sleep under a roof."

"Oh, Maeve." A mortified Alice rolled her eyes heavenward. "You say such things."

"I'm serious," I protested. "I'll need to need to make my own way, but I don't know how, and what *I* want—"

I paused.

"Yes, Miss Merritt?" prompted the Girton mistress.

"I don't know, ma'am," I told her. "What I *want* to do in my life doesn't seem to need education."

She watched me thoughtfully. "I am a firm believer, Miss Merritt," she told me, "that women, and that includes young women, ought not to hesitate to speak aloud *what they want*." She smiled. "It's been my experience that no one else will do it for you."

I decided I liked Miss Welsh. Even if she was a schoolmistress. My past experience with schoolmistresses was bleak to say the least, but this one might just be worth keeping.

I met her gaze. "I want to travel the world," I told her. "And I want to start a cricket league for girls."

Her eyes narrowed. "Is that so."

It wasn't a question. There was almost, in her eyes, a flash of...I couldn't say what, quite.

Perhaps I'd grown too easy with her too soon. Too comfortable. Now I waited tensely for her disapproval. Surely a headmistressy sort of woman, who peddled in propriety, and controlled the conduct of dozens of young ladies, would be scandalized by the thought of a cricket league for girls.

"Girls *ought* to be allowed to play," I blurted out. "I'm as good a bowler as any lad. There's no reason why cricket should only be for boys."

Miss Welsh watched me closely. "And what does your mother say to that?"

A punch in the stomach. "She loathes it," I admitted.

"And what are her views," asked Miss Welsh, "on higher education for young women?"

I gulped. "I doubt she has any," I said, "but if she does, they probably aren't good."

Miss Welsh digested this information, then took in the three of us with a welcoming smile. "I am so glad you've come," she said. "You must be fatigued from your journey. I hope you will join me for tea. But might you find it refreshing to take one quick circuit around the building? It's shady once we reach the Woodland Walk."

We all nodded. Mrs. Bromley and Alice raised their parasols, and Miss Welsh beckoned to us to follow her, giving me an especially pointed look, then strode along the path the led toward, and then veered around, the building.

Mrs. Bromley hurried to catch up with her friend. Alice and I tagged along behind. Miss Welsh chatted excitedly as we walked, pointed out flower beds, trees, and shrubs she had planted, tea rose bushes she had donated, fruit orchards she had designed, a pond she had deepened. It seemed Miss Welsh had had a hand in nearly every aspect of the grounds. Perhaps Alice, if she wanted to run a school herself, would need to study horticulture.

"It's like a fairy wood," whispered Alice. "I expect to see gnomes popping out any minute."

I laughed, then caught myself. If there were djinnis, perhaps there really *were* gnomes and fairies. Who could say? I watched each rustle in the underbrush a bit more closely, though they were proba-bly just squirrels.

Miss Welsh was saying something to Mrs. Bromley about build-ing projects—kitchens, a dining hall, a chapel, and more dormito-ries, classrooms, and laboratories—and how to raise the funds to do it, as we came around a bend. There the walk opened onto fields behind the main building, toward the pond.

I stopped and stared.

If you'd told me I'd died and gone to heaven, I might have believed it.

Great grown-up girls on bicycles crisscrossed the paths, while, to one side, girls played vigorous games of lawn tennis in doubles, and to another side, two teams of girls battled it out in a fierce game of hockey. Some distance away, a few clusters of girls practiced their swings on a small golf course. Crowning it all, upon a bit of rise in ground, stood a cricket pitch, with a team in the field and two batters at the ready.

I turned to see Miss Welsh looking at me with eyes twinkling.

"At Girton, Miss Merritt," she said, "we believe a vigorous body stimulates a vigorous mind."

"Golly," was all I could say.

"Our cricket club formed a few years ago," she went on. "We compete with Newnham, the other women's college here at

Cambridge, and we're working on setting up competitions with women's colleges elsewhere. What do you think, Miss Merritt?"

There was *already a cricket league* for girls in Britain.

To play, you had to go to college.

Go to college. How could I possibly go to college?

"I think I need to study my Latin," I told Miss Welsh.

She looked quizzically at Mrs. Bromley. Alice only laughed.

"Who's that?" I blurted out, as a young woman swung her bat and connected with a decisive *crack*. We watched the ball sail over the perimeter. "That's a ruddy six!"

Alice and her grandmother looked at me as if I'd just started babbling in a foreign tongue.

"A six," I explained. "is the best hit you can make."

The batter struck a triumphant pose while her teammates under the pavilion cheered.

"Who is that, Miss Welsh?" I inquired once more. "She's a terrific batsman. Er, batswoman."

Miss Welsh shaded her eyes with her hand. "Ah. I thought so. That would be Philippa Northam."

Alice ventured a question. "Is participation in sport, er, required, Miss Welsh?"

The Girton mistress smiled. "Every afternoon is dedicated to athletics," she said, "though for those less inclined to take up bats and rackets, we do have clubs that take walks through the country-side, and a bicycling club, which is quite popular." She turned to Mrs. Bromley. "Adelaide, did I tell you, part of my building program includes an indoor swimming pool? These girls should learn to swim, and once they do, they can play water polo, do competitive laps..."

She strode off once more, this time back toward the building, with Mrs. Bromley and Alice hastening to catch up to her.

It took all my self-control not to run straight for the cricket pitch, but Alice, knowing me well, turned and gave me a look. At any rate, I was hungry, and tea awaited us, where there were sure to be sandwiches. I wondered, was the food good at college? Only one way to find out.

The shady interior of Miss Welsh's study was a welcome change after the blinding sun of the playing fields. When we'd surrendered out hats and washed our hands, we sat down to eat. Miss Welsh did the honors with the teapot.

"Adelaide," she said, "we have much to discuss. About the build-ing committee and our fundraising efforts."

"I want to hear everything," said Mrs. Bromley.

Miss Welsh handed her a steaming cup and saucer. "How long can you stay?"

"Our schedule is flexible," Alice's grandmother replied. "The girls' tutor is on holiday for over a week."

Miss Welsh's expression grew hopeful. "Could you stay at least till the weekend? We're having a building committee meeting, and I'd love to introduce you to the others. Your championing of what we're creating here at Girton makes such a difference."

Mrs. Bromley glanced at us. "I'd love to," she said, "but what will the girls do for so long?"

Miss Welsh, it was clear, already had a plan for this. "I propose," she said, "that we engage a young woman—one of our pupils—to lead Miss Alice and Miss Maeve around the college grounds and into Cambridge proper. As a hostess and a bit of a tour guide to college life. They can accompany her to lectures and other activities."

Mrs. Bromley clapped her gloved hands. "What an inspiration, Elizabeth," she cried. "I should like nothing better than for them to be able to see college classes and ask a real 'undergraduette' their questions. This student you have in mind is...?"

"Philippa Northam," replied the headmistress. "The cricketer. Remarkably bright. From a hardworking family in Manchester." She lowered her voice. "One of our scholarship pupils."

"I should like to meet her," declared Alice's grandmother.

"Me too," I cried. "I want to know where she developed such a swing."

Miss Welsh handed me my tea. "She'll be glad to tell you."

A servant arrived with a tiered tray of sandwiches, cakes, and cold canapés.

"Now then," said Miss Welsh, "food first, and then future plans."

We tucked in eagerly. There's nothing like a long day of travel, followed by a walk in the heat, to work up an appetite. The food at Girton was delicious. Another mark in its favor, not that it needed any more after I saw that glorious spectacle of girls engaged in sport.

I was just thinking about sandwich number two when a knock sounded at the door, and a butler entered with a few letters on a tray.

"Telegrams, ma'am," he said apologetically, "for your guests. I thought perhaps they might be urgent in nature."

Mrs. Bromley's face paled. What could telegrams from home mean? She reached for the envelope with a trembling hand, tore it open, and scanned the lines quickly.

"Oh, thank heavens," she said. "It's only a burglary."

Miss Welsh's eyebrows rose. "*Only* a burglary?"

Mrs. Bromley sagged against the back of her chair. "I thought... Theodore...some misfortune..."

Alice hurried to her grandmother's side. "It's all right, Grandmama," she said softly. "Papa is safe and well."

"Of course," said Miss Welsh soothingly. "What a blessing that it isn't that."

"Things are only things," declared Mrs. Bromley.

"Was anything valuable taken?" asked her friend.

Mrs. Bromley scanned the lines of the telegram again. "A few things missing," she read aloud, "some small ornaments and household items. No art or jewelry. Nothing of great value." She fanned her face with her hands. "I declare, I'm still somewhat in shock at it all."

"Gregson," said Miss Welsh to the butler, "would you be so good as to excuse us? And to bring some cold water for Mrs. Bromley?"

Gregson, for that was apparently the butler's name, bowed. "Of course, madam," he said. "I beg your pardon. Is one of you a Miss Maeve Merritt?" He held out another telegram.

Now it was my turn to wonder who could possibly want to send *me* a telegram, and what ill omen it might contain. I took the envelope, and Gregson left the room.

I felt all eyes upon me as I slit open the envelope. I read the telegram quickly.

"It's from Tom," I told Alice.

"Tom?" inquired Miss Welsh.

"A family friend," explained Alice's grandmother.

I tore through the message on the telegram. "He says..." I realized I must choose my words carefully in the Girton College mistress's hearing. "He says when he and his father rode home from Grosvenor Square this morning, a pair of men with scarves across their faces, and with pistols, robbed their carriage." I gulped. "The bandits took *both of their carpetbags.*"

Alice's eyes grew wide. Our magic carpetbags, magic *flying* carpetbags, stolen? Lost to us forever?

Mrs. Bromley's brow creased with worry. "But what does all this mean?"

I wished I had an answer to that question myself.

"Adelaide," said Miss Welsh, "didn't you say your luggage turned up missing at the train station?"

Mrs. Bromley's eyes grew wide. "Surely you don't think—"

"I'm beginning to think," said Miss Welsh wryly, "that this is the American West, and not civilized Britain." She sighed. "But, yes. It does seem as though they could be connected." She stirred a lump of sugar thoughtfully into Mrs. Bromley's tea. "What might you have had at your house," she wondered aloud, "that so many people were determined to find?"

"Oh dear," said Mrs. Bromley.

"Oh dear," said Alice.

I took a worried bite of a roast beef sandwich. Oh dear, indeed.

CHAPTER
6

We emerged from Miss Welsh's study and followed her through the corridors until we reached a back door that led out into a leafy garden basking in the glow of late afternoon. The heat of the day had passed, but I couldn't admire the weather. Mrs. Bromley and Miss Welsh strolled the grounds once more, with the latter pointing out more of her botanical achievements, and Alice followed, listening, while I sat on a stone ledge, stewing over the baffling problem of burglars. Our carpetbags, gone! Alice's home, burgled! Our luggage, stolen! By two men with *scarves*? What on earth?

It hit me then: my trunk had held my diary, and my diary held my scrap of magical map. I'd never find it again. So much for Scotland and magical treasure.

So much for more madcap flights, skimming over treetops on our frisky, frolicsome carpetbags.

It was bitter, bitter, my disappointment. At least everyone is safe, I told myself sternly. And those fiends hadn't managed to steal Mermeros, the djinni, or surely Tom would have found a cryptic way of telling me so.

Maybe Mr. Poindexter was right. Maybe magic was too much danger and burden to bear.

"Maeve?"

Alice's voice in my ear startled me out of my thoughts and back into the sunshine.

Miss Welsh and Mrs. Bromley stood before us, with someone who must be a Girton student. She wore the long black skirt and white blouse most students here seemed to wear, but soft and open at the collar instead of stiffly buttoned up. Her dark hair was pulled back into a loose bun. She looked like an athlete but smelled like pear soap, which is no small achievement. If she'd just been playing sports, she must've have quickly had a bath. Her air of calm politeness didn't fool me. She had the look of one who always finds the hidden joke. I know a mischief-maker when I see one.

"You're Philippa Northam," I said.

She arched an eyebrow at me. "And you're a spy. Perhaps a fortune-teller?"

"Neither one," I told her. "I saw you bat a six."

She threw back her shoulders with obvious pride. "Saw that, did you?"

I nodded. "You wouldn't have gotten such a hit if I'd been bowling," I told her. "You had it far too easy."

Her eyes narrowed. "Is that so?" she said. "We'll have to test that theory, won't we?"

Miss Welsh coughed slightly. "Adelaide," she said, "may I present Miss Philippa Northam, one of our star pupils? Philippa, this is my dear friend, Mrs. Adelaide Bromley, and her granddaughter, Alice Bromley, and Alice's special friend and companion, Miss Maeve Merritt."

"Enchanted," said Philippa affably, shaking our hands. "Please, call me Pip." She shook my hand last. "Maeve Merritt, is it? We'll see if you have any *merit* in a game."

I liked her immensely. "Whenever you're ready."

Alice's eyes were wide. "*Maeve,*" she said in a low voice, "Miss Northam—"

"Pip," corrected she.

"Pip," repeated Alice, "has several years on you. And quite a bit of height."

"Her height," I said, "won't affect my bowling in the slightest."

"Aha," retorted Pip, "but it has everything to do with my swing."

"Rubbish," said I. "I'll bowl you, right enough. Send your wicket flying."

Pip leaned forward. "Care to put a bet on it? A little flutter, if you're so sure?"

"Now, Philippa." Miss Welsh rolled her eyes ever so slightly. "These are my *guests*."

Pip ignored the note of gentle warning. "The only thing flying," she told me, "will be the ball, after I've smacked it straight out of the pitch, and you know I can do it."

Miss Welsh looked quietly scandalized, but Mrs. Bromley only laughed. "What are you studying here at Girton, Miss Northam?" she inquired.

"Physics, ma'am," she said. "I want to study the atom. Like they do at the Cavendish."

"Physics?" inquired Alice. "You mean, medicine?"

Pip suppressed a smile. "Not that kind of physic," she said. "Natural philosophy. Physical science. Experimental research into the nature of matter itself."

"Do you mean the planets?" I asked. "The cosmos? That sort of thing?"

She shook her head. "That's old stuff," she said. "I want to study the forces at work all around us. Magnetism and electricity. I want to see what they both do to atoms. The tiniest bits of the material world." She jutted out her chin defiantly. "I'll take a degree in natural philosophy here at Cambridge."

Miss Welsh pressed her lips together. "So we dearly hope," she said, "though at present, our hopes depend entirely upon Friday's vote."

Mrs. Bromley nodded knowingly. Pip looked defiant, but neither Alice nor I had any inkling of what she meant. Pip read it in our faces.

"Cambridge University is holding a vote," she explained, "to see whether university degrees should be granted to women."

Alice spoke up. "Is the motion likely to pass?"

Miss Welsh looked away.

"They *have* to grant degrees to us," declared Pip. "How can they not? Women students have taken top honors in several recent tripos examinations. Outscored the men. Proven we can do anything those *precious* boys can." She grinned. "Caused no end of a row."

I poked my friend with my elbow. "That'll be you someday soon, Alice," I told her. "Mr. Abernathy says no lad can hold a candle to you for scholarship."

Alice blushed.

"I'll show you all around," Pip promised. "Give you the full tour. You can keep me company this week." She looked up at the mistress of Girton College. "What shall I do, Miss Welsh, when I need to attend lectures?"

"Bring them with you," advised Miss Welsh. "Where you go, they may accompany you."

"I'd like nothing better," Mrs. Bromley said. "I'd like them to have a real university experience. Of course, I'll pay you for your time."

Pip curtsied slightly. "Thank you, ma'am. I'm obliged to you."

"The obligation is all mine," insisted Mrs. Bromley.

"Why don't you start," suggested Miss Welsh, "by taking them to dinner? I'll ask Jason to bring some cots and bedding to your room for their sleeping arrangements tonight." She frowned. "Their luggage has gone missing," she told Pip. "We'll have to see about loaning them some nightclothes."

"Not to worry," said Pip. "My girls and I can get them outfitted for now."

Miss Welsh smiled. "Always resourceful, is our Pip."

My girls and I. I liked the sound of that. Perhaps, at a women's college, it wasn't dull and miserable as it had been at Miss Salamanca's School for Upright Young Ladies. Perhaps, at college, you found the kind of friends you'd really like to have. Other bright, ambitious girls doing something bold and brave. *And playing cricket every afternoon.* I could pinch myself.

Mrs. Bromley pulled some pound notes from her wallet and handed them to Pip. "This isn't your pay," she said apologetically. "This is just for any expenses you may incur, showing the girls around."

Pip's eyes grew wider, but she took the money philosophically and stuffed it into her pocket. "I do think some ice creams may be in order."

Alice's smile met mine. After a long day of travel and an afternoon of harrowing news, finally we were in for some fun.

"This is Alice," Pip told her roommate, one Miss Beatrice Wolverly, who went by Trixie, apparently. "And this is Maeve."

Trixie set down her spoon and hurried over to give us both a squeeze as if we were her favorite cousins. "Aren't you both adorable? Of course you are. Adorable."

Alice was adorable. I'm positive no one has thought me adorable, at least not since I swam in my lace christening gown as a baby, once upon a time. Trixie, on the other hand, was certainly likable. She was as short and soft as Pip was long and rangy, and overflowing with cheeriness.

"Bertie!" Trixie squealed to a girl crossing the high-vaulted dining hall. "Bertie, come meet these *adorable* girls!"

Heads turned from each table. So much for slipping quietly into the dinner experience at Girton College. "Bertie" came, and soon after, a Lizzy, a Megs, an Eileen, one Violet, one Barbara, one Charlotte, and two Sarahs. Before I knew it, we were literally encircled by college girls, who gazed upon us as though we were a pair of fluffy orange kittens with satin bows about our necks. If we'd been surrounded by a horde of spear-bearing Amazons, I doubt Alice would have felt more intimidated.

We'd just been served our supper—soup, a fillet of sole, roasted chicken, mashed turnips, creamed tomatoes, and cooked greens, which looked and smelled quite appetizing—and we were about to tuck in when Trixie discovered us and the Amazons descended.

"They're visiting," explained Pip. "Chumming around with me for a few days."

"Whatever for?" one of them inquired.

"Alice's grandmother is a friend of Miss Welsh," said Pip, "and Maeve plays cricket." As if that summed us both up to a tee, and perhaps it did.

"May we do your hair?" cried one "undergraduette," possibly Megs, but I was having a hard time remembering. "I always longed for a sister so I could arrange her braids."

"There's a lot more to sisters than braids," I said darkly, thinking of my frivolous, flighty sister Deborah. "I have three of them. Sisters, not braids."

Titters of laughter swept around the circle.

"You may do my braids," ventured Alice, "if you really want to." Her face turned scarlet. She glanced sidelong at me. Alice has always wished for an older sister, and has rather envied me my first-rate oldest sister, Polydora.

"You're darlings," declared Trixie. "Both of you."

Coming from Miss Salamanca's School for Upright Young Ladies, which had been ruled with an iron grip, I marveled at how free these girls were to move about the meal room, talk as they pleased, and gather to greet a pair of young visitors, if they chose. College girls were boarders, it seemed, but college felt nothing like boarding school. *Very* interesting.

"You'll bring them tonight, won't you?" a student asked Pip. Charlotte, I thought. "To our cocoa party?"

Alice and I looked at each other. A cocoa party? It sounded wonderful.

Pip eyed us both appraisingly. "I don't know," she said slowly. "Do they have anything to contribute to a cocoa party?"

I felt certain she was teasing. Mostly certain. Somewhat certain.

"We've got biscuits," offered Alice. "Maeve and I each brought a tin of biscuits with us."

Murmurs of approval sounded around the circle. *How* had we forgotten to eat our biscuits on the train?

"Store-bought?" inquired one suspicious college student.

"Homemade," Alice said.

"That settles it, then," said Pip. "They're definitely invited."

We ate our suppers, though they'd grown notably colder by the time Pip's circle of friends had finished deciding unanimously that we were completely adorable and positively darlings. The food was quite good overall, though the cooked greens I could have done without.

Afterward, Pip and Trixie led us through corridors and up stairwells to the dormitories and their room. They bid us make ourselves quite comfortable and at home, while they hurried off to assist with the cocoa-making and whatever other mysterious preparations went into a cocoa party.

Two cots had been set up before the fireplace, one for Alice and one for me. Despite the cots, the room still felt airy and open. Each girl had a bed, a desk and chair, shelves for their books, an armoire for their clothing, a trunk for other belongings, and a plump easy chair with a matching ottoman to relax in at the end of a long day. Pip's cricket bat leaned against the wall in one corner, and Trixie had what looked like an artist's easel propped up in another.

The small traveling knapsacks Alice and I had each brought with us lay upon each of our cots. No other luggage lay underneath. I remembered our lost bags and the mystery behind them. But was there a mystery? Could it be a coincidence that our luggage went missing, and Tom and his father's was stolen from their carriage?

Possibly. Probably not. The incompetent burglary at the

Bromleys' home was the clincher. Someone was after Mermeros, yet again. But who?

"Remember the biscuits," Alice said, and we each opened our bags to pull out our tins. I was just then thinking that an advance taste of biscuit couldn't hurt anyone, when I heard a clink of metal on metal, and my pair of silver mirrors, wrapped in paper, slid out with the biscuit tin. I unwrapped them, picked up a mirror, and studied my face in the glass.

"Feeling vain, are we?" Alice teased. She picked up the other mirror and gazed at her own reflection. "Come to think of it, we should freshen up a bit. After a day's traveling—*oh!*"

I didn't need to ask. I knew why she cried out.

Gazing back at me from the silvered glass was not my face, but Alice's.

Which must mean the image gaping back at her was mine.

A lice and I stared at each other, then back into our mirrors, then back at each other again.

"Do you see me in yours?" she whispered.

I nodded.

She gasped. "How does my mirror know you're *nodding*?"

It was truly astonishing. I knew people with cameras could pull off some amazing tricks—we'd seen some of them, to our horror, from that odious Professor Fustian, who had kidnapped Mr. Poindexter. But these mirrors weren't some newfangled technology. They were something else altogether.

Alice spoke first. "Do you think, Maeve...?"

"Yes," I told her. "I think they must be magic. But...I don't understand. I'd heard of djinnis, though not in sardine tins. I'd heard of flying magic carpets, though not in carpetbag form. But both of those twists are, er, modernization." I scratched my head. "Have you ever heard of a magic mirror?"

She considered. "Well, yes," she said. "In *Snow White*, remember? I said it earlier today. 'Mirror, mirror, on the wall, who in the land is fairest of all?' And then the mirror would answer?"

I groaned. "That would just be my luck. What a useless waste of magic. A mirror that decides who is the prettiest."

"Like Paris," said Alice.

"How do you mean, like Paris?" I asked. "Do you mean, it's the prettiest city?"

She laughed. "No, silly. Paris, as in, the Judgment of Paris. Paris was a prince of Troy who was told to decide which of three goddesses was the most beautiful—Hera, Athena, or Aphrodite."

I sighed. "I remember something about it," I said, "but why should I pay attention to a ridiculous beauty contest?"

She gazed into the mirror in her own hand. "Perhaps because its outcome launched the Trojan War. Don't you remember the *Iliad*?"

Right. Mr. Abernathy would be dismayed at me, though he was used to that by now.

I held up my mirror. "Um, mirror, mirror, in my...*hand*, who's the fairest...in the *land*?"

In reply, I only saw Alice's face, waiting expectantly.

"I see you," I told her. "But you could be the fairest in the land."

"Rubbish!" she declared.

"You ask the question," I said. "If you still see me, we'll know it's not the wicked-stepmother-queen kind of magic."

Alice sputtered in protest. "We won't know any such thing."

"Yes, we will," I told her. "If it says I'm the fairest in the land, we'd better smash it and risk the seven years' bad luck, because that's bad magic. Clearly defective."

I watched Alice roll her eyes as she asked the question.

"I still see you," she said.

"Then that settles it," I told her. "What we have is no talking mirror, nor a judge of beauty, but a set of mirrors that show you what the other mirror sees. And that's more than magic enough." I turned the mirror over and over in my hand. Just an ordinary, somewhat tarnished, somewhat worn-down hand mirror, such as many people owned. With mirrors, as with people, looks don't tell you much about what goes on inside.

Alice shook her head in wonder. "There's something about you, Maeve," she said. "I've said it before, and I'll say it again. You're like a magnet for magical objects. You don't even have to go looking. They come and find *you*."

"They may find me," I muttered, "but then they leave me." Mermeros. The carpetbags. My magic map. It hurt too much to think of it.

"The carpetbags?" Alice murmured. "Don't lose heart, Maeve. We'll find them yet."

I doubted it, but it was kind of her to try to cheer me up. That's Alice for you.

"Let's test these mirrors," I said. "We'll do a proper science experiment."

Alice caught on immediately. "Here," she said. "You stand behind this armoire, and I'll stand behind the other one." We both scurried into our hiding places.

I called to her softly. "Can you see me? Other than in the mirror?"

"Why are you whispering, Maeve?" she asked. "No. I can't see you."

"Right," I said. "Mirrors up. How many fingers am I holding out?"

"Four."

I let out a low whistle.

"I take it I was right," said she. "How many am *I* holding?"

"Two," I told her.

"Which ones?"

"Ring man and little man."

I saw her smile in the glass. "Just like the song."

"But was I right?"

Her smile faded into seriousness. "You were."

We returned to our couch and sat, staring into the empty fireplace grate.

"How could mirrors be magic?" I said. "*Why* would they be?"

We heard footsteps in the corridor. "I don't know why," Alice said quickly, "but we'd best hide them."

I stuffed them both back into my knapsack and hid it under my pillow. If I could've shoved the whole cot into the armoire and locked it, I would have.

Pip thrust the door open and leaned in, her feet still planted in the hall. "Come along, my little coconuts," she said. "You're our guests of honor. Your proper Girton College cocoa party awaits."

CHAPTER
8

We followed Pip's long strides along the corridors until we reached the door of another dormitory room, and she gestured us in. The smell of cocoa, starched linens, and eau de cologne met my nose.

A chorus of "Come in, come in!" greeted us from several directions. The entire cohort of "Pip's girls" that we'd met earlier, plus at least half a dozen more, had crammed inside the room, perched upon beds, chairs, trunks, bureaus, and even a piano bench, for this room had a little spinet piano along one wall.

Propriety? What was that? No longer Amazons, these Girton college girls lounged like Cleopatras. They lay back with their legs draped over one another or propped up on any old thing—the ottomans, the mantelpiece, the bed frames. Sitting upright with ankles crossed? Good heavens, no. I saw stockinged legs in various shades of brown, black, and gray, but none of these academic bluestocking girls' legs were *blue*, which seemed like a missed opportunity to me.

Two girls had their noses buried in novels. A pair of students were already engaged in a game of cards, while two others made the opening moves in a game of chess, on a board perched atop an inverted laundry hamper. The rest fizzed with conversation and bursts of laughter.

"Here they are," cried Trixie. "Our youngest bluestockings! Joining Girton College any minute now."

"Any year now, you mean," corrected another girl, who had introduced herself as Maud.

A low table had been commandeered from somewhere, and clustered upon it was a trio of cheerful teapots wafting out the fragrance of hot milk and chocolate, surrounded by wildly mismatched cups and saucers, with plates and tins loaded with biscuits, bonbons, and small pink-iced gâteaux. We produced our biscuit tins, which were met with much delight and passed around immediately.

The girl named Megs arranged a stool in front of her chair and patted it. "Come sit," she cried. "I want to do your braids."

I hung back, but Alice took the stool gladly, untying the bows on her ordinary daily braids. Megs immediately got to work, oohing about Alice's butter-colored hair. Alice's hair was quite nice, if you liked that sort of thing.

"How about you?" Bertie, a.k.a. Roberta, asked me. "Are you ready for a new hairdo?"

I shuddered. Tending to my own hair once a day was bad enough.

Pip laughed. "Little Miss Bowler? Rather not."

Trixie handed me a cup of cocoa. "Little Pip Junior, you mean."

I took my cocoa and smiled. Both names suited me just fine. Pip made room for me on the piano bench, and I sat beside her.

"Lizzy," cried a girl whose name I hadn't caught. "Give us an update, will you? Shall we win this Friday? Will Girton carry the day?"

Lizzy, who had been caught midbite, hesitated in answering.

I perked right up at the word *win*. "At cricket?" I asked. "Do you have a match Friday with that other girls' college?"

Pip shook her head. "Newnham College? I wish." She popped an entire iced gâteau into her mouth and talked through her chewing. "There'd be no question of who would win. Those girls don't know a bat from a fence post." She took a sip of hot cocoa, then paused to blow on its surface. "Tell Maeve what Lizzy means, will you, Trix?"

Trixie nodded and swallowed her bite of biscuit. "It's the Cambridge University vote," she explained. "They're deciding whether or not to grant us women students our degrees."

Ah, yes. That.

The room stilled. All the side conversations paused, and all eyes swiveled toward Trixie, Pip, and Lizzy.

Lizzy, whose angular face was spattered with freckles, stirred her cocoa with her spoon so rapidly it slopped over the sides of the cup. "We have to win," she said. "We've gathered supporters. We've canvassed and canvassed. We've joined in debates, written anonymous letters to the paper, passed out pamphlets..."

Her voice trailed off.

"Why wouldn't you win?" I asked. "How could they seriously object? If you can do the work and pass the examinations, why shouldn't you take your degrees the same as everyone else?"

Pip and Trixie exchanged a knowing look. Pip spoke first.

"You can't imagine what we put up with here," she said. "Some of the dons act as though we don't exist."

Lizzy could see that I didn't understand. "There was a professor who showed up one day to give a lecture," she explained. "None of the male students had come. Not one. All sleeping, face-first in their bed pillows, I imagine, after a night of carousing. But there were several of us girls there, from Girton and Newnham, on time, poised and ready to take notes. And what does the professor do?" She paused for effect. "He walks in, turns around, and walks out, saying, 'As there is *no one here*, I shall not lecture today.'"

"No one here?" I cried. "What a toad!"

Alice sighed. "*Maeve.*"

Several of the girls laughed. "A toad is right," declared Lizzy. "A bloaty, warty toad."

"If he were only one toad," said Pip darkly, "we could handle that.

We could handle anything. But there are profs like that everywhere. Some won't even allow women in their classes at all."

"Some of them are lovely," said Megs, between a mouthful of hairpins. "My poetry don is quite a dear and treats us girls every bit like the boys. Nicer, even."

"That's no help," insisted Lizzy. "If he's nicer, the boys cry favoritism and say that we girls can't cut it on our own, without special treatment. As though studies were made easier for us."

I chewed on a biscuit. It had never occurred to me how complicated this might be.

Trixie poured cream into her cocoa. "It's the same at Oxford. My cousin goes there. They're both so proud of their blessed *tradition*. Everything staying the same as ever."

"For nearly seven hundred years," said Lizzy darkly, "Cambridge has been a man's oasis. An island of males, with no irksome females to pester them. A sort of loafer's paradise, where they can swish around in their black robes and smoke their vile cigars, with no sensible females present to point out to them how utterly ridiculous they are."

Alice made a strangled sound. "Loafers?" she said. "You think Cambridge University is full of *loafers*?"

Low titters of laughter ran around the room.

"You'd be surprised," said Lizzy darkly. "Oh, Cambridge collects many of the smart ones, it's true—half the geniuses of 'this blessed plot, this earth, this realm'—"

"Shakespeare," Maud explained, seeing my bewildered look.

Lizzy continued as if Maud had never interrupted. "But a whole lot of lazy ne'er-do-wells," she said. "Sons of money who come here to waste a whole bunch of it."

Pip, whose cocoa had finally become drinkable, watched this with high amusement.

"Don't mind Liz," she told us. "Cambridge's academic merits are excellent, lazy loafers notwithstanding."

Liz snorted into her cocoa cup.

Pip continued. "That's why we all came here, instead of going to one of the many schools already offering degrees to women."

"It's a wonder they don't kick us out," said Trix. "Apparently we distract them with our 'feminine wiles.'" Several girls laughed.

"While also being hideous, unmarriageable hags," added Lizzy.

"Quite an accomplishment, that." Pip rolled her eyes. "It takes talent to be so alluring and so repulsive, both at once."

"At least they let us stay," said Trixie. "We get to learn and take the exams."

"It's why Miss Welsh and the others must be so strict about our rules," added Megs, from her post plaiting Alice's hair. "We have to walk such a very fine line. College boys are wild and rowdy all they please, but if a Girton or Newnham girl gets into the least bit of trouble, causes the slightest bit of scandal, they'll all say, 'See? See? We told you it would never work. We told you girls weren't serious-minded enough for study. We told you university study would corrupt your daughters' morals and distract our sons from learning.'"

"Surely... Oh!" Alice gasped as Megs twisted her hair a bit too tight. "Surely they wouldn't go so far as to say that?"

"They already do," said Lizzy grimly. "Show of hands, girls. How many of your parents worried that college would corrupt you?"

At least three-quarters of the girls raised their hands.

"How many of you had to promise you'd be ever so good and never set one foot out of line?"

Still more hands.

"How many of you," said Bertie with a wicked grin, "have set a foot out of line anyway?"

The room erupted in laughter.

"Bertie," scolded Trixie, who couldn't hide her own laughter. "The things you say!"

I tried one of the pink gâteaux myself. It was nice, but not as nice as Mrs. Tupp's coconut cakes.

"In any case," I said, "all that will change after Friday's vote. They'll award you degrees, and, by and by, they won't be able to treat you that way anymore."

"That's the spirit," said Pip. But the pause before she'd answered, before anyone answered, showed me they were none of them, for all their talk and pamphlets, very sure.

"Pip," said Megs, twisting strands of Alice's hair at the base of her neck through nimble fingers, "tell us about your new job. Wasn't today your second day?"

The tension left the room almost immediately.

"Third," said Pip. "I'm learning. Coming along. Some of the chaps are absolute prigs, but some are nice." She nodded in satisfaction. "It's more than a bit all right, if I do say so."

"Where's your new job, Miss, er, Pip?" asked Alice.

"I'm a typist at the Cavendish," Pip said proudly.

Alice winced as Megs inadvertently gave her braids a firm twist. "I'm sorry," she said. "What's 'the Cavendish'?"

"The Cavendish Laboratory," Pip said proudly. "I type up reports at the very same laboratory where Maxwell developed his equations. Maxwell! Who worked with *Michael Faraday* himself!"

She paused to let us all contemplate the deep significance of what she'd just said. As for myself, I was at a loss.

The girl called Maud was the first to speak. "Are Maxwell's equations, er, difficult to solve?"

Pip chucked a small cushion at Maud. "They *only* revolu- tionized our understanding of electricity and magnetism," she said. "Don't worry, duckie. They won't show up on your end-of-term exams."

I could tell she was just teasing. Her words got me thinking. Jobs. Her job at the Cavendish. I would need a job of my own someday, most likely.

"Is typing a hard job?" I inquired. "You seem like you like it."

She smiled. "It's not the typing I like," she said. "If I'd known what terrible handwriting these science chappies had, I might have thought twice." She set down her cup. "If I type their papers, I get to *read* their papers. I'll know about their discoveries before even the science journals and newspapers get to learn about them."

"I never thought of that," I said. "Typists get the first bite at the world's secrets, don't they?"

Pip took another sip of cocoa. "Besides, it's a chance for them to get to know that I'm dependable and smart. When I apply to do research there, Professor Thomson won't be able to say no."

This made sense. Typing was a stepping-stone for Pip. She, like Alice, knew what she wanted in life, and both of them had a plan to accomplish it.

Perhaps I'd better get moving, myself.

Megs finished Alice's elaborate braids and presented her handiwork with a flourish to the entire room. "Behold!" she cried. "Lady Alice is ready for the summer soiree, where she shall dance with the grand duke."

I didn't know anything about summer soirees, but Alice did look, suddenly, quite grown-up. She's never welcomed much attention, however, and the sight of so many girls admiring her hair made her blush. She reached upward to gingerly feel at the sculpture in braids coiled and piled atop her head.

"None of that!" cried Megs. "You'll muss them all up. Here." She rummaged through the items on a nearby dressing table and produced two handheld mirrors, which she held up angled in such a way as to give Alice a view of the back of her head.

The sight of the mirrors made me reach out for them, as if to snatch them back, as if they were my own mirrors and they'd been stolen from me. I almost squeaked out some protest, a "Give them back!," but in half an instant I caught myself. They weren't my mirrors. All was well.

"All you all right, dearie?" asked Trixie anxiously.

"I'm fine," I told her.

"We're just tired," Alice explained, giving me a look. "It's been a long day. Wonderful, but long."

"Of course you are," Trixie said. "Nothing like a cup of hot milk to make you sleepy, too. Come on. I'll lead you back to our room, and you can get yourselves settled down for the night."

We said our goodbyes and followed Trixie back to the room they were sharing with us. She produced two nightgowns for us to borrow, and Alice and I quickly changed and got into bed.

Any other night, I would have stayed much longer at that cocoa party, but Alice was right. I was tired. It had been a long day, filled both with new places and friends and college possibilities, and even new magic, but also filled with awful losses. Mermeros. The carpetbags. Our luggage. My magical map.

Stop it, I told myself. *There's nothing you can do tonight. Get some rest, and let tomorrow bring what it will bring.*

CHAPTER
9

We sat at breakfast in the half-empty dining hall, Pip, Alice, and me. Breakfast at college, I could see, was hardly the cheery affair supper had been the night before. What girls were present drifted to their tables like haggard ghosts, clutching cups of coffee in both hands.

Alice was hard at work tapping the shell of her soft-boiled egg, while I tried to get the better of a grapefruit half, when a small cough sounded at my elbow. I turned to see Gregson, Miss Welsh's butler, standing in respectful silence.

"Good morning," I told him.

"Good morning, Miss Merritt, Miss Bromley, Miss Northam," said he. I wondered if he knew the name of every girl in the college. "Pardon my interruption, but Mrs. Bromley asks if you would please join her in Miss Welsh's private study for a moment."

"After breakfast?" inquired Alice.

"I believe your grandmother's hope was that you would come now," replied the butler. "Miss Northam also."

Pip rose and drained her coffee cup. "She probably wants to discuss our plans for the day," said she. "Thank you, Gregson. I'll bring the girls there myself."

"Very good, miss," said he, and he turned heel and left.

"His feet don't even make a sound on the ground," I observed.

"We've nicknamed him the Vampire," said Pip. "We think he doesn't even cast a shadow."

Alice's mild expression grew concerned. "Isn't he nice, then?"

"Nice as raspberry jam," said Pip. "As silent as raspberry jam, too."

Gregson let us into the private study. The sight that greeted us stopped me in my tracks. Seated beside Mrs. Bromley on the sofa was Mr. Bromley, Alice's grandfather, and in chairs opposite him sat Mr. Poindexter and Tom.

"What are you doing here?" I cried.

Tom grinned. "Nice to see you, too, Maeve."

Alice ran to give her grandfather—Papa to her—a hug. I introduced Pip to our newcomers.

"When did you get here?" I cried. "How did you come?"

"We drove," explained Mr. Bromley. "I hired an automobile and a driver."

"You drove in a *car*?" I cried. "A horseless carriage?"

"You'd love it, Maeve," said Tom. "We got in last night. We're staying at a hotel in Cambridge."

"We've brought you some clothes," added Mr. Bromley. "We knew you needed them."

I turned to Mr. Poindexter. "What made you decide to come, too?"

Mr. Bromley answered for him. "I asked Mr. Poindexter if he would like to come with me," he said. "Frankly, neither of us wanted to remain in London, where we didn't know who—" He paused, glancing up at Pip, and seemed to reconsider how much he'd been about to say, probably about our mysterious thieves.

"Traveling together just made sense," said Mr. Poindexter smoothly. "Safety in numbers. I thought we might as well get out of the city for a spell."

A wicked thought tickled my brain. "Did you also ask Mr. Wilberforce if he'd care to take the drive?"

Mrs. Bromley looked away, pretending to use her handkerchief. Her husband coughed faintly. "Under the, er, circumstances, I felt he might better remain in town," he said. "To visit friends and see to his meetings. That sort of thing."

Meetings that weren't due for another fortnight, but I let it pass.

Alice gave me a look. She knew exactly what I'd been thinking. She might scold me, but I knew she was glad her papa's cousin Eugene hadn't come along to spoil our visit to Cambridge.

Mr. Poindexter carried on speaking as though I'd never interrupted.

"We also came," he said, "because your words, ma'am"—here he gestured toward Mrs. Bromley—"very much got me thinking. We could use a little holiday, and Tom ought to see Cambridge as well. Oxford, too, at some point. He should think more about his education and future, just as these girls are doing."

That reminded me. "Tom," I cried, "Girton College has a *girls' cricket team*! Pip, here, is its top player."

Pip smiled. "I don't know about that," she said. "But I do like to play."

"Miss Northam will lead us on a tour of Cambridge," said Alice. "We're going to visit her lectures with her and see the Cavendish Laboratory, where she works."

Mr. Poindexter sat up taller at the mention of the Cavendish. "You don't say," he said. He looked over at Mr. and Mrs. Bromley as if seeking permission. "Miss Northam. Would it be too much to ask for my son, Tom, to accompany you today?" He paused. "That is, if Mrs. Bromley does not object?"

"Of course I don't object." Mrs. Bromley laughed. "Where Alice and Maeve are, Tom is always welcome."

"It's fine with me," said Pip. "The more, the merrier." She gave Tom a look. "Provided you'll behave yourself better than some of these Cambridge undergraduate lads."

Mr. Poindexter stifled a laugh.

Tom gulped and nodded. "On my honor," he said, "er, ma'am."

"None of that," replied she. "No *ma'am*. Just Pip."

"Yes, ma'am," said a flustered Tom. "I mean, yes, Miss Pip."

She glared at him.

"Pip," he choked. "Only just Pip."

"That's better." She nodded. "Right, then. Are we ready? Have you eaten? The tour begins shortly. Lectures won't keep."

"Before you go, girls," said Mr. Bromley, "I was just about to say I received a telegram last night from Mr. Abernathy."

We paused and turned back at the door.

"Our tutor," Alice explained to Pip. She turned to her grandfather. "Did he reach Scotland safely?"

Mr. Bromley rubbed his chin. "Yes..."

Something in his reluctant reply caught my attention. "Don't say *his* luggage was stolen, too?"

Mr. Bromley exchanged an uncomfortable glance with his wife. Her face paled. Clearly, this hadn't been something Mr. Bromley had wished to discuss in the presence of others, meaning Pip. But just as clearly, Mr. Abernathy's luggage *had* been stolen.

"It has," said Mr. Poindexter quietly.

Pip's brow furrowed. "That's an awful lot of stolen luggage," she said. "Either that, or train station porters just aren't what they used to be."

Her joke, if that's what it was, failed to lighten the mood in the room.

"It's all behind us now," said Mr. Bromley. "We shall hope the pieces turn up somehow." He nodded at me and Alice. "I've put in a call to our dear friend Mr. Wallace."

Inspector Wallace of Scotland Yard had accompanied us on our last magical expedition, when Mr. Poindexter had been kidnapped, and we'd had to use the flying carpetbags, as well as a good deal of quick thinking, to fetch Mr. Poindexter and Mermeros, the djinni, back. He'd started out skeptical, to say the least, of our magical claims, but after all he'd seen, he'd become a reluctant believer.

"He says he'll join us," Mr. Bromley continued. "He's got a bit of a delay at work—apparently his secretary has just quit—but as soon as he's able, he'll make his way here."

I was relieved to hear it. I wasn't sure if Inspector Wallace knew how to catch our thieves, but at least he wouldn't think we were silly for talking of magical things and magic thieves.

An idea hit me. A great, big, colossal idea walloped me in the solar plexus. I don't know why I hadn't seen it before, though I'd certainly been busy.

"Mr. Wilberforce," I told the room.

They all stared at me.

"What about him, dear?" asked Mrs. Bromley gently.

I turned to see Pip watching me in curiosity and realized my terrible blunder. How rude!

"I'm sorry, Pip," I told her, "but would you give us just a moment?"

She shrugged good-naturedly and left the room.

I turned back to the others, gathering my bubbling thoughts. "All the trouble began," I said, "when Mr. Wilberforce arrived upon the scene."

"Yes, but," Tommy began, "wasn't he at the house still when Dad and I were burgled in our taxicab?"

He was. I had to admit it.

"Could he have been one of your railway porters in disguise?" continued Tom.

I shook my head. "Certainly not," I said. "He's a much larger person than they were. But he could have *accomplices*." A wonderful word, one which I'd acquired from my reading of the Sherlock Holmes stories. Of course someone like Cousin Eugene would need help to pull off a grand theft. He'd probably need help to tie his shoes.

Alice's eyes bulged. "Surely, Maeve," she said, "you don't suspect my grandfather's cousin of being involved in a plot to steal"—she let her voice trail off—"you-know-what?"

I turned to Mr. Bromley. "I'm sorry, sir," I told him, "if this idea gives any offense. If you tell me there's no possible way under heaven that your cousin Eugene could be involved in a money-grabbing plot—for that's always what motivates these scoundrels—then I'll drop the ideal and never mention it again."

All eyes turned to Mr. Bromley. He swallowed once or twice. "Well," he said at length, "one never wishes to think ill of another person," he began. "Especially one's own relations." He glanced over at his wife, who was viewing him with pursed lips as though she was sucking on a lemon drop, and a sour one at that.

We waited.

"I mean to say," Mr. Bromley continued, "one can hardly even imagine Eugene having the gumption, and the follow-through, to carry out such a scheme."

"So he definitely would never attempt it?" prodded Mr. Poindexter.

Mr. Bromley tugged at his collar in some desperation. "Does any of us," he said vaguely, "ever really know what another is capable of?"

It took all my powers of restraint not to say "Aha!" and "Eureka!" Instead I said, "So it does seem at least hypothetically possible?"

Poor Mr. Bromley wore a hunted look. (To be fair, I can have that effect upon people.)

"Hypothetically," he admitted faintly. "Poor Eugene. He has had, shall we say, some unfortunate tendencies from time to time. I would never like to suspect him of ill intentions. But," he glanced at his wife, "upon consideration, I shall pass this idea along to Inspector Wallace."

The distressed look on Alice's face made me wonder if I'd gone too far, but I had a feeling, from the satisfied expression on her grandmother's face, that I'd hit upon her own thoughts precisely.

"Now," Mr. Bromley said, "let's not keep Miss Northam waiting or make her late for her engagements."

Alice, Tom, and I collected hats and jackets and left the room to find Pip waiting for us in the hallway.

"Everything all right?" she asked.

We nodded, and she was satisfied. No Nosey Parker was Pip. She took off striding down the hall, and we hurried to follow her. She led us out through a back door to a paved area where several bicycles stood, leaning against the building underneath a brick arch.

I gestured to the bicycles. "Is this how you get around Cambridge?"

Pip nodded. "Do you lot know how to ride?"

"I don't," said Alice apologetically. "Maeve and Tom do, though."

"Pick out bikes, then, you two," instructed Pip. "Alice, hop aboard this three-wheeled contraption, will you?"

She led Alice to a large three-wheeled bicycle, one wheel in front, and two in the back, with a comfortable seat in the middle of the two wheels, high above them.

"Now, can you reach the pedals?" asked Pip. "That's right. Now, a good push forward and down with your right foot, and then the same with your left. Good, good. This one has some speed to it, doesn't it? Take the handlebars! Don't forget to steer!"

She spent a few minutes instructing Alice in the finer arts of riding a tricycle, for I supposed that was what such a thing must be called, including how to brake and slow it to a stop. It required no special balance and thus was quick to learn.

While Alice practiced for a moment, under Pip's watchful eye, I pulled Tom aside.

"Are you all right, Tom?" I asked him. "After yesterday? When you were robbed?"

Tom was still for a moment. "The worst part was afterward," he said eventually. "When it happened, it was all so fast. We're riding along, and suddenly both doors to the cab yank open. One on either side."

I tried to picture it. It sounded terrifying.

"They climbed up into the cab, faster than you can snap your fingers," he said. "One of them had a pistol. They threatened us with it and told us not to make a sound."

My skin went cold. A gun? Pointed at Mr. Poindexter and Tom?

"But at the moment," Tom said, "you're not thinking about that, you know? You're just thinking, *What is happening? This can't be happening.*"

A thousand questions bubbled through my brain.

"They took our bags," he said, "from inside the cab and from the carriage rack. They made us take off our jackets and turn out our pockets."

I let out a whistle. "It's a wonder they didn't find Mermeros," I said. "Are you sure they didn't?"

"I'm sure." Tom wore a curious expression. "But they got our carpetbags, Maeve!" His face fell. "No more flying, ever again. That's what I mean when I say it was worse after it was over. When it's done, there's plenty of time to think about how you could've been killed. And how wrong, just horribly wrong, it is for people to treat other people that way—to treat you that way. You think about all that you've lost to the thieves. And how cruel it is that they would take your carpetbags, thinking they're just taking any old bags, not knowing they're making off with *magic flying carpetbags.*"

"I'm sorry, mate," I told him. "It sounds awful."

Tom wasn't done. "And how unfair it is that out of all the cabs on the streets that day, ours was the one targeted."

"Cheer up, then," I told him. "You surely won't the only one. You could probably fill a country chapel with just the morning's victims of London cab burglaries."

"Ha," he said, rolling his eyes. "Very funny."

"But I don't think it was random," I said. "I don't think you were robbed by chance."

"I suppose not." His face was grim. "Do you really think it was that awful Eugene?"

I paused to consider. "I think he could be behind it," I said. "He's just that nasty sort. But I can't say that it *is* him. Only that it could be."

I peered around just in time to see Alice's three-wheeled bicycle careen into the brick wall of the Girton College building with a thump. A faint "Sorry" in Alice's voice's came from the contraption, and a laugh from Pip. The cycling lesson, it seemed, was nowhere near done.

"In any case, it's over now," said Tom, shaking himself as if shaking off the bad memory.

He needed some help changing the subject, I thought. And I knew just how.

"Tom," I whispered. "We've found something magical. Look."

I pulled the mirrors out from my knapsack and showed them to him. It took a minute for him to realize what he was seeing, but when he did, his eyes grew wide.

"You're sure?" he whispered. "Sure this isn't some sort of trick?"

"Positive," I told him. "We tested it out yesterday, Alice and me. We found them at a little stall at the train station, here in town."

He shook his head in wonder. "There's something about you, Maeve," he said. "You'll be finding magical objects all throughout your life. As for me, my only option is to steal them."

I started to laugh, then stopped as he pulled his jacket open. I saw a bulge in the inner breast pocket. A rectangular bulge in the approximate size and shape of *a sardine tin*.

I blinked. "Is that Mermeros?"

He nodded.

I looked side to side to see if anyone was watching us. Pip and Alice were busy, and I saw no one else around.

"Does your father know you have him?" I whispered.

He shook his head. His eyes were wide, his face flushed with both fear and excitement.

"When did you take him?" I asked.

"This morning."

I gulped. "Tom," I whispered, "he'll be furious!"

Tom nodded. "I know," he said. "But, Maeve, he's determined

to get rid of Mermeros. I had to take him before something awful happens."

"Your dad will think he's been robbed again," I said. "He'll be distraught."

"I know, but Maeve—"

"He's your *father*," I said. "He trusts you. Don't you trust him?"

Tom looked down at his shoes. "I do trust him," he said. "Completely. With anything. And I feel terrible about doing this. But this choice he's making—it's wrong."

I opened my mouth to reply, but Tom kept going.

"I don't mean it's *morally* wrong," he added quickly. "Dad's heart is in the right place. And I know the dangers of having a djinni are real. But to throw away a power like this is a mistake. To leave it where others might find it is a mistake." He patted his pocket protectively. "To do something that would harm Mermeros would be the worst mistake of all."

I watched Alice laugh as she pedaled faster around the paved area. Pip grinned, watching her, then poked her head indoors, probably to look at a clock.

Tom spoke again. "You won't tell my dad, will you, Maeve?"

I fixed him with a look. "What do you think I am, a snitch?"

He sagged with relief. "I knew I could count on you."

"Just because I'm not a snitch," I told him, "doesn't change the fact that I have a very, very, *very* bad feeling about this."

He clapped me on the shoulder. "Cheer up, Old Mother Hen," he said. "It'll be fine. I know what I'm doing."

"Ha," I said. "I've heard that before." Chiefly from myself. "Old Mother Hen?"

He grinned and stuck his hands underneath his armpits, flapping imaginary wings.

"Just do me a favor, Tom," I said. "Don't make your wishes too quickly. Think about them. Really think."

Tom rolled his eyes. "From the moment I first laid eyes on Mermeros, Maeve—when you first summoned him behind your girls' school—I haven't thought about much else."

It made sense, but somehow, it brought me no comfort.

"Are you two ready?" called Pip. "Alice can now ride better than quite a few girls at Girton. We need to get moving."

"Ready," I said. "Let's go."

CHAPTER
10

Pip hopped on a bicycle, and Tom and I did the same. We set out down the path toward the road, in a formation with Pip in the lead, Alice following behind her, and Tom and me flanking Alice in the rear. We pulled out onto the road and took off toward the city of Cambridge and Cambridge University itself.

We passed through the village of Girton, past houses and small shops we'd seen the day before on our ride from the train station. We had to travel slower than we otherwise might, since Alice's tricycle couldn't get up to the speed of a proper bicycle, but that meant more time for thinking and admiring the scenery. We rode along a stretch of farmland, with sheep grazing in pastures and fields shimmering with young green stalks of something, I wasn't sure what. Wheat? Barley? Vegetables?

I hadn't grown up around farmland, nor even around such clear, fresh air. Breathing it into my lungs felt marvelous. I could see why many favored the country over the city. On a day like this, who wouldn't? It was a glorious morning, bathed in golden sunlight, with just a few fleecy clouds swimming in a bright blue sky. The kind of morning that might almost let one forget that one of her best friends had just robbed his own father of a magical djinni, one that other thieves were determined to snatch as well.

Soon the blur of a small city appeared on the horizon. Towers, steeples, and spires came into view as we pedaled up small inclines and coasted down gentle slopes.

"There she is," Pip called back to us. "The city of Cambridge. We're about to cross the River Cam."

Sure enough, we crossed a wooden bridge over a smooth, sleepy river shaded by willow trees and found ourselves surrounded by stone and brick buildings, some faced with ivy and all with tall, stately windows. The sidewalks were filled with students dressed in black robes, some on foot and some on bikes. All of them, young men. Not a woman student in sight, except Pip, and she wore her usual black skirt and white blouse. No robes for young ladies, apparently.

"This is St. John's College," said Pip. We pedaled faster to catch up and hear her words before the wind snatched them from her mouth.

She signaled to us to turn off the main road onto a winding thoroughfare. Medieval-looking churches and stately academic buildings were everywhere, with their wings, like outstretched arms, enfolding smoothly mown lawns of green grass. It felt like an altogether different world, with a magic all its own. I thought of what Trixie had said the night before, about how fond they all were here of tradition. I could see why. It was everywhere. These ancient buildings and statues, these stately paved walks—the whole place was positively sticky with tradition.

"That college," Pip said, pointing to her right, "is Trinity. Where the science chaps tend to go. And all the science dons. All the way back to Sir Isaac Newton."

I pedaled faster still to ride alongside her.

"Do you wish you went there?" I asked.

She made a face. "Well, I can hardly live in a men's dormitory, can I?" she said. "I'm a Girton gal through and through. But it's no secret that the dons favor the lads from their own colleges. So the lads at Trinity have another advantage over me. Besides being able to earn degrees."

I marveled at the gray and tan-colored stone edifices, each embellished with elaborate decorative stonework. Like castles. Like monasteries. Dignified, beautiful, and rich. And exclusive—only the lucky could get in. Lucky, and male.

Yet girls were here, and surely, surely they'd carry the day at tomorrow's election and earn their degrees like anyone else. Then more women would enroll. They'd spend years living in this magical place, taking classes in these beautiful buildings, and playing cricket every afternoon without worrying about their mothers catching them do it.

We passed a vast church. Here and there, little shops and cafés clustered together. I noted a stationer's, selling paper goods of all sorts; a chemist's shop; a pub, promising cheap dinners; and more than one bookshop, offering new and used books. I'd have to stop in when I had a moment.

"This one's King's College," continued our tour guide, who seemed to take her role quite seriously. "Oldest of all the colleges."

And the most opulent, it seemed. The sense of grandeur and ancientness filled its courtyard, as did black-robed students and a few men in even more pompous robes. Professors, I supposed.

"What's that huge building?" Tom pointed to a long, high-walled church that seemed to extend in a straight line as far as the eye could see. Tall stained-glass windows ran the entire length of it.

"It's the chapel," Pip explained.

"It goes on forever," Tom exclaimed.

"So do the sermons," was Pip's reply. "This one's St. Catharine's College, and beyond it is Queens'."

"They sound like women's colleges," I said hopefully.

"They're not," said Pip. "Left turn."

We cycled after her, turning onto a narrower street called Pembroke, and from there another left onto Free School Lane.

"And here it is," announced Pip, dismounting from her bicycle. "Across the street is Corpus Christi College, but this whole row, here, is the Cavendish Laboratory. The greatest laboratory for the study of physics in the world."

We surveyed the long stone building. It was no cathedral, but no less imposing for that.

"Are we coming in with you?" inquired Alice.

"For now," said Pip. "We'll stick our bicycles inside, in the corridors, but I have a lecture starting soon at Corpus Christi. Latin."

I groaned.

"What's the matter?" asked Pip. "You don't care for Latin?"

I sighed. I knew I needed to do better at it. And apply myself more.

"I could be wrong," said Tom, looking around, "but this feels like the part of town where our hotel is. We came from there, just this morning, and drove up to Girton College."

"What's your hotel?" asked Pip.

"The Lion," replied Tom. "On Petty Cury."

"Why, that's just around the corner," she said. "You're only a few minutes away."

We entered the Cavendish Laboratory. After the bright morning light, its halls felt dim, almost damp. Everywhere you looked, bicycles lined the corridors, propped against walls, even cluttering stairway landings.

"What a mess," I observed.

"Wait till you see some of the labs themselves," answered Pip darkly.

Finding a corner suitable for stowing Alice's tricycle proved challenging, but eventually we found a small supply room, barely more than a closet, underneath a stairwell.

"Let's take a chance on this one," said Pip. "We can leave all our bikes here. If I'm late to Latin, Miss Welsh will have my hide. You can be sure she hears about it if one of those 'flighty Girton girls' disrupts a class by being late. Boys are late constantly, yet nobody seems to mind."

"I can't wait to see what a real college Latin lecture looks like," Alice said. "I've only ever studied it with Mr. Abernathy."

This gave me an idea. "Pip," I said, "why don't you and Alice go to Latin, and Tom and I will stay here, right in this room, and keep an eye on the bicycles."

Her eyes narrowed. "You won't leave this room?" said she. "On your honor?"

I nodded.

"And you won't go prowling and nosing about, getting into trouble?"

Tom and I shook our heads. "We promise," I said.

"What will you do, then?"

I pulled my copy of *Jane Eyre* from my knapsack. "Read."

Pip folded her arms across her chest like one not about to be fooled "You'll read."

Tom pulled a copy of *Great Expectations* by Charles Dickens from his shoulder bag. "Me too."

Pip wasn't having it.

"Fine," I admitted. "We'll probably also talk a bit."

"And that's *all*?"

Alice intervened, trying not to laugh. "They won't be, er, canoodling," she said. "You can trust them."

If Alice's words weren't enough to win Pip over, possibly the fit of horrors, coughing, and shuddering that came over me did the trick. *Canoodling?* Did Pip actually imagine Tom and I would sit here *kissing*?

The chime of bells began sounding across the city. Pip's face fell.

"Come on, Alice," she cried. "We need to make a run for it. You two?" She pointed a stern finger at Tom and me. "*Behave yourselves.*"

She took Alice by the hand and dragged her out the door.

When their footsteps had faded, Tom and I found rickety chairs and tested our weight upon them. Tom's face, I noticed, had turned bright red. No wonder he was embarrassed. Honestly, Pip! We were good friends, and that was all.

The room we sat in was only barely lit by an electric bulb

dangling from a cord overhead. Along one wall was a series of wooden cabinets. Shelves lined the other walls, cluttered with dusty apparatus of some sort, though what any of it did for the cause of science, I couldn't guess. Our bikes, and Alice's tricycle, lay on the floor in a jumbled heap.

Tom pulled Mermeros's sardine tin slowly from his inner pocket. The sight of that familiar enameled cover, colorfully painted with "Sultana's Exotic Sardines, packed in salted oil, imported exclusively by the Eastern Trading Company, Liverpool," filled me with that same old longing I'd always felt. Magic. Wishes. All the thousand possibilities, and all at my command.

Now, all at Tom's command.

"What will you do with it?" I asked. "What will your first wish be?"

Tom rotated the sardine tin slowly between his finger and thumb. "I'm not sure." He took off his cap. "Do I wish for pots of money to help orphans? Do I wish for, oh, lots more families to adopt kids?"

"Be careful how you word it," I advised. "Mermeros is a stickler for following your wishes to the letter and excluding anything he can exclude if you didn't specifically ask for it."

Tom nodded grimly. "That's what I mean," he said. "It's hard to know how to get it exactly right. Even a good wish can have awful consequences that you never saw coming. Especially where people's lives are concerned."

How well I knew it. Wishing was a serious business.

"Maybe," I said aloud, "you shouldn't think in terms of money, or even individual orphans and their potential families. Maybe you should think of something that would be a mechanism for helping lots of orphans."

Tom stared at me. "A *mechanism*?" he said. "An orphan-helping machine?"

I laughed. "No, silly. I mean, a system. A process. Something that could go on helping kids long after the magic has ended, so to speak."

"Do you mean, an orphanage?" Tom scratched his head. "London alone is full of them, and they're all wretched places."

The door to our little closet banged open, and a man came sweeping in. He was tall and broad, quite filling the doorway, but young. His hair was sandy-colored and his face mustached and ruddy, but he seemed friendly.

"Hullo hullo, what's this, a secret luncheon party, and nobody invited me?" He nodded toward the sardine tin and playfully jammed his fists into his hips, as if he was indignant about missing out on sardines. (If he knew what type of "sardines" these were, I'd wager he jolly well would be.)

"Pardon us," murmured Tom. "We can go somewhere else. Get out of your way." He slid Mermeros's sardine tin back into his pocket.

"Nonsense," declared the newcomer. "You're not in my way." He crossed the small room, navigating around the bikes, and pulled open one of the tall cupboard doors. "Just need a few supplies." He grinned. "Didn't know they kept fish and kids in here."

A joker, this one. His manner of speech was curious, with an accent like nothing I'd ever before heard.

"What brings you two here? To the Cavendish, I mean?" he asked us. "If I may pry."

I hesitated. Could an answer be bad for Pip?

"We have a friend," I said slowly, "who works here at the Cavendish."

"And he locked you in the supply closet?" the young man teased. "Not a nice chap. Is it one of the research assistants? Good chance I know him." He pulled a curious-looking glass object from the cupboard, some sort of tube.

"It's a she," I said. "Philippa Northam."

"Ah," said he, recognition dawning. "The typist. She's helping me with my latest paper. I just finished writing it out last night." He extended a hand toward me. "I'm Ernest Rutherford. You can call me Ern."

I shook his hand, and Tom did the same.

I couldn't resist. "Miss Northam wants to be a researcher here," I said. "Not just a typist."

He considered me thoughtfully. "Is that so? Does she have her MA?"

At our blank expressions, he tried again. "Her BA? A college degree?"

"Not yet," I said. "She's working on it, at Girton College. Of course, Cambridge won't award women their degrees." I was very curious to see how this "Ern" might respond to that.

"It's barbaric," he said cheerfully. "Right here in the cultured heart of Old Mother England."

"What is?" I demanded. "Women wanting to study?"

"Heavens, no." His booming laugh felt twice as loud in our narrow room. "Keeping them out."

I decided I liked Ern Rutherford.

"Say, where are you from?" inquired Tom. "I've never heard an accent like yours."

The tall man grinned. "I'm from New Zealand," he said. "You won't find many of us around here." He gave me a wink. "Folks at Cambridge are about as welcoming to us colonial blokes as they are to women." He peered down the length of his glass tube as if it were a telescope. "No, I shouldn't say that. They've started letting us colonial 'aliens' in. It's quite new, but at least they're doing it. So I guess we foreign fellows do have a bit of an advantage." He pulled a handkerchief from his pocket and polished a bit of the glass. "But I say it's a crime, keeping the women out. At my old alma mater, women were admitted right from the start."

Satisfied at last with whatever the glass thing was, he turned to leave. "Pleasure meeting you both... Say, we didn't actually meet, did we? What are your names?"

"I'm Maeve Merritt," I told him.

"Tom Poindexter," said Tom.

Ern shook our hands once again, very solemnly, but with a twinkle in his eye. "Tell your friend, Miss Northam, that next time she needs to deposit you somewhere, she can bring you right up to the lab, and I'll put you to work. And tell her we can always use more help in the lab, if she'd really like to gain some research experience." He blew out his mustache. "Come to think of it, she's due here in under an hour. I'll tell her myself. Good morning to you, Maeve, Tom." And with that, he pulled the door shut behind him.

We'd barely drawn two breaths when the door opened again, and another young man stuck his head in. He jumped when he saw us, as if we were a pair of rats. I suppose kids were as rare as rats at the Cavendish Laboratory. Possibly rarer.

"What are you doing here?" he demanded.

"Sitting," I told him. Tom coughed to hide a laugh.

Our new visitor was not amused. He was slimmer in build than Ern Rutherford, with pale blond hair combed back off his face. He stared at me as if expecting an apology. I stared right back.

"Well?" he said.

"Well, what?" said I.

He gritted his teeth. "What is this, the nursery? Where's Rutherford?"

Tom and I looked at each other before I spoke. "He isn't here."

The young man rolled his eyes. "Obviously. But he *was* here, wasn't he?"

I nodded. "He was."

The young man nodded as if this had confirmed his worst suspicions. "And what did he get from here?"

I began to wonder if I was in the presence of a police detective. "I don't know."

He let out a groan of disgust and left, pulling the door hard shut behind him.

"Criminy," muttered Tom. "What was eating him?"

"Science fever, I imagine," I said.

"I liked the first chap better," said Tom. "Rutherford." He paused. "What are you doing?"

I had wedged my chair under the doorknob, and was sliding a heavy wooden crate in front of the door.

"Buying us some privacy," I explained. "Sounds like Pip and Alice will be back in half an hour, maybe forty-five minutes. That gives us just enough time for a little tête-à-tête with Mermeros."

Y ou want me to summon the djinni?" whispered Tom. "Here,
now? At the Cavendish Laboratory?"

"Why not here?" I said. "Why not now?" I considered. "I
doubt any of their laboratory instruments, or whatever they're called,
will be able to detect the presence of an ancient magical djinni of
infinite power."

That caught Tom's attention. "My dad told me on the drive up
here that they do have all sorts of machines for studying electricity
and magnetism," he said. "He reads a lot about science in his newspapers. Suppose the appearance of a djinni makes the instruments all
go haywire?"

"Then it will be a banner day for science." I laughed. "Magic is
something they've never studied properly. Now, come on. Open that
sardine tin."

Tom needed no further persuasion. He pried the key off the
bottom of the tin and fit the slit in the tin's lid into the hole in the

key, then cranked the whole apparatus back, twist after twist. His fingers fumbled a bit. First-time jitters.

At first, nothing happened. My stomach dropped. Was this the wrong sardine tin? I'd been known, more than once, to pull that trick upon others who were trying to steal Mermeros from me. But then, all doubts vanished. Billows of noxious yellow smoke mushroomed out from the opened tin, in wave after wave as if pumped by a bellows. The smoke gathered into a giant, twisting, cyclonic form that all but filled the cramped space of our little supply closet. Green glaring eyes shone out from a green face set in a green billiard-ball-shaped head, the whole of him emanating a ghostly green glow.

"What's this?" cried that familiar, malevolent voice. "A new master? Oh. It figures. It's *you* two."

"Hullo, Mermeros," I said. "Fancy meeting you here."

It was Mermeros, yet not as we knew him. His usual attire was a vest of fish scales, a shark's tooth about his neck, and a skirt of some sort belted at his waist and hiding his trailing, disappearing (nonexistent?) legs. When last I'd seen him, just this past Sunday evening, he'd worn, on a bit of a dare, a quite ludicrous purple suit of menswear. Now he lay reclined in the air, as if resting in an unseen easy chair, in a pair of mauve silk pajamas with an embroidered housecoat worn over them, a pair of half-moon spectacles perched on the tip of his nose, a long, pointed stocking cap, and a book dangling open in his hand. My book. The book I'd given him: *The Arabian Nights' Entertainments.*

"You're turning into quite the English gentleman, aren't you, Mermeros?" I said. "Good to see you."

He ignored me and peered appraisingly, up and down, at Tom. "So," he said with a wicked smile curling across his fishy lips. "The son has stolen the djinni from the father. Excellent. Did you slit his throat to do it?"

Tom's face paled. "Of course not!"

Mermeros's great fishy eyes narrowed. "All in good time. The day will come. I've seen it countless times before. There's nothing like jealously over my power to call forth a blood feud."

"I'm not going to hurt my dad," Tom said flatly. "Enough of that."

"Ignore him, Tom," I said. "He's just trying to rile you up."

Mermeros turned his watery eyes my way. "Have you come to steal me back from this weak-willed comrade of yours?"

Tom let out a howl of protest. "I'm not weak-willed!"

"You're ruthless and clever enough to do it," purred Mermeros. "You still have one more wish, you know."

Tom cast a doubtful look my way, as if the thought had made him pause, as if he believed the old liar. Honestly!

"Don't listen to him," I told Tom once more. "He likes to sow doubt and mistrust between us." To Mermeros, I said, "Cease and

desist, if you please. Tom is my friend, and I would never rob him."
(Which, it must be said, is a far cry from how our friendship began,
when either of us would rob the other blind in a heartbeat.)

"Why wouldn't you take from him what is rightfully yours?"
Mermeros closed his book and tucked it into the enormous pocket
of his djinni-sized housecoat, and his spectacles along with it. "Does
some strange tie bind you? Is he your betrothed?"

Twice in one day! And twice in one day, Tom's face flushed as
red as a tomato. He must be growing strangely sensitive to what
others said.

"Don't be revolting," I told Mermeros. "Tom, as you know
perfectly well from our many adventures together, is my friend."

His bushy brows furrowed. "Males and females do not
make *friends*."

"Of course they do!"

He peered haughtily at me. "I've been around for thousands of
years of human history, you shrimp of a girl, and I know of what
I speak." He sniffed disapprovingly. "Males and females are either
related, or romantically involved, or they avoid one another in a
proper spirit of mutual contempt."

"You're a backward old caveman," I told him. "A prehistoric
brute. These are modern times, and 'males and females,' as you so
crudely put it, get along as friends just fine."

"Name two."

Tom snickered. "Ignore him, Maeve," he said, parroting my words back at me. "He's just trying to rile you up. We don't have time for this."

"He's right," agreed Mermeros. "There's no time to waste. Make your wishes before you lose the chance, Fish Spawn."

"Meaning me?" Tom teased.

"Meaning both of you."

Tom glanced my way. "I don't think I'm quite ready to make my wish, Maeve," he said in a low voice. "Were you thinking I should?"

I shook my head. "No. I just thought perhaps you and Mermeros should get better acquainted."

Mermeros reopened his book and donned his glasses once more. "You bore me, Hatchling," he said. "This youth—practically still in his larval stage—is no stranger to me, nor I to him. We have nothing to discuss. If he lacks the spine to make a wish, then I don't wish to waste my morning making small talk with him. You see, I don't delude myself into thinking I'm his *friend*, unlike *some* young persons I could name." And with that, he buried his nose back in his book.

"Are you enjoying *The Arabian Nights' Entertainments*?" I inquired.

He looked up. "The authors got a great many details quite ludicrously wrong," he said thoughtfully. "But yes, I must say, I do find it diverting. This is my third reading of it. It almost takes me back to..." His voice trailed off.

"Back to what?" I prodded. "Back to growing up in Persia?" I considered. "Back to when you were human?"

He gazed off into space. "Human..." he mused. "It's been a long, long time."

"Some would say that makes you lucky," I pointed out. "To live forever and never die; to be free of the pains and illnesses that come with being mortal."

He scowled. "Those who would say it," he said, "speak from ignorance."

His tone made me pause. Was Mermeros unhappy? Of course, nothing about him had ever seemed particularly *happy*, but I'd always assumed he was content with his role. There must be some advantages to having such spectacular power.

"What do you miss, Mermeros?" I asked him. "About being human?"

He stopped and looked at me, peeling his spectacles off his face and polishing them thoughtfully with his mauve pajama cuffs. "The night sky," he said. "How the stars fill the dark void as far as the eye can see."

I certainly never expected an answer like that from Mermeros. It almost had a sort of poetry to it. The night sky? I suspected that if

I left human life behind, what I might miss most would be teatime sandwiches. Besides my friends and family, of course. Well, some of my family.

Mermeros returned his glasses to the bridge of his nose and peered through them as he turned a page in his book. "I ask you again," he said, "what do you want? You say you're not ready to cast a wish. Fine. But why, then, did you disturb me?" His eyes traveled slowly down the length of the page. "I've reached one of my favorite twists in the tale of Ali Baba and the Forty Thieves, and I'd be grateful for silence."

Intriguing. Mermeros the reader.

"I only wonder, Mermeros," I said. "Tom wants to use his wishes to help orphans. Perhaps you have some advice..." I let my voice trail off. "Oh, never mind."

"Advice about what?" the old fish demanded.

I demurred. "I wouldn't wish to trouble you."

"Liar," he said. "Advice about what?"

I shrugged. "Since you insist," I said, "I wondered if you had any advice on how best to use wishes to do the most good in the world."

"How precious." Mermeros returned to his reading. "The reprobate has become a philanthropist."

"None of your sarcasm, please," I told him sternly.

He snapped his book shut. "My apologies," he purred. "You wish me to impart to you some advice?"

Tom jumped up from his chair. "No! No wishing!"

Mermeros sulked and turned away.

Phew! That had been a close one. I should know better than to ever let my guard down around the old sea snake. That slippery old eel.

Tom panted as though he'd just avoided a deadly blow. Wishes are dangerous business, I've always said.

Mermeros floated back over to Tom. "Is what the girl says correct?" he asked Tom. "Do you truly wish to use your wishes to do some sort of pathetic good in the world? Or did the meddlesome girl make you say that?"

Tom found himself cornered, his back to the wall. "I won't answer," he said, "if it means you'll trick me into making a wish."

"I won't," said Mermeros. "I'm only asking."

Tom spoke slowly, using his words carefully. "I'm an orphan," he said. "Or, I suppose, I was. My dad only recently adopted me. Before that, I lived in a dismal orphanage. The only good thing about it was how much they ignored us." His voice took on a different tone. "But then my dad met me, and he ended up adopting me. I guess you could say I got very lucky."

Mermeros watched him through unblinking eyes.

"I haven't figured out yet how to do it," Tom said, "but I would like to use my wishes in a way that helps a lot of orphans. To find homes or families; or, if that's not possible, at least to help them make their way in life. Getting education. Learning to read, and write, and cipher. Learning skills that would help them with a job." He frowned. "But not like the horrid Mission Industrial School and Home for Working Boys."

Mermeros got a gleam in his eye. "You could wish for wealth beyond imagining," he told Tom. "With money, you can help as many orphans as you like."

Tom shook his head. "I don't think it's as simple as all that."

"You told me yourself, Mermeros," I reminded him, "that gold lust would consume and destroy the mortals who wield your power."

He sneered at me, then shrugged and returned to his book. "Suit yourself."

I reached into my bag and pulled out my copy of *Jane Eyre*. "Here, Mermeros," I told him. "I hadn't realized you'd be such a reader. Try *Jane Eyre*. It's a classic, or so they say."

He watched me narrowly. I could tell he was working hard not to show any excitement, but his eyes stayed riveted on the book.

"A book about a *girl*?" he sniffed. "Does she complain and irritate her elders as much as you do?"

"I couldn't say." I pulled it back. "If you'd rather not..."

He swooped forward and snatched it out of my hand. "I suppose," he said, as if he were doing me some great favor, "I have time to read even a book about an ill-tempered girl."

Tom, who had watched this whole exchange with a grin, pulled a book from his bag. "I have one for you, too," he told the djinni. "*Great Expectations*. By Charles Dickens."

Mermeros looked like a tot in a candy shop. A colossal green floating tot in mauve pajamas, but I digress. He seized the second book and flipped through its pages. It had a few illustrations, which made his eyes bulge right out of their sockets.

"You'll like this one," I told Mermeros. "It's about a boy. Hardly any ill-tempered females to be found." I stifled a laugh, thinking about Miss Havisham and Estella. They were nearly as ill-tempered as he was. Mermeros should love it.

A rattling came from the doorknob. "Maeve?" came Pip's voice— our Pip, not the boy Pip from Mr. Dickens's novel. "Tom? Are you in there?"

Tom rose and began cranking the key back on Mermeros's sardine tin.

"Just a moment," I called through the keyhole. "The door's a bit stuck." Which was technically true, as I'd stuck a chair underneath the knob.

Mermeros began to shrink, his form condensing and being tugged back into the tin. He clutched the novels to his barrel chest as though we might change our minds and snatch them back from him.

"This is a fine farewell," the djinni muttered. "Stuffing me away without so much as a by-your-leave."

I held up a warning finger to shush him. "We'll see you soon," I told him. "We'll bring more books next time."

And with that, he seemed satisfied. He slid all the way back into the sardine tin, which sealed itself shut with a *ping*, just as I pulled away the chair and opened the door.

CHAPTER
12

Pip stood there with her arms folded across her chest, eyeing us both with an arch expression. "How was reading time?" she inquired pointedly. "I suppose it must've been riveting, if you needed to bar the door. Why don't I see any books?"

Tom gulped.

"People kept stopping by," I said smoothly. "One, er, person seemed so envious of our books that we gave them to him."

Pip frowned. "You *gave* your books *away*," she said slowly. "To somebody who stopped by."

She waited for us to crumple and confess to—*yuck!*—romantic misbehavior.

"Precisely," I told her sweetly.

"I have my doubts," said Pip darkly. "Come on; we've got to get upstairs to the office where I work."

As we left the room and climbed the stairs, Alice, the peacemaker, tried to intervene on my behalf. "Maeve is a great one for loaning books," she said soothingly. "She gives them away like candy."

"To *physicists*?" demanded Pip Northam, interrogator. "They're not usually the literary type. Which ones did you meet?"

"Ern Rutherford," replied Tom, as coolly if he and Ern went way back to their good old boyhood days together.

Pip forgot herself and goggled at us. "You met Ernest *Rutherford*?" she hissed. She glanced left and right to make sure no one in the corridors could hear her. "He's only the golden boy of the department. J. J. Thomson's right-hand assistant! Everyone's so jealous of him. Especially the old Cambridge crowd that's studied here forever. He comes sweeping in from the colonies and turns the Cavendish on its head. Every project he touches turns to gold. You're saying, you loaned him your copy of *Jane Eyre*?"

"Not to him," I said. "One of the, er, persons who came afterward."

Alice gave me one of her *What are you up to now, Maeve?* looks.

"Maeve put in a good word to Ern for you, though," said Tom. "Told him you hoped to be a research assistant."

"Good *night*," moaned Pip. "What must he think of me now? Sending schoolchildren to recommend me to the top minds at the Cavendish!"

We reached the top of the stairs, and a big voice greeted us.

"Miss Northam," cried Ernest Rutherford, coming into view.

"Miss Maeve. Master Tom. I was just looking for you." He shook our hands again heartily. A great handshaker, was Ern Rutherford. "You brought another companion along?"

"This is Alice Bromley," I explained. "My dear friend."

"Charmed, Miss Alice." And another handshake.

"Mr. Rutherford," Pip gulped. "I hope I haven't kept you waiting."

"Not at all, not at all," cried he. "Miss Northam, I've left the longhand notes for my paper in the locked cabinet by the typewriter. I thought perhaps, while you typed, your young friends could join me in the laboratory this morning?"

Pip nodded with a strangled, helpless expression.

"I also understand," he went on, "that you're interested in physics yourself."

Pip drew herself up tall. "That's right. I am." She hesitated. "But I'm only in my second year of undergraduate studies."

Ern Rutherford brushed this aside. "That doesn't matter a trifle." He entered the office and we followed, watching as he unlocked the cabinet with a key from his pocket and handed the sheaf of papers to Pip. "When your typing is done, let's look at your schedule, shall we, and we'll see if we can find times for you to work alongside me and Mr. Thomson?"

"Thank you." Pip's cheeks flushed pink. "It would be my honor, sir."

Ern grinned. "No 'sir,' if you please," he said. "Not until I'm a great deal older. Going gray, perhaps. And don't thank me yet. There's a great deal of rigorous work to do."

"I'm ready for it," declared Pip.

He nodded. "I believe you." With that, he strode off down the corridor, whistling the familiar tune of "Onward, Christian Soldiers." He paused and looked back at us. "Well, you lot? Are you coming?"

Pip waved us forward. "Go," she said. Before I could leave, she rested a hand on my shoulder and gave it a squeeze. I turned to look at her face.

"Thanks, Maeve," she said.

I smiled. "Don't mention it."

CHAPTER
13

We followed Ern Rutherford down the corridor to a laboratory door and entered in. The room was empty, other than two young men hard at work at a table in a far corner on what looked like many pairs of bottles full of water, connected by tubes. They seemed deep into making measurements of some kind and took no notice of us. I gazed around in wonder at all the apparatus clustered upon tables, desks, and shelves. Glass tubes, cords, hoses, bits of metal, and miles of wire. Machines, pumps, valves, and I didn't know what else. I'd never been in a proper laboratory before. It made me think of a wizard's lair.

"Right, then," said Ern, rubbing his hands together. "Want to see something fun?"

He produced an ordinary light bulb from a drawer and held it up for our inspection. "Do you know how a light bulb lights up?" he inquired.

"Electricity," said Alice.

"Right," he said. "But *how* does electricity make this bulb light up?"

We looked closer.

"It travels along the wire," I said, hoping I didn't sound silly. "The electricity, I mean. When it does, that thin, little coiled part—"

"The filament," supplied Tom.

"That's it. The filament, it glows," I said. "It gets orange or yellow, and hot."

Ern Rutherford nodded. "Exactly," he said. He put the bulb back in its box and pointed to the same odd tubular contraption he had pulled from the cupboard in our little supply room. "Now, what would you say if I told you that I could shoot a beam of light across this tube with no wire or filament at all?"

"Light moving through the air?" asked Alice. "Like the northern lights in the Arctic sky?"

Ern's hands, which had been tinkering with his apparatus, froze. He turned slowly toward Alice. "The aurora borealis," he said softly. "I wonder..."

He seemed lost in a sort of dream for a moment or two, then snapped out of his reverie. "You, young lady, might be onto something there."

"Onto what?" I demanded.

"What are the, er, aurora boraxos?" asked Tom.

"*Borealis*," I told him. "Not hand soap. Beautiful bands of colored lights that dance in the northern sky."

"And the southern." Ern smiled. "Don't forget those of us from Down Under, though ours are called the aurora australis." He pushed the tube he'd be fiddling with toward us. "As I was saying, except for lights we sometimes see in the sky, we *usually* need wires to make electrical light."

He clipped wires to two metal prongs emerging from the tube in different places. The wires seemed attached to a battery of some sort.

"Ready?" he said. "Gather close so you can see."

We came nearer.

"This is called a cathode ray tube," he explained. "We've pumped all the air out of it, as best we can, though we can't do it perfectly." He pointed to a small disk of metal at the left end of the tube. "This part, here, is called the 'cathode.' It's attached to the negative end of the battery." He pointed toward another small metal disk suspended inside the tube, a few inches away, with a tiny hole in it. "This bit, here, is the anode, to which we're adding a positive charge."

I held only the littlest speck of knowledge about positive and negative charges, whatever they were, but I did know that electricity had a positive and negative aspect to it.

"Now, other than those two bits of metal and the wires that go from those bits to the outside of the tube," Ern said, "do you see any wires anywhere? Anything connecting the cathode and the anode to each other?"

We shook our heads. The tube looked otherwise quite empty. The far side of the glass seemed painted or coated with some whitish substance, but we could clearly see that nothing connected the cathode to the anode, nor to any other part of the tube.

"Now," he said, "watch." He flipped a switch on the battery. A wavering arc of green light appeared along the whitish face of the tube. The entire tube glowed green, but the arc of light seemed to sizzle brightly, like a slow, sustained bolt of lightning.

"Blimey," whispered Tom. "You did that with science?"

Ern Rutherford grinned. "Like magic, isn't it?"

Tom, Alice, and I looked at one another thoughtfully.

"Not exactly," I told him, "though I did like the shade of green."

Ern looked momentarily deflated. "Usually people are astonished by that," he said. "You three are hard to impress."

Tom ignored this. "So, the glass tube itself made the light?"

"The electricity connected to the cathode and the anode made the light," corrected Ern, "though the light you're seeing is just a side effect. The electricity created *cathode* rays. The real rays can't be directly seen. The rays cause the fluorescent paint on the side of the tube to light up. That's what you're actually seeing." He waved a hand through the air at the end of the tube. "Believe it or not, these cathode rays, when they hit the glass at the far end of the tube, produce another kind of ray. Roentgen's rays, or X-rays."

"I've heard of those," said Tom. "My dad has told me about them."

"Then you'll know this one," said Ern with excitement. "What would happen if I held my hand still here"—he held his hand upright just past the far end of the tube—"and placed a photographic plate behind it?"

Tom's eyes grew wide. "The X-rays would make *a photograph of the bones in your hand.*"

Alice shook her head. "I don't believe it."

"It's true," said Tom excitedly. "I saw a picture of it in a magazine."

Ern strode over to a drawer and pulled it open. He pulled out a folded magazine and thrust its cover image at us. The shadowy image of a ghost-hand filled the page, with flesh dimly showing where hand and wrist flesh ought to be. In sharp detail inside the ghost-hand lay all the hand's bones, and, overtop the ring-man finger, a metal ring.

We stared at the image. It was horrible and wonderful, both together. Chilling and astonishing. It reminded me of a time, months before, when the three of us took a magical journey to Persia and opened the sarcophagus containing the bones and rings of Mermeros's father, the sorcerer king. This photograph, if one can imagine it, was even more chilling. At least the sorcerer king was centuries dead. The bones in the photograph were from a living hand.

"These X-rays, and the effects they produce on gases, are what I'm studying now," Ern said. "We've discovered that when you point X-rays at gases in a tube, they produce *ions*—atoms containing electric charge—and the jolly little buggers allow the gas in the tube to carry electric current. Just as if it were a wire, and not a gas."

I paused to digest what he'd just said. "X-rays turn gases into ... things that conduct electricity?"

Ern nodded eagerly. "Amazing, isn't it?"

"Amazing" wasn't the word I would've chosen. "That sounds dreadful," I said. "If electric current traveled through the air, wouldn't we all get zapped and burned?"

Ern let out a booming laugh. "Not quite," he said. "To produce the effect, we have to isolate small quantities of gases in tubes and focus X-rays quite carefully. I think you're safe."

"So you use a cathode ray tube like a gun," said Tom, "and point its scary X-rays at another tube, full of gas..."

"And measure the strength of the electricity produced, using this electrometer," finished Ern.

Alice's brow furrowed. "But why?" she asked. "If X-rayed gases conduct electricity, or if they don't, so what?"

"An excellent question," cried Ern. "With our knowledge of how conductive gases can become, we were actually able to help with some very important research, just recently."

A laugh sounded from behind us. I looked over to see that the two young men had left the table where they'd been working and come over to investigate. "What are you on about now, Rutherford?" said one in a thick Irish accent. "Recruiting new assistants? Or just boasting?"

The other joined in his laughter. "He's looking to put us out of our jobs." This second young man's Scottish accent reminded me of Mr. Abernathy's.

Ern Rutherford grinned. "Pardon me, gentlemen," he said good-naturedly. "These are my new friends, Maeve, Alice, and Tom." He gestured to his comrades. "Allow me to introduce John McClelland."

The Irishman shook our hands warmly.

"And C. T. R. Wilson."

The Scotsman did the same.

"Tell me, now," said C. T. R., "does anything this big, booming New Zealander's been babbling at you about make a bit of sense to you?"

Tom, Alice, and I exchanged glances.

"Not really," admitted Tom, "but I wish it did."

C. T. R. Wilson laughed. "So do we, laddie," he said. "So do we."

John McClelland elbowed him. "You'll have the kiddies here thinking we're imbeciles."

"That's already been proven through repeated experiments," said Rutherford, and the other two laughed.

"Kiddies?" I said. "You're not that much older than we are."

John bowed. "I stand corrected," he said. "C. T. R., here, has only just started shaving."

He received a cuff in the shoulder for this from his Scottish friend. "Have not!"

I liked these three fellows right away.

"Do you mean to say, Mr. McClelland," I ventured, "that you *don't* understand what Ern—I mean, Mr. Rutherford—is talking about?"

"Please, call me John," he said. "Oh, we understand *him* well enough," he said. "But the truth is, we're all just scratching the surface of forces and phenomena none of us understands as well as we'd like to."

"It's an exciting time in science," added C. T. R. Wilson. "We're on the brink of great breakthroughs. Unlocking the atom will explain all of nature to us. Absolutely everything! From clouds and thunderstorms, to the electricity that powers the world, to the treacle tart you ate for lunch. It's like a mad race, all over the world, to see who'll find the big answers first. Right now, there are far more questions than answers."

"Where'd you get a treacle tart?" John McClelland found an apple in his pocket and took a bite, then spoke between chews. "The Germans think they'll beat us."

Ernest Rutherford nodded. "Don't forget the French."

"And the cocky Americans," added C. T. R.

"Why don't you all work together?" asked Alice. "Why does it have to be a competition?"

The three researchers exchanged a laugh. "Because we all desperately need promotions," said Ern, "to keep bread on the table and roofs over our heads. If we say that our discoveries come from international cooperation—"

"Which, in fact, they do—" interjected C. T. R..

"Then who'll get the next research job or teaching post that comes available?" asked Ern. "The globe?"

There came a knock at the door. We looked over to see Pip standing in the doorway, watching us and holding a sheet of paper in her hand.

"Come in, come in," bellowed Ern, loud enough to raise the dead.

Pip entered the room. "I'm sorry to interrupt," said she, "but I had a question about your notes. About something you'd written." She handed the paper to Ern Rutherford and pointed at a phrase. "I can't tell, is that 'sulfate' or 'sulfide'?"

"It's his chicken-scratch handwriting," C. T. R. told us in a mock whisper.

"I'll bet mine's worse," said Tom.

Ern peered at the scribbled chemical formula and scratched his scalp. "Well, I'll be jiggered," said he. "That should say 'sulfate,' but it seems I'd written 'sulfide.'"

Pip rocked back and forth on her heels. Her expression was that of one trying to hide a smile of triumph, and failing.

"You knew that, didn't you," Ern told Pip. "It wasn't my handwriting. It was my *error* that got your attention." He shook her hand heartily. "Miss Northam, I'm very impressed and much obliged to you."

She looked down at her boots, then back up and smiled. "Thank you, Mr. Rutherford."

"Please," cried he, "call me Ern."

On her way out the door, Pip cast a glance my way. It needed no interpretation. Its meaning was clear. *Behave yourselves.* I nodded and waved her away.

"Now," said Ern, "where were we?"

"I think, Rutherford," said C. T. R., "you'll need to start with a bit of a lesson first before you get these young people taking notes on electrometer readings and such."

Ern Rutherford pulled up a chair and sat on it backward, straddling the seat.

"Right," he said. "What do you lot know about atoms? Do you know what they are?"

Alice, Tom, and I looked at one another to see who wanted to go first. No one else did, so I chimed in.

"Little bits of stuff," I ventured. "The smallest bits that exist. Hard little indestructible bits of—copper, or iron, or sulfur. Of matter."

"Right you are," declared Ern. "And also wrong."

This caught me off guard. "Well, which is it?" I said. "Right or wrong?"

"You're right," Ern said, "that atoms are the smallest bits of any pure substance. As you say, copper, iron, and so on. Even the gases, like hydrogen and oxygen, are made of atoms. All the stuff we see, feel, touch, and weigh is made of matter, and all matter is made of atoms. Atoms are the smallest bits of what makes a substance itself." He picked up a short rectangular bar of metal. "This is aluminum." He tapped it on either side. "This bar is *all* aluminum." He took a knife from his pocket and pared off a tiny curl of the silver-colored metal, then held it out in his hand. "This is all aluminum, too."

He beckoned me over and held out the tiny curled sliver of metal to me, then handed me a magnifying glass. Looking at it under the glass, I saw that it wasn't anything near so smooth as it appeared at first glance but had all sorts of texture and jagged edges. I didn't know something so small could be so intricate.

"Now tell me," said Ern. "If we cut that little sliver in half, would it still be aluminum?"

"Of course," I said.

"And if we could get tiny knives and cut it in half again, and again, and again?"

I paused to consider. "Yes," I said. "Though it would get to a powder at some point."

"So it would," he said. "And if we still could cut those bits of powder again, and again, and again—if we had minuscule knives and tiny little fingers; let's say, tiny little elves or fairies could do it for us—would it keep on being aluminum, all the way down, forever?"

I paused to consider. "Yes," I said slowly. "Until you got to a piece that was two atoms thick. When you cut that in half, you'd be left with one atom each. After that, you could cut no more."

"Aha," cried Ern. "That's where things get very, very interesting."

"Meaning," laughed C. T. R., "here's where we start making things up."

"Theorizing," said Tom. "Hypothesizing."

"Spoken like a true scientist," said Ern. "There's room for you at the Cavendish someday."

John McClelland chimed in. "By using our imaginations," he said, "and some mathematics, and a bit of Sherlock-style detective work, and reasoning"—here he held up the magnifying glass before his eyes—"we form hypotheses. Ideas about why things are the way they are and behave the way they behave. We test the ideas here, in the laboratories."

"Back to our aluminum," said Ern. "You're right, Maeve, that we could cut no more and have it *remain aluminum*." He tapped the side of his forehead. "The question is, if you cut an aluminum atom, do you get anything at all? Is an atom cuttable into something that, perhaps, is no longer aluminum, but is still *something*?"

Alice frowned. "The word 'atom' itself means uncut," she said. "Indivisible."

"We have a scholar of languages," cried McClelland. "She knows her Latin and Greek."

"Yes, but don't let words fool you," said Ern. "Nature is in charge. Not human words."

"But if you cut the uncuttable," I said, "wouldn't you get...I don't know...an explosion? A puff of smoke?"

Ern, C. T. R., and John exchanged sober glances.

"I hope not," said Ern. "I hope not an explosion. It does seem possible. And if so, some fool in a laboratory might blow up the world one day."

The room seemed to grow cold.

"Don't listen to Gloom and Doom Rutherford," said C. T. R. Wilson. "Science has gotten along this far at the Cavendish without blowing up much more than a laboratory room or two."

I smiled. "You're joking, right?" I said. "About blowing up laboratory rooms?"

John McClelland coughed and looked aside.

"I wish we were, lassie," said C. T. R. Wilson. "Things do get a bit singed around here, now and again."

"Things and people," added John.

"Blimey," said Tom. "I wouldn't mind going to college if I got to blow things up."

C. T. R. grinned. "You have a bright future in research." He jabbed a thumb in the direction of Ern Rutherford. "The important thing, and what Mr. Humble over here is trying to get at, is that right here at the Cavendish, our director, a Mr. J. J. Thomson, has recently, with a bit of help from yours truly—the three of us, and a few others—demonstrated that there *are* particles smaller than atoms."

"Using these very same cathode ray tubes I've been showing you," added Ern proudly.

"Or so we believe," added John McClelland. "We're pretty certain. The data, and the mathematics, all point to that conclusion."

"Corpuscles," said Rutherford. "Little bits much, much smaller than the smallest known atom, which is hydrogen. And carrying a negative electric charge."

"That's the part we proved for sure at the Cavendish," added John proudly. "The Germans couldn't get that far with their inferior vacuum tubes."

"But they would have eventually," argued Rutherford. "Our real

breakthrough was the charge-to-mass ratio, showing that these particles must be very lightweight."

"It's quite taken the world by storm," said C. T. R. "It's the biggest
thing since Roentgen's X-rays. A particle much, much smaller than
the smallest-known atom."

"You mean, you're now a famous scientist?" demanded Tom.

"Heavens, no," said Ern with a smile, "though I plan to be someday."

"Mr. Humble," teased C. T. R.

"Mr. Thomson believes all matter is made up of these tiny
corpuscles," said McClelland. "He thinks atoms are just made up of
lots and lots of corpuscles."

"Do you believe that?" I asked.

Ern Rutherford stroked his mustache. "It's too soon to tell," he
said. "We have a lot more research to do to understand the atom
better." He nodded to his friends. "But we'll get there, won't we?"
He smiled at us. "We'll need more researchers. Bright young minds
like yours."

The door to the laboratory opened again, but this time Pip didn't
knock. She looked pale, almost green about the gills.

"Mr. Rutherford," she said breathlessly.

"Come in, come in," said he, "but do call me Ern."

"I don't understand how this could have happened, but—" Pip
paused as though trying to gather her words, then swallowed hard. "I

had finished your paper. I had it all stacked on my desk, along with your original notes."

"Wonderful," said Ern. "You made excellent time."

Pip shook her head in desperation. "I'm afraid you don't understand," she said. "When it was all done, I stepped out for just a moment, just down the hall to fetch a drink of water, and when I'd returned—not even thirty seconds later, I could swear it!—all the papers were gone."

The next ten minutes or so were awful. There was nothing Alice, Tom, or I could do but watch as Ern and Pip hurried back down to the office where she'd been typing and tore it apart searching for the mislaid papers. They lifted the typewriter and shifted every pile of books and folders. They searched rubbish bins and file drawers. They looked inside and underneath cabinets, all to no avail.

Ern's cheerful manner had gone rather quiet. Whatever this paper contained, it was evidently very important. And it was gone.

"You don't have another copy of it, do you?" Alice ventured to ask.

He shook his head distractedly. "The draft contained all the data I'd collected," he said. "Both the data and the mathematic equations and conclusions existed solely in the notes that I'd clipped to my draft." He scratched his head. "I guess that was daft of me. But it's why I kept it in the locked cabinet."

Pip looked like one about to be sick. "I am so sorry," she said. "I–I didn't think anyone would even know what I was working on, much less have any reason to take it."

"Could someone have made a genuine mistake?" I asked. "Maybe they saw the paper and thought it was one of their own?"

Pip sank into a chair. "I suppose it's possible," she said without conviction. "But it had Mr. Rutherford's name in capital letters right across the front."

Ernest Rutherford's expression was grave. He looked like someone who dreaded what they were about to say.

"Miss Northam," he said, "might I ask permission to look through your own personal bag?"

"Of course," Pip said quickly. She snatched the bag from its place near the door and handed it to Ern willingly—almost too willingly—but her cheeks flamed red in mortification. To be suspected of taking the paper must have stung her pride to no end.

Wordlessly, Ern pulled a sheet of paper from her bag and held it up for our inspection. "Some Preliminary Findings on Conductivity of Gases Ionized by X-Rays," he read aloud. "By Ernest Rutherford, the Cavendish Laboratory."

The color faded from Pip's cheeks. "That's not possible," she whispered. "I haven't touched my bag since arriving here. I would *never*, never take your work."

Ern said nothing. He looked back and forth from the paper to Pip's stricken face.

"Mr. Rutherford," she pleaded, "I assure you, on my honor, that I did not put that there."

I knew this was something I should stay out of, but I couldn't bear it. "Is the rest of the paper in the bag?"

Ern held the bag open for us to see. It held a few smaller books and notebooks and a pencil case, but nothing that could hide a typed scholarly document.

"If you think Pip took it," I asked, "then why would she only have one page of it?"

The room was silent.

"If I used the bag as a means of handing off the paper to an accomplice," Pip explained in a hollow voice, "the cover page could have been inadvertently left behind."

"Or," I said, "someone could have put the page there on purpose to throw suspicion on you."

Pip hadn't the heart to take up this argument in her own defense. "I'm afraid that doesn't seem very likely."

Ern Rutherford cleared his throat. "It was good of you to let me know right away that the papers had gone missing," he said carefully. "Under the circumstances, I fear..."

"Of course," Pip said quickly. "I'll go."

Ern nodded, though his face was grim. He slid a notepad and pencil in her direction. "Would you be so good as to write your address here?" he asked. "In case anyone wishes to contact you with further questions?"

Pip scrawled her name and address at Girton College on the notepad. She collected her things and passed silently out of the room.

We rose to follow her. I wanted to say something to Ern Rutherford in parting—to thank him for the laboratory lessons, to tell him there must be some mistake—but I couldn't find the words. He wasn't watching us leave anyway. He sat behind the desk, running his hand through his hair, his head hanging down, his gaze on the desk blotter.

Silently, we left, and followed Pip down the stairs and out the Cavendish Laboratory's main front door.

P ip shaded her eyes against the sunlight or, perhaps, from our view. She stood in the middle of Free School Lane as if she wasn't sure where to go next, with bicycles weaving around her on either side. All over the college, peals of church bells in discordant tones began chiming the noon hour, but she didn't seem to hear them at all.

I felt awful for her. Of all the dreadful days to be tasked with shepherding young visitors around the campus, it was just her luck that today would be the day she lost her new job—the new job that meant so much to her future plans and hopes—while needing to play host to the three of us.

A bit of commotion caught my attention at the corner of Pembroke and Free School Lane. Three young ladies stood holding placards on poles high above their heads, placards that read, "DEGREES FOR WOMEN." They were surrounded by at least a dozen university students, undergraduates, I would guess, from

their robes, and, of course, all of them young men, loudly jeering
at and heckling the women students. One of them—I'm ashamed
to say it was likely a cricketer, based on his throwing form—took
a large tomato from a grocer's bag and hurled it straight at one of
the placards. It smashed on the sign right in the middle, shattering
against its supporting pole. A perfect shot, frankly. Wet tomato pulp
rained all down the sign and onto the hair and blouse of its bearer.
The other young men cheered.

I clenched my fists and took a step toward the fracas, ready to
bowl my way into those brutes myself, but Alice seized my wrist and
pulled me back.

"Leave it, Maeve," she said gently. "They far outnumber you, and
they're young and strong. There's nothing you can do. Not here."

That wouldn't be enough to stop me, but Alice continued.

"We won't do any favors for Pip," she said, "or for Girton, if we
cause a scene and get ourselves into trouble,"

"They're the ones causing the scene." But she was right. I left off
trying to charge into battle.

I turned back to see Pip had been watching the whole exchange
with an expression I couldn't read.

"Pip?" I asked her. "All you all right?"

She didn't turn to look at me, but kept her gaze on the group at
the corner.

"I need my scholarship if I'm to stay here," she said in a low voice. It felt as though she was speaking more to herself than to us. "I need this education."

I waited, unsure of what she meant.

"My family needs me to get it," she continued. "To secure a proper job and help my brothers and sisters get a leg up, too. To get them into schools and jobs. To make connections my parents can't ever make." Her voice began to choke with emotion, though she fought to hold it off. "They're factory workers, did you know that?"

We shook our heads. I remembered something Miss Welsh had said about Pip coming from Manchester, but it hadn't registered at the time.

"I need a *degree*," she continued, "but those pigs"—here she pointed at the little mob of male students—"will make sure I don't get one. Did you know," she went on, "they've lined up extra trains to bring in alumni from all over Britain, just so they can cast their votes *against* Cambridge granting degrees to women?" She shook her head. "They're that determined to keep us in our place."

I tried to think of something comforting to say. "They're not all that way," I said. "Ern Rutherford believes women should receive degrees. They did at his old college in New Zealand."

She let out a bitter laugh. "Ernest Rutherford is an exception," she said. "But what of it? He's the reason I'll be chucked out of here."

Her face fell. "*How* could that title page have ended up in my bag? How? Who would be so cruel to me as that?"

Alice spoke gently. "Is there any way you might have placed it there by mistake?"

Pip shook her head. "I never touched the bag after I got there."

"I don't understand," said Tom, "how Ern Rutherford is the reason you'll be chucked out."

Pip sighed and tore herself away from the spot where she'd been rooted to the pavement. She started walking up Free School Lane, away from the sorry scene of picketers and their tormentors. "When word reaches Girton that I've been dismissed from my post under suspicion of losing or, worse, stealing original research," she said, "and you can be sure Miss Welsh will be notified, I'll lose my scholarship. It's based on both my grades and my 'sterling character.'"

"That can't be so," I protested. "Miss Welsh thinks very highly of you. She'll believe you when you tell her you didn't do it."

"Will she?" asked Pip. "Protecting the respectability of Girton College is her top concern. She can't abide any of us girls getting into trouble." She shook her head dejectedly. "Even if she might believe me, no one at the Cavendish ever will. And that's where I had hoped to study. My name is worthless there now."

We had reached the end of Free School Lane. Tom, who'd been looking about intently, now spoke.

"Miss North—er, Pip," he said. "We're quite near the hotel where my dad and I, and Alice's grandfather, are staying."

He paused. "I wonder if you'd like a bit of time to yourself?"

I'm sure Pip didn't mean to look relieved.

Tom spoke quietly. "What if Alice, Maeve, and I stopped at the hotel and had some lunch," he said, "and, er, amused ourselves for a while, and then we met up with you later?"

I took a second look at Tom. What a thoughtful, considerate suggestion. Every now and then the lad surprises me.

Pip took a deep breath. "I–I do have a class soon."

Alice rested a hand on Pip's arm. "A bit of lunch would do you good, too."

Pip nodded absently. "Are you sure I'm not faulting at my post? I told your grandmother I'd look out for you."

"Let's all go to the hotel," I suggested. "You can see us deposited in the care of Tom's dad and know that you've managed your duties properly."

"After my next class, I'm done for the afternoon," she said. "I could meet you here, and we can collect our bikes and all ride back to Girton together."

"Excellent," said Alice. "Let's do that."

"The Lion Hotel, you said?" inquired Pip. "Follow me."

She turned to the right and strode off to the end of that short street, took a left turn by the town hall, and then her first right onto Petty Cury. A sign with a magnificent red lion carved into its faded oak boards dangled above the door of the Lion Hotel.

"There he is," cried Tom, pointing to Mr. Poindexter, who stood on the front landing, talking to someone. "There's my dad."

"I recognize him," said Pip. "All right, then. It seems you're in good hands. Suppose I come back and collect you here in, say, two hours?"

"Two o'clock on the nose," I told her. "We'll be here. And Pip?"

She turned back toward me. "Yes?"

"I'm sure the situation at the Cavendish will work itself out," I told her. "You'll still be able to study there."

Pip's smile was sad. "That would be nice," she said. "I hope you're right." Then she turned heel and disappeared into the press of people and bicycles clogging the street.

We watched her leave, then made our way toward the Lion Hotel. I hoped that a bit of lunch and time to clear her head might cheer her up.

"Let's surprise my dad," whispered Tom. We snuck up behind him, careful not to let ourselves be seen. He was engaged in conversation with a stout, middle-aged woman wearing a black dress and cap. Both of them seemed on edge, somehow, and I wondered if this little surprise of Tom's might be a mistake.

But Tom went ahead with it. He tapped his father on the shoulder and cried "Boo!" when Mr. Poindexter turned around.

Mr. Poindexter jumped as if he'd seen a ghost. It would've been a most gratifying surprise prank, but the look on his face stopped me in my tracks.

"Got you!" cried Tom.

In response, Mr. Poindexter pulled Tom toward him and hugged him fiercely. "Thank God you're all right."

Tom pulled away from him. "Why wouldn't I be, Dad?" he said. "What's the matter?"

Mr. Poindexter's expression was hard to read. Grim, grief-stricken, baffled, maybe even on the brink of tears. "Our hotel room was burgled this morning."

We gasped.

"Another burglar?" cried Alice. "When will it stop?"

"*Another*?" demanded the stout woman. "You've been burgled before? Recently?"

We turned and got our first proper look at her. Her clothing was all a widow's black, complete with black lace trimming around her ruffled cap. Her steel-gray hair was pulled back in a tight bun, as though hair was something she couldn't abide. The only bit of color about her was her tomato-red face, and her pale blue eyes glaring at us.

"What have you done?" she cried. "Brought a plague of crime to my hotel? I'll thank you not to invite a scandal to my very door!"

Alice stepped back in horror at what she'd inadvertently done, but Mr. Poindexter didn't seem to notice the landlady's scolding.

"Alice's grandfather's room was robbed as well," Mr. Poindexter continued. "Both our rooms were raided. Torn apart like someone was searching for a diamond in a bed of straw."

"Oh, no," Alice moaned. "How dreadful!"

My mind spun. I knew this wasn't my fault, and yet, I felt responsible. I'd ignored the warnings. I hadn't paid enough attention to the serious danger we were in. I suppose, since my loved ones were safe, and appropriate measures, I thought, had been taken, I hadn't let yesterday's burglaries worry me much. I'd let college and cricket and Mermeros and the Cavendish occupy my mind.

The spinning gears in my brain began to click into place. Robbed at Grosvenor Square. Robbed on a cab ride back to the Oddity Shop. Robbed on the trains heading north—ours, and Mr. Abernathy's. Robbed in a Cambridge hotel. If there was any possibility, yesterday, of believing—hoping—this was all just a string of coincidences, that was over now. Someone was desperate to lay hold on what we had.

Of course they were. We had a magical djinni of limitless power. We already knew, all too well, what that did to people.

"When you say 'everything,' Mr. Poindexter—" I began.

His sorrowing gaze met mine. He leaned forward and whispered so only the three of us could hear. "The tin is stolen," he told us. "Mermeros is gone."

CHAPTER

16

Tom pulled away from our little huddle and stared wide-eyed at me. I knew what he was thinking. His dad didn't know he'd stolen Mermeros, and now his father believed Mermeros was gone from them forever.

But he wasn't. He was safe in Tom's jacket pocket.

"A scandal!" the stout landlady was saying. "I scrimped and saved to buy this hotel—and me, a widow!—and I've run a highly respectable establishment for years. And here you come, bringing thieves in your wake!"

I needed to draw that irksome lady away from Mr. Poindexter. He had enough to worry about without her.

"How do I know you're not one of them?" she sputtered. "How do I know you're not part of a gang of thieves?"

I saw my opening. "Like Ali Baba?"

She blinked. "How's that?"

"A gang of thieves," I said, "like Ali Baba and his Forty Thieves?"

The landlady thrust her nose up high in the air. "I'm sure I haven't the faintest notion of what you're talking about, Miss Impertinence."

"Maeve Merritt," I told her, holding out a hand. "Pleased to meet you."

She regarded me as though I had three heads. "Alison Moyes," she said in reply, "though under the circumstances, I'm not sure I can return the compliment."

"Fair enough."

She seemed to decide I was the one worth complaining to, perhaps because I bothered speaking to her at all. "See here," she said. "Your party can't just waltz in here and attract the criminal element."

I gave her my most severe look. "Your hotel can't be so lax about security, allowing rooms to be burgled as easy as pie."

Her eyes bulged. "I'll have you know," she said, "I could replace you guests in a heartbeat. I've had to turn away a dozen inquiries just this morning."

I caught myself just before *Then do it* escaped my lips. The last thing Mr. Poindexter and the Bromleys needed was to be evicted.

Mrs. Moyes seemed to realize, suddenly, that she was spending her noon hour arguing with a young teenage girl. She threw up her hands in a huff and sailed back inside her highly respectable establishment.

I turned back to where Tom stood, speaking earnestly to his father, with Alice looking on, gravely worried.

Mr. Poindexter didn't look well. His face was ashen. He stared off into the distance with unseeing eyes. He twitched at loud noises coming from the street. It had only been a couple of days, I reminded myself, since his horrible ordeal of being kidnapped by that rotten professor. He had seemed mended when he left the Bromleys' London home, but perhaps the shock of this latest burglary was much too much for him. The last straw. The breaking point.

"We'll move far away." Mr. Poindexter began mumbling to himself. "We'll live off the land in the wilds of northern Canada. Chop wood. Catch fish. No one will ever come looking for us there. No one will rob my son right out of the carriage he's in. And point a gun at him. And break into his room." He began to choke up. "And kidnap his father."

"We're safe, Dad," Tom told him. "You're safe, and I am safe. We're here together. Maeve and Alice are here. Everyone is fine."

His father shook his head. "We're *not* safe," he protested. "We're *not* fine. Wherever we go, they'll find us."

Alice and I exchanged a look. This state of mind was serious. Terribly so. Far worse than stolen belongings. Chopping wood and catching fish?

Then again, was he wrong?

If it really was Cousin Eugene, I thought, I doubted he had the intelligence to track Tom and his father down in the Yukon wilderness, or the Northwest Territories, or wherever it might be. But whoever his accomplices were, they might be cunning and determined enough. Or anyone else who might learn about Mermeros in the future. Enough people had already learned about him in the past. Where magic was concerned, people became ruthless. Ruthless and reckless.

"Come inside and take some food, Dad," Tom said in a low voice. "Come lie down. Some rest would do you good."

"Yes, do, Mr. Poindexter," urged Alice. "This must have come as quite a shock."

They each took him by the arm and steered him indoors. He allowed himself, reluctantly, to be led.

I followed after, blinking in the dim light of the dark oak-paneled hotel. It was empty, as far as I could see, mostly draped in shadow save for the few squares of brilliance where window light from the street poured in. Warm, beefy smells mingled with woodsmoke wafted from the kitchen. It had more of the feel of a public house and tavern than an elegant hotel. Homey. Comforting. I hoped it would do Mr. Poindexter some good.

"Won't you sit down at a table," Alice asked Mr. Poindexter, "here in the restaurant, and we'll get you some food? Some soup?"

Mr. Poindexter shook his head. "I don't want food. I think...I think perhaps I'd better lie down after all."

"I'll take you to the room," said Tom. "Here. Lean on me. I've got you."

They hobbled off together, with Mr. Poindexter's broad arm resting on Tom's shoulder, the father's bald head leaning toward the son's bright-orange hair.

"The poor man," whispered Alice. "He's lucky to have Tom."

"Tom's lucky to have him," I said. "I remind myself of that so I don't feel I've ruined both their lives by introducing them to Mermeros and magic." I looked around to make sure no one had heard me. There seemed to be no one else around, except Mrs. Moyes, far off in the kitchen, scolding a dishwasher.

"Mermeros and magic brought Tommy and his dad together," Alice said, not for the first time.

I nodded. "I only pray that they won't also tear them apart."

She looked at me curiously. "How can they," she said, "if Mermeros is gone now?"

I had no answer for that. Should I tell her that Mermeros wasn't gone? But Tom hadn't told Alice that bit of secret information. Only me. Was it my place to tell her?

"You don't seem to be as bothered by it as I would have thought you'd be," she said.

I took a deep breath. "I'm just glad everyone is all right."

She nodded earnestly. "We've got to do something, Maeve," she said. "We're under attack, all of us. It feels as though something dreadful is about to happen."

"Hasn't it happened already?" I asked.

She bit her lip. "I'm afraid not," she admitted, "and that's what scares me."

I had nothing to say to that. I certainly couldn't say she was imagining things or worrying too much.

Mr. Bromley entered the hotel common room from the street door. Alice saw him first and ran to greet her grandfather.

"Papa!" she cried. "Have you heard?"

He embraced her. "How did you get here?"

"Pip brought us," she told him. "We thought we'd visit you for lunch. We had no idea..."

Her voice trailed off. Mr. Bromley looked her over gravely, as if searching for any sign of injury.

"I'm fine, Papa," she told him. "I wasn't even here."

"I know." He held her close to his heart. "Oh, my dear girl. What a terrible business this is." He stroked her hair. "It must have happened while we were visiting you and your grandmother this morning at Girton. We took our time coming back, only to discover the fiends had been at their devilish work while we were away."

We shook our heads. What else was there to say?

"I called Inspector Wallace again, as soon as we discovered the burglary," Mr. Bromley continued. "He was planning to come meet us tomorrow, after he'd sorted out some business at his offices at Scotland Yard, but he's rearranged his schedule to come join us here this afternoon. I expect him presently."

"Scotland Yard!" came the indignant voice of Mrs. Moyes, from behind the front counter. "I don't need them dragging the good name of the Lion Hotel in the mud."

Mr. Bromley was gracious and didn't retaliate and torment her as I would've done. "Our friend, the inspector, is the soul of discretion," he said. "He will be quiet and tactful in making his inquiries. Might I reserve a room for him?"

The landlady looked offended by this question. "No, you may not," she said. "I'm booked full, with a waiting list as long as my arm."

Alice beckoned us over to a table, where we all sat.

"Papa," she said, "why don't you stay at Girton College, with Grandmama? Then Mr. Wallace can have your room."

Her grandfather nodded. "A good idea. I'll do just that."

She leaned closer to whisper, given the sharp hearing of the landlady. "Does Grandmama know? About this new burglary?"

He shook his head. "Not yet," he said. "I plan to tell her when I return there this afternoon. It will be better for her to hear it from me, in person. I'm afraid the strain of this will be hard on her."

"It's been hard on Mr. Poindexter," Alice said. "He doesn't look well. He's in his room, resting."

Mr. Bromley sighed. "How did we ever get tangled up in all this dreadful business?"

Too late, he realized his mistake.

I was how.

He looked over at me. His expression melted.

"My dear Maeve," he said warmly, "you must know, you are family to us. We couldn't imagine our home, nor our lives, without you."

I swallowed down the lump in my throat. "Thank you, sir," I told him. "I feel the same way. I'm most grateful to you, for everything."

He patted my hand. "No one blames you at all," he said warmly. "We all know that none of this is your fault."

An awkward silence fell over our little table. Other hotel guests began to appear in the common room, taking seats at other tables.

"Why don't I order us some lunch?" cried Mr. Bromley, jumping up from the table as though he couldn't get away fast enough. He hurried over to the counter and hailed Mrs. Moyes.

Alice watched me with eyes full of concern.

"He means it, Maeve," she said warmly. "My grandparents love you."

I didn't know how to look at her. "I love them, too," I said. "But I keep bringing danger and disaster upon them, don't I?" I swallowed down the rising tide of sadness. "On everyone I love. Again, and again, and again."

"It's not your fault," Alice protested.

"That's debatable," I said. "But fault or no, it's still my curse."

CHAPTER

17

om came down the stairs from his father's hotel room and
rejoined us in the common room just as Mrs. Moyes brought
over a pot of tea and a tray of brown crockery bowls of beef
stew. Its dark, savory fragrance made me begin to forgive her, just a
bit, for being so unpleasant.

"Just in time, young Thomas," said Mr. Bromley cheerfully. "Pull
up a chair."

Tom slid out of his jacket, sat down eagerly, and grabbed a spoon.

Mr. Bromley smiled. "I thought we'd find a need for a fourth
bowl. Can we send some up to your father, too?"

Tom shook his head. "He's sleeping."

"Sleep will do him good," Mr. Bromley declared.

I tried to make eye contact with Tom, but he avoided my gaze.
I wanted very much to know if Tom had told his father he still had
Mermeros to ease his mind.

Finally I kicked his shin under the table.

"Ouch!" cried Mr. Bromley.

My cheeks burned. "I'm sorry, Mr. Bromley," I told him. "I must've just, er, had a spasm."

He bent over and rubbed his shin. "That was a very forceful spasm," he said ruefully, then held up a hand with a laugh when I tried to apologize still more.

I glared at Tom. Finally he returned my gaze with a silent *What?*

Speaking silently is quite a nightmare to describe, but I managed, I believe, with eyebrows and half-mouthed words, to convey my meaning to Tom: *Did you tell your dad?*

He knew what I was asking. I'd bet my eye teeth. But he ignored me and returned to his food.

Alice, who never missed a thing, saw me trying to get his attention and wondered silently at me. I shook my head slightly. Explanations, if there were to be any, would have to wait.

We dug into the food, but hadn't gotten far when a messenger boy entered the hotel and bawled out, "Telegram for a Mr. Theodore Bromley!"

Mrs. Moyes came swishing over, brandishing a rolled-up newspaper in the air as though the delivery boy were a pesky horsefly.

"How many times have I told you," she growled, "this ain't Paddington Station! This here's a *genteel* establishment. My guests are dining, and you can't just come in here and holler at 'em!"

Mr. Bromley dropped his napkin and rose. "I'm Theodore Bromley," he told the lad, who trotted over to our table and away from the landlady's swinging arm. Mr. Bromley pressed a coin into the boy's palm, took the message, and ripped the envelope open. The boy gaped at the coin in his hand, then bobbed his head in a grateful bow and left the Lion Hotel, thanking us four more times on his way out the door.

Mr. Bromley patted his pockets to locate his spectacles, put them on, and read the note quickly. "Oh, dear," he said. "I need to make another telephone call."

"Everything all right, Papa?" inquired Alice.

"Fine, my dear," her grandfather replied. "Just a small matter at the factory requiring my attention."

Alice gave me a look, then spoke to her grandfather. "Why don't I come with you, Papa?" she asked. "I can keep you company."

"Why, don't you want to eat?" he asked her.

"I've had some food," she said. "And the rest will keep. I haven't gotten to see you much these last few days."

He beamed and held out his arm for her. "That would be lovely." He glanced down at us. "Would you two like to come?"

Tom shifted in his seat. "I'd rather be here," he said, "in case my dad needs me."

"We won't leave this table," I promised Mr. Bromley. "We'll be here when you get back."

My motives were far less pure than Tom's. I was hungry, and I didn't want the stew to get cold.

Mr. Bromley hesitated for only a moment, then rose and left the table with Alice at his side, bidding us to "be good." Alice sent another glance my way before letting her Papa lead her out of the hotel. That was Alice. A true friend. She knew I needed time to grill Tom, so she gave it to me. Or perhaps she was more anxious to protect her grandfather's shins.

When the door had swung shut behind them, I delivered my urgent question. "Did you tell your dad?"

Tom's spoon hung suspended in midair. He looked at me for an uncomfortable moment.

"No."

"You *didn't*?"

He gave me an annoyed look. "No."

I gaped at him.

"What am I supposed to say, Maeve?" he said. "'Don't worry, Dad; all is well, because I—'"

"*Shh!*" I hissed.

He lowered his voice to a bare whisper. "'Don't worry, Dad; all is well, because I robbed you first'?"

I considered this while chewing a bite of stew.

"All right," I said. "I can see how that would be awkward." I swallowed. "But I would think you'd want to set his mind at ease, if you could."

Tom said nothing but kept on eating.

Conversation, I saw, was to be my job. "How was he," I asked, "when you got him upstairs?"

"I didn't know what to do with him," Tom admitted. "He seemed in such a bad state. But once I got him lying down, he soon settled."

"It's terrible," I said, "all he's gone through, and in so short a time. No wonder it got to be too much."

Tom stirred his stew thoughtfully. "I can't help but think," he said slowly, "this is a blessing in disguise."

I stared at him. "Being robbed? A blessing *in disguise*?"

"That part's a shame," Tom admitted, "but don't you see, Maeve?" He leaned across the table and whispered so softly I could barely hear him over the background murmur and clinking of lunchtime eaters. "Now my dad will never know I swiped Mermeros from him when he wasn't looking!"

I did not approve of his cheeriness on this point. "What had your plan been," I asked him, "when you first pocketed Mermeros?"

He shrugged. "Make a few wishes, then slip him back before Dad ever even noticed."

"Perhaps you should've given that a bit more thought," I said, "before robbing your own dad?"

He bristled. "Turns out to be a good thing I did, don't you think?" he said. "Otherwise it, er, *he* actually would be lost to us by now."

I didn't know what to say to that. Of course I was glad Mermeros wasn't lost. I was definitely glad he wasn't in the grip of whatever fiends wanted him now. But how could I be glad of any of this? All this crime, and danger, and greed, and fear?

"Besides," said Tom, "now my dad can relax. His fears can fade away. We can get on with normal life. He doesn't know, and he doesn't need to know, that I still have, er, you-know-who."

I glanced around me at the restaurant area of the hotel's first-floor common room. Nobody looked familiar. Nobody seemed to be paying us the slightest attention. But still, we ought to be more careful.

And so should Tom.

"You don't see it, do you, Tom?" I whispered. "Look at the number of attempts. The outright attacks, in *just the last two days*."

Tom took a big bite of stew and spoke right through it. "Sscho?"

"Nice manners." I tried to figure out how to say it. "Whoever is after, er, him, will stop at nothing," I said. "Whether it's Mr. Wilberforce, or his helpers, or someone else altogether. Perhaps your dad does now believe the worst of it all is behind him. That this horror has now passed to someone else." I took a sip of tea. "He wouldn't have wanted it to go this way—he wanted to find a more responsible solution to the problem, one that wouldn't let Merm—er, *him*, fall into dangerous hands."

Tom held out his own hands indignantly. "He's not in dangerous hands!"

"Not yet," I said. "But don't you see? Your dad didn't want it to go this way. He's got principles. He cares about others. About the greater good. But now that, as he believes, the deed has been done, it's out of his hands, and it can't be helped, he probably is getting the first good sleep he's had in a while because he *thinks* he's not in danger anymore."

Tom stopped chewing midbite. He saw it.

But just in case he didn't, I supplied the rest. "How long do you think it will take him to figure out the truth when another burglary attempt is made?" I said. "And how much do you think that next one will terrify him, coming when he least expects it and is already so fragile?"

Tom looked down at his stew with unseeing eyes.

"That's not all," I said. "Perhaps we've been lucky thus far. Nobody's gotten hurt. But what if the thieves we're up against are willing to stop at nothing? What if, the next time, someone *does* get hurt?"

Tom closed his eyes. His fingers curled into fists on the dark wooden table.

"It's like we're rats in a trap," he whispered angrily. "Fish in a barrel. We don't know what we're looking out for, and we can't see it coming. We can't protect ourselves, and we can't outmaneuver them. We just wait until they nab us."

I nodded. "I know. It's awful. There's nothing, no weapon, no shield, that would help us."

A muscle in Tom's jaws twitched. "Except one."

My skin prickled, and the room certainly wasn't cold.

"No, Tom," I said. "No, no, no. You can't. You mustn't."

"Mustn't I?" he said darkly. "Who's to say?"

Desperately, I tried to think what to say. "Is *this* all your wishes are worth to you?" I whispered. "Revenge? Anger?"

He wasn't listening.

"I wasted a wish that way," I told him. "It was a terrible, awful mistake. It only made things worse for me. Far, far worse."

"I'll be smarter than that."

I chose not to sock him for that insult today, but to save that pleasure for another time. Mrs. Moyes might not approve.

"We're not just rats in a trap," I told him. "We're not powerless. If we work together and draw on Inspector Wallace's help, we can figure out who keeps coming after us, and we can outwit them. You know we can."

He made a face. "No, I don't," he said. "It's like they're invisible.

They come without warning. They know where we're going. They leave no trace."

"It only feels that way to us now," I said. "Everyone leaves a trace. There's a way to catch them. There must be!"

"And what is it?" said Tom. "What's your plan?"

Oh, I wanted to break something. Instead, I took a deep breath. "I don't have one yet," I admitted. "But I'll make one."

He dug back into his stew. "Well, let me know when you do."

"Tom," I pleaded with him. "If you spend a wish just to punish these criminals, whoever they are, then what? You've seen for yourself. Look at the number of people who've heard there's a... Who've heard about, you know, and who have made our lives an absolute mess? One right after another."

"So?"

I wanted to scream. "So, you only get three wishes. You're going to spend them all *defending your wishes*. And then they're gone, but people will likely still hound you for a while to come. It won't be easy to prove to the criminal underworld that your...your you-know-what is gone."

"You lack imagination, Maeve," Tom said haughtily. "Just because you can't think of a way out of this pickle doesn't mean *I* can't."

"Well, bully for you," I snapped.

He made a show of ignoring me, buttering a roll placidly

as though he hadn't a care in the world. Personally, I found the idea of buttering my own roll and smearing it in his face extremely tempting.

But my better angels, if I have any, intervened. I took a deep breath and tried another approach.

"What about all the orphans you wanted to help?" I asked him. "Would you throw that all away just for the chance to get back at some rotten burglars? Like a common schoolyard bully?"

He let out an aggravated breath. "I know what I'm doing, Maeve," he said. "You seem to think I only ever make rash, stupid decisions. *You* were apparently smart enough to manage your turn at—you know. But I guess I can't handle myself without your constant supervision."

I fired my better angels.

My skin felt hot. What was happening to Tom and me? Why were we fighting all of a sudden? We, who used to be such pals— well, we had started off as enemies, but that was only at first—fought now like wild dogs over lunch in a Cambridge hotel.

Was this what happened when people got older? Was this what growing up meant?

No. This wasn't growing up. This was Mermeros's doing, whether intentional or not. What had he said, those many months ago? How had he warned me?

Greed will take hold. Gold lust will consume you. It will infil-trate you like a cancer until it owns you, body and soul, and drives you to madness and ruin.

Tom didn't seem to be full of gold lust, but surely anger and pride were close cousins to greed. Weren't they all the same in the end? Weren't they working their poisonous effects on Tom, just as I'd feared they would?

"Maeve."

I looked up to find Tom looking at me with a more thoughtful expression than before.

"Maeve, I—"

"Excuse me," said a voice. We looked up to see an aproned serving girl, probably not much older than we were. "Are you Master Tom Poindexter?"

Tom nodded.

"Your father has asked me to fetch you," she said.

He stood up quickly. "Is he all right?"

"He is," she replied. "I'm sure he's fine. He just... He rang his bell, and I came, and he asked if I'd be so kind as to come get you."

Tom didn't seem much reassured. "I'll go now." He hurried off to the stairs and took them two at a time.

I wondered what he'd been about to say. But I didn't wonder long. There, draped over the back of his empty chair, was his jacket.

I looked around me to make sure no one at all was watching, then leaned across the table, slipped my hand into the inside pocket, felt the cool, smooth metal of Mermeros's tin, and took it.

CHAPTER
18

Once upon a time, the quivering, tingling feeling of magic emanating from that sardine tin would have thrilled me down to the tips of my toes. Now it felt hot and heavy, like a lump of molten lead in my hands. I slipped it into my travel valise and went back to eating, but the dark, rich stew became bitter ashes in my mouth.

What was I doing?

Saving Tom.

What right did I have to do it?

Mermeros was mine long before he was Tom's. I could see this matter more clearly than he could.

Wasn't I betraying a friend?

No. I was protecting him from disastrous mistakes he would regret for life.

Wasn't I being selfish?

No. I wasn't going to make that last wish for myself. Definitely not.

I turned, and turned, and turned it over in my mind, and no matter how I examined the dilemma, my actions felt justified.

Why, then, did I feel so guilty? Why, in the pit of my stomach, was I sure I'd become a traitor instead of a friend? Instead of an ally, a thief?

I poked chunks of potato with my spoon, moving them around in the gravy of my stew, barely seeing what I was doing. I looked up and noticed a few hotel guests gazing at me strangely and realized how I must have looked—one thirteen year-old girl sitting all alone at a table with four bowls of stew. Oh, well.

A large group of men in bowler hats entered the hotel, clutching valises, and asked to be checked into their rooms. They seemed to be in their mid-twenties or thereabouts—fully adult, but still young. From their loud laughter and conversation, it was clear that they knew each other, that they'd gone to Cambridge University together, and that they were having a reunion of some sort.

"Good thing the girls have gone mad, or we wouldn't have seen each other till Christmas," one of them was saying.

"We'll squash their folly, then have our own bit of fun," laughed another.

I glowered at them. Eight or nine of them, come to make a holiday out of dashing the hopes of girls like Pip and Trixie, Megs and Lizzie. And even, someday, me. It took all my self-control not to hurl a crock of stew at them. My fingers crawled toward the strap of my travel bag, where Mermeros lay hidden.

I caught myself short. I'd swiped the sardine tin from Tom because he was growing too vengeful, and here, only moments later, was I any different?

A man sitting at a table opposite me turned the pages of his newspaper, and the motion caught my eye. I glanced up, and for a moment, he seemed familiar to me. I peered more closely at him. He noticed and favored me with a smile.

"Good day, miss," he said. "Do I know you?"

"I was just wondering that myself," I told him. "I thought you looked familiar, but I was mistaken."

"You'd be surprised how often I hear that," he said. "I must just have one of those faces that looks like everyone's brother-in-law."

And indeed, he might. He seemed like an affable enough fellow, but I was in a sour temper toward all males just then, or at least, all males in Cambridge that I didn't personally know, seeing as they held Pip's fate, and someday, mine, in the grip of their dastardly votes.

"Are you one of the men who's come for the Cambridge University vote?" I asked him.

He blinked at me. "Pardon?"

I saw my mistake. "Never mind," I said, relenting only slightly. "Just a bit of local conflict surrounding the college."

"You seem young to be worried about that," he observed.

"What difference does age make?" I retorted.

He nodded, almost like a bow. "Indeed," he said. "My apologies." And with that, he resumed his perusal of the newspaper.

Well done, Maeve, I told myself. Snapping at strangers, stirring up trouble where there was none, being ill-tempered toward harmless travelers who were perfectly polite.

The traffic in the hotel steadily increased as diners came from off the street for lunch, and as hotel guests checked in and out. Mrs. Moyes was in full sail, escorting people back and forth, and ringing for her staff to help with luggage, linens, laundry, and other necessaries. In the ebb and flow, I didn't realize Alice and her grandfather had returned until they resumed their seats at the table.

"Where's Tom?" Alice asked, settling into her chair.

"His father rang for him," I explained. "Everything all right at the factory, Mr. Bromley?"

"Fine, fine," he said. "Just the ordinary wrinkles of doing business."

They resumed eating their now-tepid stew.

"Are you all right, Maeve?" Alice inquired, noticing my barely eaten bowl and watching me with a worried look.

"Hmm?" I stalled for time. "Perfectly fine. Just...thinking."

"Goodness knows there's enough to think about," she said sympathetically.

We all tried to eat, and for a while our little trio was quiet, until a man's shadow fell across our table, and we all rose gladly.

"Inspector Wallace!" Alice cried.

"Andrew," Mr. Bromley said, shaking the man's hand warmly. "I'm grateful to you for coming."

The man with the newspaper, seated opposite us, dropped some coins on his table and left while Detective Inspector Andrew Wallace, of Scotland Yard, sat in Tom's seat at our table. Mr. Bromley called for another crock of stew.

Inspector Wallace was the son of one of Mr. Bromley's friends from their old school days. He'd been a great support to us during the recent crisis of Mr. Poindexter's kidnapping by the repellent "Professor" Fustian. And now here he was, back again after only a few days. He knew all about our magical treasures.

Inspector Wallace, I supposed, was in his young thirties, old enough to be taken seriously but not so old as to be stodgy and dull. He was, I supposed, the kind of man women might call handsome, though why they favored so many whiskers on the male face, I couldn't fathom. At least his were neatly combed. He was intelligent, and I liked that about him. No nonsense. The active sort. Less of a talker and more of a doer.

"What's all this, then?" he said after shaking all our hands. "Burglaries every hour, on the hour? By cab, by train, by hotel room? It seems I can't leave you alone for a minute without you stirring up trouble."

Alice glanced around the busy dining area. "Should we talk about this here?" she wondered aloud. "Doesn't it seem...unwise?"

Inspector Wallace surveyed the room. "You're right, Miss Alice," he said. "Some privacy, and a quiet room where we may speak freely, would be better."

"We could send the food up to my hotel room," suggested Mr. Bromley, "though the thieves have left it a terrible mess."

"I'd rather see it as it is," replied the detective. We rose and followed Mr. Bromley up the stairs. He paused to ask the landlady to put our dinner on his tab and to send Mr. Wallace's food up when it was ready.

On the way up the stairs, we ran into Tom, headed down. He was pleased to greet Inspector Wallace and agreed to follow us back upstairs to join the conference. He urged us to visit his father's room, where his father, now seated upright in bed, could join the conversation. We all filed in there.

The hotel room, I could tell, had been modest and comfortable, at least until the thieves found it. Then they took it apart, bit by bit. Personal items were strewn about everywhere. Mr. Poindexter greeted us and tried to get up, but Tommy urged him to stay in bed, to which we all agreed. Inspector Wallace shook Mr. Poindexter's hand, then wasted no time getting down to business.

"No signs of forced entry," he murmured, studying the door, lock, and frame. He picked his way across the rubble and examined the windows just as thoroughly. "Whoever robbed you walked in through the door without difficulty."

"We locked the rooms this morning when we left," Mr. Poindexter said. "I saw Theodore lock his, and Tom saw me lock mine." The two men nodded to corroborate this.

"What do you know to be missing?" asked Inspector Wallace.

Mr. Poindexter shook his head sadly. "A sardine tin."

The room fell silent. Tom cast a sidelong gaze my way. Softly, he clapped a hand to his chest, where his jacket pocket was, or rather where it would be. Then his eyes grew wide as clocks.

A knock sounded at the door. Inspector Wallace, who had crossed the room, opened the door. A serving maid stood there, holding the stew we had ordered for the inspector, and something else draped over one arm.

"Here," she said, holding out Tom's coat. "You left this downstairs, didn't you, young sir?"

Tom sagged with relief and almost snatched the jacket away from the woman. He clutched at where the pocket would be, and his face paled. He felt it again, and again, then pulled the jacket on and patted down all its pockets frantically.

My travel bag hung on its strap over my shoulder. A quarter pound of sardines had become a thousand pounds of lead. And guilt.

Alice, ever thoughtful, found a coin in her own purse to give as a gratuity to the servant, who bobbed a curtsy and left. The men in the room took no notice. Their eyes were on Tom, still searching feverishly through his coat.

"Did you lose something, Tom?" asked Mr. Bromley kindly. "Some money gone missing while your coat was left downstairs?"

Tom had no words. Alice's grandfather pulled a crown from his pocket and flipped it airborne with his thumb. It spun in an arc through the air. Tom made no move to catch it, but watched vacantly as it hit him in the chest, then clinked to the floor.

"Excuse me," Tom said, and slipped out the door, no doubt to search under the table and through the corridors for a sardine tin he'd never find.

"The djinni is gone," his father continued. "It's a terrible loss, and one that may prove dangerous, extremely dangerous. But there's nothing more we can do. We must hope a merciful Providence spares us any further trouble arising from the djinni and magic. We're better off without it."

Inspector Wallace coughed. "Ahem. Did the thieves take anything else at all?" He scrubbed the eraser tip of his pencil through the hair over one ear. "You must understand, I can hardly mobilize the resources of Scotland Yard to investigate the theft of a tin of sardines."

"But that's not what the tin truly contained," protested Mr. Poindexter.

The detective sighed. "You know that, and I know that," he said, "but the rest of the department doesn't, nor do they believe in such things."

"But surely, if *you* told them, they'd believe you," said Mr. Bromley.

Inspector Wallace shook his head. "If I tried to persuade them that an ancient, magical djinni had been stolen," he said, "they'd give my job to someone else and bring me to a nice warm bed in a mental asylum." He shoved his pencil back in his pocket. "You wouldn't believe how creative I needed to be when I wrote my last report for the bureau's files. I worked all night on it, and I still fear I said too much."

Inspector Wallace sat down at a small table and took a bite of stew. "Is there nothing else of value that was taken?" he asked once more. "It would make my job easier."

Mr. Bromley was able to name a few small valuables that the thieves had taken from his room, and Mr. Poindexter got up and began looking more thoroughly around the items in his bedroom. Before long, they'd given the detective enough losses to satisfy his requirements.

"Inspector Wallace," I said breathlessly, "before you go any further, you should know, none of this business started until Mr. Bromley's cousin, Mr. Eugene Wilberforce, arrived at the house, saying all sorts of odious things. He's just the sort of rude, greedy, unpleasant person who—"

"Maeve."

I looked up to see Alice regarding me with a small frown.

"Maeve," Alice said, "Grandpapa telephoned home and spoke to Mr. Linzey. He says Cousin Eugene hardly stirred from bed once yesterday, but rang for meals all day long, and most of this morning, too."

I froze, trying to process this new information. On the one hand, it wasn't hard to picture Eugene Wilberforce being so lazy and selfish. On the other hand, it would make it hard for him to carry out multiple burglary attempts.

"He could still have accomplices," I insisted.

"He's received no messages, and no telegrams, and sent none," added Alice, "nor did he make or receive any telephone calls."

I chewed on my lip.

"The telephone call Grandpapa received," Alice added, "was from the foreman at his factory. Apparently Mr. Wilberforce applied there today for a management position, claiming a family connection. The foreman wanted to know how Grandpapa wished to proceed."

I let this information settle. It couldn't mean the repellent Cousin Eugene was innocent. It just couldn't.

Or perhaps it could. I realized, then, how much I'd been out for blood, and that of my host's own cousin. Was I any less boorish and rude than frightful Cousin Eugene?

I hung my head. "Mr. Bromley," I said. "I owe you an apology."

Mr. Bromley rested a warm hand on my shoulder. "Nothing of the kind, dear Maeve," he said gallantly. "My cousin does, in many ways, seem like an ideal candidate. I confess that the thought did cross my mind. But I felt certain he lacked the resolve to actually pull off such a bold scheme."

Inspector Wallace's eyes twinkled. "Cheer up, Miss Merritt," he said. "It's a blow, finding out your golden suspect can't have done it. The disappointment gets easier with time. Don't let it get you down."

I blew out a breath. "Do you plan to hire him at the button factory, Mr. Bromley?" I inquired.

A rather greenish cast came over Mr. Bromley's features. "I think... perhaps...my cousin's, er, talents would best be utilized elsewhere."

Alice gave me a wink, and I knew that I was forgiven. But this demanded much consideration. If Cousin Eugene really and truly had nothing to do with these burglaries, then who did? Who was out to get us?

I liked it better when I thought I knew where to look for our villain. Now, we were back to the beginning and no wiser.

While this was happening, Tom slipped quietly back into the

room. I remembered his errand and the ruse I had to maintain. I met his gaze with an unspoken question—another lie, without making a sound—*Did you find it?* When, of course, I knew he hadn't.

While the men spoke, Alice and I sidled over to the window where Tom was standing.

"Cheer up, Tom," Alice said in a low voice. "Mermeros has been stolen before. He has a way of coming back home to roost."

Tom shook his head morosely. "He's gone forever. I don't deserve anything better than that."

"Now, see here," I protested. "What does that even mean?"

It took Tom a while to answer. "I thought I was ready to govern the djinni and dictate my wishes to it." He wiped his nose with a handkerchief, one of the few treasures his pocket search had yielded. "It turns out I wasn't even ready to keep an eye out for it for one day."

Alice looked puzzled. "But how could you have looked out for it," she asked, "when you were at the Cavendish with us? You couldn't know thieves would come here in broad daylight."

I opened my mouth to speak, but Tom gave me a short shake of his head.

"Don't lose hope, Tom," Alice said. "Let's put our faith in the inspector. If we work with him, and help him find the...er, clues and things, just like in the Sherlock Holmes stories, perhaps our trail will lead us to the thieves, and we can find Mermeros again." She smiled at me. "Whenever Maeve knows who's stolen Mermeros, she's a crackerjack at getting him back."

I gulped. Alice was more right than she realized. Fortunately, her words didn't seem to give Tom any new ideas about who might have Mermeros.

My conscience skewered me with a jagged ice pick. With a rusty sword. With a plumber's drill. What kind of a traitorous fiend was I? Even now, I could pull Tom aside, explain the truth, and show him the sardine tin without anyone noticing. I could keep his secret safe from his father. I could pretend I'd done it to keep Mermeros safe. He would believe me. He would forgive me for not telling him instantly. He would be so relieved that all hard feelings would disappear. Even now, I could set things right.

Except that I couldn't. Tom was right. He *had* been careless with Mermeros. With the caliber of thieves we faced, we couldn't afford to be careless again.

I turned my attention back to what the adults had been discussing.

"We need to find out who may have checked out of the hotel late in the morning or right around noon," said Inspector Wallace.

"Why is that?" I asked.

"We also need to find out if any of the staff are missing any sets of keys," the inspector continued. He turned toward me. "Whoever robbed these two rooms came in through the front door with a key, which wouldn't be too hard for a skilled pickpocket to nick from the pocket of a careless maid or footman. Having found what they were looking for, they would certainly leave the hotel behind as quickly as possible. Don't you think?"

It would've been a reasonable line of thought, if it hadn't been based on faulty information. The thieves certainly had *not* yet found what they wanted most. All these secrets and lies were wasting everyone's time. Even Scotland Yard's.

"Shall I go ask the landlady?" I volunteered. Anything to get me out of here and away from Tom. "She and I have struck up a bit of an acquaintance, you might say."

"I'll go with you," offered Alice.

We left the room. Once in the carpeted corridor, I felt I could take my first breath in a very long time. Alice watched me with concern. "Are you all right?"

I didn't know how to answer her just yet. Keeping secrets from both my friends!

You're doing this for a reason, I told myself. *Stop fussing.*

"I'm fine," I told her. "Just worried, is all."

She nodded. "Of course you are."

On the landing of the stairs, we came upon the gentleman I'd crossed words with at lunchtime. He seemed intent on passing by me without even acknowledging me, not that I could blame him.

"Excuse me, sir," I said.

He paused and looked at me curiously. "Yes?"

I took a deep breath. "I fear I wasn't, er, my best self when we spoke at lunch."

His brows furrowed. "Oh?"

I don't know what I had expected, but it wasn't this.

"Well," I said, "I just wanted to apologize, is all. For being rude."

He nodded slowly. "Good of you," he said. "Think no more of it." He turned to continue on up the stairs.

"I'm Maeve Merritt," I called after him, though why I suddenly felt the need to make friends, I couldn't say. He didn't seem inclined to be friendly.

He paused a few stairs up and turned back. "Yes," he said. "I mean, pleased to meet you. I'm Samuel Haley. Good day." And on up the stairs he went.

We reached the bottom of the stairs, and Alice tugged at my sleeve. "I can't leave you alone for ten minutes without you getting into some kind of trouble," she teased. (She barely knew the half of it!) "What did you do to that poor man?"

I sighed. "Nothing much," I said. "I just thought he was one of the men coming to Cambridge to vote against women taking degrees."

"Even if he was," said Alice sternly, "that's no excuse for being impolite."

I nodded. "I know. I did say I was sorry."

She turned toward the front counter, the lair of Mrs. Allison Moyes. "He forgave you quite readily," she said. "Whatever you said didn't appear to leave a deep impression on him."

"Then that would be a first time," I said, "that my crimes and mistakes—and even my mere presence—didn't destroy someone's life today."

"Oh, Maeve." Alice sighed. "You do overdramatize at times."

19

"I f the inspector gentleman from Scotland Yard wants information from me," Mrs. Moyes hissed, "he can jolly well ask me for it
himself and not send an impertinent schoolgirl to vex me with
questions."

"Good afternoon, madam," came a familiar voice from behind
me. "Andrew Wallace. Scotland Yard." I turned to see him holding
out an identification badge and smiling disarmingly at the landlady,
who suddenly needed to fan her face.

"Well," she said breathlessly, "how can I help you, sir?"

"I wondered," he said, "if we might speak privately? Just a few
questions. Strictly routine."

"Privately," breathed the proprietress of this respectable
establishment.

He leaned conspiratorially across the counter. "No need for your
other guests to get...*suspicious*, wouldn't you say?"

Her eyes grew round. "Come with me, would you please?" And

she beckoned him to follow her behind the counter and through a swinging door.

"There you are."

We turned to see Pip standing behind us. Pip! I'd almost forgotten her dreadful morning and the ride we were to take back to Girton with her.

"Ready to ride back home?" she asked.

We hesitated.

She noted the looks on our faces. "What's the matter?"

I hated to make her aware of our troubles, but I didn't see a way around it.

"Tom's father and Alice's grandfather have been burgled, here at the hotel," I said quietly. "It's been a hard day for them."

Pip let out a low whistle. "It's been rotten all around," she said. "That's too bad. I'm sorry to hear it."

"How are you, Pip?" asked Alice. "It's been a trying day for you."

Pip shrugged nonchalantly, but she didn't fool me. "So what if they chuck me out of Girton and send me home in shame?" she declared. "Worse things have happened."

"Not many," I pointed out.

Pip declined to argue the point. "Well, do you want to ride back?"

Alice and I conferred silently, then Alice answered. "My

grandfather can drive us back," she said. "With all that's going on here, we feel we ought to stay a bit longer."

"But what about the bikes?" I asked. "You'll need help getting them home, won't you?"

Pip shrugged. "I know some girls who can help me get them back," she said. "They took an omnibus to school this morning but wouldn't mind chucking it for a ride home now. You're sure, then?"

We nodded.

"Then I guess I'd better get back in time for cricket."

I felt a pang. I had hoped to join her for cricket this afternoon.

"Though, in truth," she continued, "I'm not sure I'm up for it today."

Pip Northam, not feeling like playing cricket! Nothing was right in the world anymore.

"See you this evening," Alice said, and we both waved as Pip turned and headed out the door.

"I wish we could do something to help her," Alice said. "But it seems we have our hands full with our own troubles."

We returned to Mr. Poindexter's room and found Tom and Mr. Bromley there. Inspector Wallace soon joined us with his notebook clutched in one hand.

"I think we need to hold a council," he announced. "We must put

our heads together and to discover what we know about our mysterious thieves."

"We know nothing," moaned Tom. "That's the problem."

"Not so," said the inspector. "I think you'll be surprised. Mr.
Poindexter, may I?" He reached for a small side table and brought
it closer to the bed where Tom and his father sat so that we could
all, in a clumsy fashion, gather around it with what chairs we
could find.

Inspector Wallace spread his notebook out on the table.

"I have here," he said, "a list of names of all the guests at the
hotel, including those who checked out today or checked in today. I
cast a broad net, just to be safe."

"Do you recognize any of them?" Mr. Poindexter asked.

"No," replied the inspector, "though I wouldn't expect to. I'll
call the bureau and have some my men investigate these names
looking for any past crimes or any connection to our, er, recent
misadventures."

"That's the spirit," cried Mr. Bromley. "I like the sound of that."

"Now," said the inspector, "I ask once again, what do we know
about our thieves?"

We listened to the clock tick.

"They are...here?" ventured Alice. "Or, at least, they were
this morning?"

"Excellent," said Inspector Wallace. "He, or she, or they, were in Cambridge this morning, between the hours of, say...?"

"Eight o'clock in the morning," supplied Mr. Poindexter, "and eleven o'clock, which is when we returned and discovered the theft."

"A three-hour window," the inspector murmured. "I've dealt with worse before."

"It's 'they,'" added Tom's dad. "Two men held up our cab."

"Was a police report filed at the time?" inquired Inspector Wallace. "Did the cabbie get a good look at the fellows?"

"Yes to the police report," replied Mr. Poindexter, "and no to the cabbie."

"What did they look like?" asked Alice. "Did you see?"

Mr. Poindexter scratched his bald head. "They wore low hats and had scarves over their faces."

"Yes, but, what about their shape, their size?" I asked. "Their hair? Their coloring? The state of their clothes?"

Mr. Poindexter and Tom exchanged a look. "They both seemed... average," Mr. Poindexter said helplessly. "Neither tall nor short. Neither thin nor stout. Neither old nor young."

"That's helpful," muttered the inspector.

"Hair color?" I pressed.

Mr. Poindexter looked helpless. "It was dim inside the cab," he said. "Their hair color was the last thing on my mind."

"Could you contrast them with each other?" Alice asked. "One was taller, one was shorter? That sort of thing?"

Inspector Wallace smiled. "You're a natural investigator, Miss Bromley."

Mr. Poindexter squinched his eyes, as through trying to focus on those faraway burglars. "That's just it," he said. "I can't say that one was taller, or darker, or thicker, or any such thing."

I peered at Inspector Wallace's paper.

"We know there are at least two of them," I said. "We know they were here this morning, and they were in London yesterday."

"No, we don't," said Alice. "We know they were in London yesterday, and we know that someone burgled our rooms today. We don't know for certain that they're the same people."

"It jolly well wasn't random," I said. "Two different sets of burglars? What are the chances?"

"I doubt that's it," said Alice, "but perhaps we're talking about a larger gang?"

Inspector Wallace's mustache twitched. "Let's assume, for the moment," he said, "that our burglars are the same burglars. Though you're right, Miss Alice... We don't know that for certain. But let's keep that as our working theory." He turned to me. "Go on, Miss Maeve."

I nodded. "If they're the same people, they were in London yesterday and here this morning. We know they're more or less average in appearance." I snapped my fingers. "We know they know about us, and about Mermeros, and they knew about our travels by train and by car to Cambridge."

"That's significant," agreed Mr. Bromley.

"Some of your domestic staff?" suggested Mr. Poindexter.

Mr. Bromley shook his head. "I'll never believe it. They've been with us for years. They're like family to us."

"Family can surprise you," muttered the detective. "Believe me."

"Besides," said Alice, "none of the men on staff at Grosvenor Square have what you'd call average appearance."

"And weren't they all at home with us," I asked, "while Tommy and his dad were being robbed?"

"So they were," agreed Mr. Bromley. "So that rules them out. Besides, if they had wanted to rob us, they'd have much easier ways of doing it."

Tom, who'd sat silent and downcast for the entire conversation, now spoke. "It doesn't sound like we have much to go on. We're no better off than when we started."

Inspector Wallace looked at him thoughtfully. "I don't know that I'd say that, young man," he said. "Something is always better than nothing. Who knows? Maybe something will come of our inquiries into this guest list."

The inspector meant well, but Tom still sat deflated.

"What about a trap?" I said. "What if we tried to lure the burglar into making another attempt?"

Four pairs of eyes goggled at me. Only Inspector Wallace seemed unfazed by what I'd said.

"Go ahead," he said. "I'm listening."

My mind spun. Would I ever learn to form a plan first and *then* open my mouth, instead of the other way around?

"What if..." I collected my thoughts feverishly. "What if we made it easy for the thieves to find their way into the room? Made it seem we were all going out? Maybe the thieves would try again, and this time, we could be waiting for them?"

Mr. Poindexter frowned. "The thieves have already secured their prize," he said. "They've got the djinni. I'll bet they're long gone by now."

Everyone in the room believed that to be true. Everybody but me. My plan did look pretty flimsy through their eyes. Only the thieves and I knew that they hadn't gotten it yet. Instinctively, I slid my hand over my little bag to the bulge that was Mermeros's sardine tin. If I urged this plan upon them, would they begin to suspect me?

The sardine tin wasn't the only hard object in my canvas bag. A flash of inspiration hit.

"What if," I said, "we make it known that we have another magical object?" Carefully, I slid my hand into the bag and pulled out the silvered mirrors. I placed them on the table for all to see. "These are magical mirrors. They're a pair. They each show what the other mirror sees. Would this be enough of a fishing lure to catch our burglar?"

I wasn't prepared for what followed next. Mr. Bromley groaned. Mr. Poindexter pressed his fingers to his temples as though he had a sudden headache. Inspector Wallace leaned back at his chair and gazed up at the ceiling as if to say, *Lord, give me strength.*

"What?" I demanded.

"Maeve," Mr. Poindexter said softly, "please tell me this isn't a prank."

"It isn't," I cried, feeling more than a little stung. "I would never!"

When no one said anything, I added, "Have I *ever* lied to you about magical things?"

Other than right now, you djinni stealer, whispered my nuisance of a conscience.

"Maeve isn't lying," Alice said gently. "She found them yesterday, from a rag-and-bone dealer here in Cambridge."

At the blank stares that followed this statement, she added, "I think Maeve has a special knack for finding magical objects. They find her. Or she awakens something in them." Alice faltered. "Or something."

"Good *night*," murmured Inspector Wallace. "They'll have

to open a special bureau at Scotland Yard. The Maeve Merritt Magical Mess task force. I'll be dealing with magical mischief the rest of my life."

"I think it's good news," Tom said stoutly. "Maybe she can find us another djinni." He grinned for the first time this afternoon, and I was glad to see it. "One with nicer manners."

I patted my bag once more. *Don't listen to him, Mermeros.*

"All right," said Inspector Wallace grimly. "It can't be helped. We have these mirrors, by gum, so the question is, can we use them? Can we bait a trap and catch a magic thief?"

"How would we, um, make it known that we have magical mirrors?" asked Mr. Bromley. "Whom do we tell?"

Inspector Wallace and I made brief eye contact. "Mrs. Moyes, of course," I said. "The landlady."

"I'm not worried about that part," added Inspector Wallace. "That's easily handled. The question is, are the thieves still nearby?"

Mr. Poindexter shook his head. "I'm sure they're long gone. They're probably back in London already, making their way to Dover and a boat for the Continent."

He was wrong, but only I knew it. How could I say so without giving away too much?

"Maybe," I said, "the thieves didn't want to bolt out of town too soon because it would attract suspicion. Maybe they're staying nearby to see if there's anything more to find."

Inspector Wallace began gathering his papers. "It's worth a try," he said. "If you've no objection, let's spring our trap right now."

CHAPTER

20

The thing is," Inspector Wallace told Mrs. Moyes, leaning across the front counter at the hotel as though the two of them were longtime friends, "the thieves...they were looking for rare antiques, don't you see—Mr. Poindexter deals in them—but as I was saying, the thieves didn't even know enough to take the most valuable objects of all!"

"You don't say," gasped the landlady. "What might they be?"

"A pair of silver mirrors," the inspector said, loud enough for most in the lobby and restaurant area to hear, yet not seeming to raise his voice. "They have a long history to them. Supposedly they once were magic mirrors. Though that's all balderdash, of course."

"Of course," she agreed. "Magic mirrors! The nonsense people think up!"

"Too right." The inspector nodded. "You wouldn't believe the things we hear."

Mrs. Moyes's eyes were wide. "I shouldn't wonder."

"But magic or no," Inspector Wallace continued, "they're worth a mint. To the right sort of collector."

"There's no accounting for taste," the landlady said to her new bosom friend and confidante.

"Well, Mrs. Moyes," he said, holding out a hand to shake, "you've been a tremendous help. My friends and I are stepping out for tea, but you'll keep a close eye on their rooms, won't you? Until we return? Scene of the crime, and all that?"

Her jowls quivered. "Upon my honor."

He doffed his hat to her, turned heel, and headed for the front door.

Alice, Tom, and I followed after him, out into the street.

"That was impressive, Inspector," I told him.

He winked. "Tricks of the trade, Miss Merritt," he said. "Tricks of the trade."

We ducked into a coffee shop next door and located our table, secluded from view in the back corner. Mr. Bromley and Mr. Poindexter were already there, waiting for us. We had picked this as the place to wait and watch the mirror for entering burglars.

We squeezed ourselves into the booth, and I pulled my solitary mirror from my bag. I handed it to Inspector Wallace.

He peered into its silvered glass and shook his head in wonder.

"No sign of me," he whispered. "Just your hotel room, Siegfried. I'll be darned."

We had carefully propped the mirror's twin in Mr. Poindexter's room, in a slightly opened bureau drawer. From that vantage point, we had a clear view of the door to the room, and most of the room itself.

"I still don't understand," said Mr. Bromley, "why we're waiting here, Andrew, and not much closer by. In my room, for example. So you can be there in two shakes if you see any sign of activity."

"We needed our thieves to see all of us leave," Inspector Wallace explained. "By now they're sure to have heard that someone from Scotland Yard is in the building. This would make them extra cautious. But if they know we've left, perhaps they'll take a chance."

"If anything happens..." began Mr. Poindexter.

"I can be there in under a minute," replied the inspector.

We sat and waited, watching the mirror. A waitress came and went, then returned with tea, lemonade, and biscuits. We stared at the image in the glass. It might as well have been a painting of a hotel room door.

"When the thief enters the room," Alice began, "won't they see our faces, looking back at them in the mirror? Wouldn't that put them on alert?"

Inspector Wallace smoothed his mustache. "I confess I hadn't thought of that."

"Keep a napkin ready," said Tom. "As soon as you see anything, cover the mirror with the napkin. The thief won't have enough time to notice what's really happening. They'll think it's a trick of the light."

"Good thinking, son," said Mr. Poindexter with a half smile.

"It's dark in here, anyway," added Alice. "That should help."

"I tell you, they're long gone," said Mr. Poindexter.

"Maybe," said Inspector Wallace.

"I'll bet not," I said, trying to sound optimistic but not *too* sure. "If they know so much about us, they know there were, at least, er, multiple items of interest."

"The carpetbags," moaned Tom.

"I think there's every reason to hope they'll stick around," I said.

"All we can do is wait and see," said Inspector Wallace.

"It feels like we've gone duck hunting," said Mr. Bromley. "Sitting in a blind all day in the pouring rain, waiting for one duck to move."

"How frightful," said Alice. "I'd rather read a book."

"So would Mermeros," I said.

Several sets of eyes looked at me curiously. Except for Tom's. They flashed a warning. Too late, I realized my careless mistake.

"It's nothing," I managed to say. "We gave him a book recently," I added. "He seemed, er, to be pleased."

The subject dropped.

That was close! Careless, careless. I couldn't let it slip that I or anyone had spoken to Mermeros as recently as this morning.

Awkward silence hung like a heavy cloud over our table. I sat there sweating and wondering what else I should say, when Alice pointed at the mirror.

"Look," she whispered.

The door was opening. Mr. Wallace rose to his feet, and Tom picked up the napkin, ready to hide the mirror.

"Wait," whispered the inspector, as though the thief could hear us, too. "Let's see what we're up against."

We hung back, trying to see the glass without it seeing us, so to speak. The door to the hotel room closed, and the room grew brighter as the intruder switched on the overhead light.

"It's a woman," Tom gasped.

"Why not a woman?" I demanded. "Women can be thieves, too. Women can be anything they like."

"Ahem." The inspector sounded like he was trying not to laugh. "Watch, please."

"Is she rummaging through our things?" asked Mr. Poindexter eagerly. "Is she searching for something?"

We watched as best we could from the awkward angle we were using to avoid being seen.

"She appears to be replacing your towels with fresh ones," observed Alice. "And dusting off the furniture."

"She *is* wearing a chambermaid's costume," I pointed out.

Inspector Wallace sat down heavily. "So much for that."

"Maids can be thieves," I protested. "Maybe that's her cover."

"Shh," hissed Tom. "Look!"

The maid had found the mirror. She picked it up and peered in it. Her face loomed large in our mirror's glass. We shrank back further in the shadows and watched as she twirled a curl of hair that had escaped her frilled cap around her finger. She stopped and frowned into the mirror, her curl of hair forgotten, and, from the looks of things, tilted the mirror this way and that to find out why it didn't work.

"Does she see us?" Mr. Bromley whispered.

"I don't think so," said Mr. Poindexter. "If she had, she probably would have been startled out of her wits. The nerve of her, poking around our things!"

"She's just tidying up," said Alice soothingly. "The mirror did look very strangely placed. Everyone glances at themselves in mirrors, don't they?"

She put the mirror back down, or so we assumed, because everything went black. Facedown, most likely, on top of the bureau, or in one of its drawers.

"So much for our duck blind," laughed Mr. Bromley.

"And for our trap," said the Inspector.

Mr. Poindexter took a sip of his now-cool tea. "It was worth a try, Maeve," he said, "but our thieves are long gone."

I fumed silently. Our thieves *weren't* gone. Thieves this determined and this intelligent wouldn't stop now. Something had gone wrong with this trap, but surely a trap would still work. There was something we were missing. But what?

"What do we do now, Inspector Wallace?" Alice asked.

The inspector tapped his pencil against his notebook. "Now, we wait, and watch, and think some more," he said. "And in the meantime, I suggest we find some supper."

"I told Adelaide we would all join her at Girton College this evening for a meal," said Alice's grandfather. "Beforehand, I can talk to her privately and explain all that's happened."

"Let's go now, may we, please, Papa?" asked Alice. "I–I think I'm ready for this day to end."

"Of course, my dear," he replied. "I'll send for the car right away."

"Lend me your key, Mr. Poindexter," I told him. "I'll run and get the mirror from your room."

He handed it to me slowly. "Be sure to lock up afterward."

Before anyone could offer to join me or object to my lack of a chaperone, while everyone else was gathering their belongings, I slipped out of the coffee shop and over to the Lion Hotel.

I needed to end this. I knew the thieves were still lurking close at hand, though where I couldn't say. It was an ominous, choking feeling, knowing we were being watched by someone who could see us, but we couldn't see them. Like mice, unaware a cat was watching them play.

My first trap hadn't worked. I needed to build a better one.

In the lobby, I found a writing desk with a pen and ink. I scribbled a note, fanned the ink to dry it, then hurried upstairs. I unlocked Mr. Poindexter's room, retrieved the mirror, then left the note on the floor, just inside the doorway, with a tiny corner of it poking out in the hallway, just enough for someone watching the door closely to notice. The note, I thought, had been rather clever, if I did say so myself. I prayed it would work. If it didn't, when Mr. Poindexter found it, I would have some explaining to do.

LATE TONIGHT, it read. *GIRTON COLLEGE. THE WOODLAND WALK.*

CHAPTER
21

I'd always wondered how it would feel to ride in an automobile, and now I knew. It was loud, smelly, noisy, and bumpy. I loved it. I would have loved it more if I hadn't been worrying about catching burglars. It reminded me of the roller-coaster ride we'd enjoyed, the Topsy-Turvy Railway, at the Crystal Palace in London a few weeks ago. Fortunately, the streets of Cambridge had no loop-de-loops.

It took the Bromleys' driver two trips in their shiny, hired Daimler automobile to transport all five of us from the Lion Hotel to Girton College. Mr. Bromley escorted Alice and me first, and then the driver returned to collect Mr. Poindexter, Tom, and Inspector Wallace.

Mr. Bromley went straight to his wife, who came out to greet us all cheerfully, eager to tell us about a wonderful day of meetings with Girton College donors to review the builder's plans for the school's expansion. Mr. Bromley took her aside to fill her in on the events of the day, and Alice joined them, perhaps to reassure her grandmother that she really and truly was safe and unharmed, or perhaps just to help soothe her fears in general.

Not knowing what else to do with myself, I went upstairs to the girls' dormitory and wandered about somewhat until I had located Pip and Trixie's room. Pip wasn't in, but Trixie was.

"There you are, my poppet!" Trixie planted a kiss on my cheek as if she were my sister. "Where's your friend? Where's Alice? Oh, and aren't you with Pip? I haven't seen her all afternoon. She wasn't out on the playing fields."

"I haven't seen Pip for a while," I said cautiously, wondering how much I had the right to say. "We spent morning with her, then met up with Alice's grandfather and some, er, other friends, for lunch and the better part of the afternoon."

"How nice," Trixie said. "Perhaps Pip had extra studying to do. You might find her in the library." She handed me an envelope. "If you see her there, would you give her this envelope? It just arrived for her." She handed me an envelope made of stiff, creamy paper, with "Miss Philippa Northam" written across the front in an elegant hand, and no other writing. It must not have gone through the postal service, or it would have borne an address as well.

I took the envelope and left. I remembered Pip pointing out a library en route to the dining hall, so I went downstairs and wandered the halls somewhat until I found it. THE STANLEY LIBRARY, read the brass placard on the door. It was a large room, rimmed by bookcases full of leather-bound volumes and marble busts of important thinkers long since dead. The bookshelves were interspersed with pairs of colorful stained-glass windows, each with a pane of regular glass at the bottom, allowing views of the grassy gardens outside. Comfortable chairs near the fire seated students immersed in reading, with tables and desks full of young women hard at work, writing and studying. Over in another chair, in a corner by herself, sat Pip, her chin resting on her fist, the textbook in her lap unseen.

I approached her. "Penny for your thoughts?"

She roused like one in a stupor. "Oh, hullo, Maeve."

I sat in the chair beside her. "Are you all right?"

"Not especially, no," she said. She blinked and sat up straighter. "Sorry. Never mind me. I'm fine." She patted her knees. "Got two legs, two lungs, two hands, and some days, a head on my shoulders. I suppose that makes me luckier than a lot of folks."

Seeing Pip looking so forlorn broke my heart. What a difference a day made! Yesterday, she had been king of the mountain here at Girton College, the unofficial leader of a group of girls, their star athlete, a strong pupil, according to Miss Welsh, and an ambitious future physicist.

"Pip," I said, "may I ask you a question?"

She shrugged. "Ask away."

"Do you...*like* being in college?"

She looked over my shoulder, out the window.

"I love it." She sounded like someone making a terrible confession. "I've never had so much fun. So many times here I've thought, what will I even do when school ends? There's no going back, once you've been here. I don't ever want to leave this place. And now..."

I waited for her to continue, but she didn't.

"Did you always feel that way?" I asked. "About learning. Did you love school, too?" I watched for her reaction. "Because sometimes I find it so frightfully dull—"

She laughed, a little. "Everyone feels that way at your age," she said. "That's when you must study all sorts of things that don't appeal to you, with all sorts of girls who don't appeal to you."

I felt guilty. "I love Alice," I said, "and Mr. Abernathy, our tutor, is tops. He makes even the boring things interesting. But—"

"But you can't bear sitting still," she supplied. "You'd rather be reading stories than writing out long-form compositions about the Battle of Waterloo."

"Yes!"

A few students raised their heads to look at me. I hunched back down in my chair.

"The Battle of Waterloo sounds fun," I whispered. "It's the fall of the Roman Empire that makes me want to go to sleep."

Pip patted my shoulder. "Hang in there, sport," she said. "It's so much better once you're in college. Then, you choose what you want to study. Mostly, anyway. You choose what interests you. What you want to spend the rest of your life doing."

I sighed. "I want to spend the rest of my life playing cricket."

She grinned.

"Me too, Maeve," she said. "Some days, it's cricket that gets me out of bed." Her expression clouded. "My team will be pretty sore with me for missing today's practice. But…"

Her voice trailed off. I wanted to help her change the subject.

"Can I ask," I said again, "how you got here?"

She looked at me curiously.

"Alice's family has pots of money," I explained, "but mine doesn't. We get by all right, but…" I tried to think how to say this. "I can't imagine my dad having the funds to send me to college. I certainly don't have a rich aunt who will leave them to me in her will."

She sat up and looked at me intently. "Listen closely, Maeve," she said. "There's always a way. You may have to fight for it, but a way can be found."

It felt as though she'd grabbed me about the collar.

"Work hard," she said. "Work harder than you're used to. If you can get in, there are scholarships, and jobs, and grants. And lots of people anxious to help girls like you and me get an education. Girls with ambition and smarts, but not many shillings to spare."

I felt a little flush of pride. Did Pip Northam think I had ambition and smarts? Did *I* think so?

Her urgency crumpled, and she sank back into her chair. "It's too late for me," she said. "But it isn't too late for you."

My heart broke for her. "Surely it isn't too late for you," I protested. "You just said it yourself. There's always a way."

"For people who haven't been accused of academic theft, lying, and stealing," she said bitterly. "The record of my 'sins' will follow me wherever I try to go."

I shook my head. "That can't be right."

She didn't bother to try to enlighten me. She just stared out the window.

"Pip." I leaned in close to whisper. "*Did* you steal Mr. Rutherford's paper?"

Her eyes flashed hot, like she wanted to snap back at me. Then she grew quiet. "No," she said. "I didn't. I typed it and stacked it and turned my back on it for a minute. After that, I neither saw nor touched it."

I believed her.

"If that's true," I told her, "then why aren't you fighting for it?"

Her eyes narrowed.

"There's always a way," I echoed back to her. "You may have to fight for it, but a way can be found."

"That's true," she said, "for people whose reputations aren't ruined."

"Poppycock!" I said, then lowered my voice. "If my reputation was ruined," I told her, "because of something I didn't do, I'd fight to set it to rights."

She gave me a half smile. "You'd go down swinging, anyway," she said. "But life doesn't always let us be as brave as we think we'll be."

I didn't know what more to say. Maybe I'd said too much already. Maybe now, when her dreams were shattered, wasn't the time to give her advice.

"Here," I said, handing the envelope. "Trixie gave me this to give to you."

Pip took the envelope. Her expression, if it were possible, sank even more.

"Well, there it is," she said. "My sentence of execution."

Rather a bold statement about one plain envelope. "What do you mean?"

"It's a note from Miss Welsh," she explained. "I recognize her writing."

"But that could be anything," I said. "She could be thanking you for showing us around today."

Pip shook her head. "A note like this, in her own handwriting, only means one thing. You're in trouble." She handed it back to me. "See for yourself."

I opened the note.

"'Miss Northam,'" it read, in elegant penmanship. "'Be so good as to wait upon me in my private study tomorrow morning at 11:00 precisely.'"

I slid the note back into the envelope. "That doesn't sound sinister."

"More than you know." Pip slid the note between the pages of the book she'd been ignoring and rose from her chair. "Such notes are never invitations to a cozy gossip, or congratulations for how well one is doing." She straightened her things. "Well, it's time for supper. Even the condemned are allowed their last meal. I wonder what we're having tonight..."

I didn't get up to follow her. "Don't give up hope, Pip."

She gave me a long look. "Goodbye, Maeve Merritt," she said. "I hope you can find your way back here someday. Do it for me, all right?" She mustered one small smile. "And give those Newnham girls what-for on the cricket pitch."

And with that, she was gone.

I looked around me and realized that I was completely alone in the Stanley Library. Every other student had left, hearing, no doubt, the siren song of supper.

I examined the doors and discovered that I could lock them. Long tan-colored drapes in each window bay could be pulled to block out the light and the view. Soon there was no light in the great room save the small glow from a low-burning fire in the grate.

I reached into my bag and cranked open the sardine tin.

Mermeros slid out from the tin on his usual spume of billowing, yellow, sulfurous smoke, but unlike other times, he seemed to not even notice me. He still wore the silk pajamas and housecoat he'd worn earlier, and his half-moon spectacles were still perched on the tip of his nose, but that nose was buried so deeply in the pages of *Jane Eyre* that he didn't even look twice at me. What shocked me even more were his eyes. He was crying.

"Mermeros?" I cried softly. "Are you all right?"

He didn't respond, but turned a page. I fished into my bag, pulled out a handkerchief, and handed it to him. He took it without a glance my way and blew his nose loudly, then held the handkerchief back out to me.

"No, thanks," I told him. "Keep it."

He tucked it into the pocket of his pajamas. *Yech.*

I tried again to get his attention. "Enjoying the novel, are we?"

He regarded me coldly. "'Enjoying' is hardly an adequate word." Then, for the first time, he seemed to notice his surroundings, dimly lit by the fire and by his own greenish aura. "What manner of room is this?"

I looked around. "It's a library," I told him. "A room for storing books."

Jane Eyre hung limp in his hand. "Whole rooms set aside, just for books," he whispered. "Do mortals actually own this many?"

"Some do," I said. "The wealthier ones. This library belongs to a college. So it's bigger than what most people own. But Alice's grandparents' library is at least half this size. It holds thousands of books. Haven't you ever seen a library before?"

He held up *Jane Eyre* indignantly. "The book," he said, pointing toward the pages and the binding holding them together, "as you now know it, in codex form, with stacks of pages stitched together, was invented thousands of years *after* I was born."

Born before books were born. It was hard to fathom. I knew

Mermeros was thousands of years old, but still, the notion was full of surprises.

"Too bad we can't take you to visit a bookstore," I told him. "You'd be green with envy. Well, you're green anyway."

Mermeros was not amused. More to my surprised, he actually looked a bit stung.

"I'm sorry, Mermeros," I said. "Does it bother you? Being green?"

"What bothers me," he growled, "is my constant need to listen to your prattling questions."

There he was. His old self again. I smiled.

"Well?" he demanded. "I see you've gotten rid of the young man. Your betrothed. Did you break off the marriage?"

May God grant me patience. "He is *not* my betrothed," I said sternly, "and I haven't 'gotten rid' of him."

Mermeros's eyes narrowed. "Don't tell me he gave me to you of his own accord."

"Well, no," I admitted. "He doesn't know I have you. I'm holding on to you for safekeeping."

He scowled at me. "Lie to yourself all you like," he said, "but don't lie to me."

I wasn't lying. Was I? I gulped.

"Let's have it, then," he said. "Your final wish. I'd like to get back to my story."

My final wish. I looked around at the plush carpet, the soft chairs, and the countless books. I thought of the cricket pitch and the beautiful halls and chapels along the River Cam. The Cavendish Laboratory. Cambridge University.

Surely I could wish myself here. Then Mermeros would be gone.

And thieves would hound and harass Tom and his father for months or years to come. Perhaps the Poindexters really would relocate to the wilderness of northern Canada. Worst of all, someone else would find Mermeros someday, in a sardine tin or something else, and the cycle of greed, and crime, and danger would begin anew.

In another place, and another time, that wouldn't be my problem. But the world was different now, with bigger weapons, more powerful machines. Could a war be fought over power such as Mermeros's? Of course it could.

"Well, Girl Hatchling?"

I gulped down my hopes, one last time.

"Mermeros," I said, "can you grant yourself wishes?"

He hovered, weaving this way and that, blinking at me and saying nothing.

"For example," I said, "if you wanted to wish for more books to read, could you just wish them up for yourself?"

His eyes narrowed, but still he said nothing.

"You seem to wish yourself new clothes and things," I ventured.

In the time it takes a soap bubble to pop, Mermeros was back in his original clothes—the fish-scale vest, the sash, the skirt.

"Those aren't wishes," he said, "and they're hardly clothes."

Just an illusion of them, I supposed. More a magic trick than actual belongings.

"So, no?" I prompted him. "You can't?"

"I may protect myself," he said. "But if I could grant myself wishes"—here he darted closer to my face—"do you think I would remain as I am? Trapped forever alone? Tossed about by the whims of one greedy mortal after another?"

He drew himself back, as if he'd just realized he'd said too much.

Mermeros was miserable. Why had I not seen it before? What else could explain his constant ill-temper? I had always supposed he found it amusing to be irritable. I looked at him with new eyes.

"If you could have a wish, Mermeros," I asked him, "what would it be?"

He folded his arms across his chest and looked away from me. "None of your business."

I circled around him. "You said something this morning," I said. "About the night sky. And about immortality not being what people think it is."

With another small pop, Mermeros resumed his housecoat and

pajamas, and buried his nose in *Jane Eyre* once more. "You weary me, Fish Spawn," he told me. "I am not required to bare my soul to you."

To bare my soul to you. When he'd spoken of missing the stars at night, had he shared more of himself than he'd meant to?

"If you answer me one more question," I told him, "I'll buy you a book."

That got his attention. "Five books."

What did he think I was, made of money? With Alice's help, if I found a used bookseller, I could probably manage it.

"Three books," I told him. "That's the best I can do."

"Ask your question, then," he said. "And make the books good ones. Thick ones."

I paused to word my question carefully. "Has a djinni ever, er, stopped being a djinni?"

He gazed at me as if I'd sprouted a pig's snout and tusks. "Died, you mean?"

"No!"

A rattle came at the door of the library. I heard voices outside, wondering why it was locked. In no time, someone would return with a key.

"I mean," I whispered, "lost their power."

He let out a bitter laugh. "Don't you dare imagine that you can steal my power from me."

"I don't want your power!"

"Of course you do," he spat back.

Was he wrong? If someone gave me the power to grant wishes, but none of my own...? All that power, but no way of using it to accomplish my own goals?

Perhaps power could be a prison. Perhaps the power to make one's own choices was worth far more than magic.

More voices joined the person at the door.

"Please hurry, Mermeros," I whispered. "And please talk softly."

He heaved an exaggerated sigh and began ratcheting himself down in size.

"It is said to have happened once." Mermeros's whisper was barely more than a breath. "A young woman found a djinni, and they fell in love."

All my senses prickled. This had all the makings of a topper of a story.

"But how did it happen?"

He'd grown tiny, the size of a lapdog. "The only way it could."

"I only give one book for cryptic answers," I hissed.

He hopped nimbly back into his sardine tin, and promptly disappeared. "I skin and bone people who break their promises," his voice called faintly from the tin. "Skin them and bone them alive." The lid sealed itself shut with a *ping*.

I slid the sardine tin into my bag and had just enough time to open the drapes, sink into Pip's chair, and pretend to sleep.

"Good heavens," came a voice from the door. A woman, presumably a faculty member, stood there holding a key, with a few students behind her. "How could this have been locked? Have you been here this whole time, my dear?"

I blinked, and rubbed my eyes, and stretched. "Hmm?"

"You're one of Miss Welsh's guests, aren't you?" She favored me with a smile. "I'm Miss Jex-Blake. I'm sorry to have disturbed you. We've reserved the library for a meeting of the Committee for Nominal Degrees for Women."

I rose to make my exit.

"You're welcome to stay," she added. "One is never too young for the cause."

"I'd love to," I told her, and I meant it. Of course women ought to earn degrees! "But I think I need to go find my friends."

I left the library, patting the hard lump in my bag that was the sardine tine.

"Skin and bone me, eh, Mermeros?" I whispered with a smile. "You can lie to yourself all you like, but don't lie to me."

The sardine tin, as if in reply, gave an indignant wiggle and was still.

S upper was a somber affair.

We ate in Miss Welsh's private study, where a table had been set for all of us—the Bromleys, the Poindexters, Inspector Wallace, and me.

Miss Welsh ate with us, of course, which meant we couldn't discuss magic in the slightest, but she had caught wind of the fact that another burglary attempt had been made at the Lion Hotel. She offered up rooms for our entire party, which were gratefully accepted. In a brave attempt to stir conversation, she lamented the state of crime in the nation, but nobody was in the mood for that. Inspector Wallace, in particular, rankled at the statement. Coming from Scotland Yard, I suppose he welcomed complaints about crime as much as she would welcome Cousin Eugene Wilberforce's rants against higher education for girls.

Everyone, it seemed, was touchy about something.

As for me, I spent the meal with my mind spinning. Every tick of the clock brought us closer to dark, to nighttime, when my plan, my trap, my bait, might work—or fail miserably.

After supper, Miss Welsh had college matters to attend to and chapel services to oversee. Mrs. Bromley announced she wished to retire early. It was clear that the news of yet another burglary attempt had shaken her terribly, just as her husband had feared. Alice now volunteered to sit with her for a while to keep her company. That left the men, and Tom and me.

"Tom," I said, "shall we stretch our legs a bit, out in the gardens?"

"Don't go far," Mr. Poindexter called out to us.

We went outside to the grounds and strolled around. The sun had set, but the sky still held the pearly light of early evening. Dew had fallen, and the air felt fresh and soft. I looked across the rolling green to the cricket pitch, the hockey field, the pond, and beyond it, the Woodland Walk. The place I'd told our thieves to come. Had they seen the message? Would they be there tonight?

And Tom, walking beside me. What could I say to him? Especially after what I'd done?

He barely noticed the lovely evening. His head hung low, in utter dejection.

"I never should have stolen Mermeros from my dad," he said at length.

"If you hadn't, the thieves would've gotten him," I pointed out.

"They got him anyway," he said, "and now I must bear this guilty conscience for the rest of my life."

My own guilty conscience was hammering so loudly against my skull, I feared Tom would hear it.

"In two days," he said, "I've lost everything. The carpetbags. The djinni."

My magical map, I thought.

He looked up at me, and a fleeting smile lit up his face for a moment. "Still have my friends, though."

I was so relieved by this, I gave his hand a squeeze. "That's the spirit, my lad."

He squeezed my hand back. We walked along a moment that way, until my insides started squirming. I needed to yank my hand away without it seeming that I was yanking it away. Tom spared me the trouble, and let go.

"Maeve," he said, "do you ever think about being grown-up?"

This caught me off guard. "Mostly I try not to," I said. "Seems most adults' lives are dull beyond belief."

He smiled. "Yours won't be."

"Pah," I said. "Women's lives are all boring. Now, you, for instance," I said, punching him lightly on the arm, "will live in the wooded wild of northern Canada, and I'll be, I don't know, sorting through files in a dusty office somewhere, typing papers and eking out a meager living."

"Whatever happened to cricket?" he asked, turning to look at me, "and traveling the world?"

Indeed. What about cricket, and traveling the world?

"I still hope to do those things," I admitted. "Since coming here, I do think perhaps I'd like to attend college after all. I never would've thought so. But how on earth to pay for it, I couldn't begin to guess."

"Is this Maeve Merritt, talking to me?" Tom looked around as though searching for someone else. "Maeve Merritt doesn't admit defeat."

If only that were so.

"I don't want to live in the woods of northern Canada," Tom said eventually, "though it sounds like a fun place to visit."

We had reached the pond, and we now walked around it. It was rimmed with reeds, but the pond itself lay still, a shimmering mirror of what light remained in the sky, marred only briefly by the ripples and *plops* of frogs and fish piercing the surface.

"Where do you want to live?" I asked him.

"Here, in Britain," he said. "Somewhere with a bit of room."

"For cricket matches?" I knew Tom loved the game as much as I did.

He glanced at me sidelong. "For, maybe, a home for orphans," he said. "And a family of my own."

I knew he wanted to help orphans, but, good heavens! What was happening to us all? Here Girton and Cambridge had me thinking about college and career, Alice was planning her future as a schoolmistress and benefactor, and now Tom was thinking about being a *father* someday?

Until recently, Tom had lived without a family for most of his life. Of course he would want one.

"Tell me about your future family," I said, just to be social.

"I want twenty children."

I laughed aloud. "You do not!"

He grinned. "All right," he said. "Thirty, then."

"You'll have no place to put orphans," I went on, "with twenty children. Thirty."

"Fifty children, then," he said, "and a hundred orphans."

"You'll need to be a robber baron," I told him, "just to keep up with the grocery bills."

"Fine," he said. "A robber baron, fifty children, and a hundred orphans."

I rolled my eyes. "I thought *I* was being extravagant, wanting a pony and a pair of collies."

"Oh, I'll have ponies and horses and dogs, too," he said. "Robber barons require them."

A bird took off flapping into the air from a hidden nest as we passed by.

"Chickens and ducks, too, I'll wager," I said. "To lay eggs to feed all the children."

"Definitely," said Tom. "Chickens and ducks by the hundreds. And sheep, for wool to make their clothes."

I was glad to see Tom smiling again. He'd had me worried today.

"Is that what you would've used your wishes for?" I asked him.

He looked around at the now-darkening air, the color of an amethyst. Amazing, how quickly the colors of twilight could deepen, and one didn't even notice it, even while walking along under that bowl of sky.

"Of course I wouldn't use wishes to gain a family," he said seriously. "A family you used magic to get wouldn't be much of a family, would it?"

"I suppose not."

"Maybe that's true of everything," he said. "Maybe wishes were always a bad idea."

I wasn't quite ready to go that far. I kept my mouth shut.

"I don't really want fifty children—or twenty," he said. "Just a nice little family. I want my kids to have brothers or sisters to play with."

That made sense, especially for someone who had mostly been alone. I tried to think if I had ever "played with" Deborah, the sister closest in age to me. Not that I could recall, nor would I want to. But still, I'd always had Polydora, looking out for me, and even, on good days, Evangeline.

"Make sure you find a wife I can get along with," I told him. "I can be Auntie Maeve and bring presents to your kiddies."

He gave me a funny look. "I'll try to keep that in mind."

The sky was dark now. We'd circled the pond, and we aimed our steps back toward the Girton College building.

On the terrace, we found Inspector Wallace seated alone in a chair, studying a sheaf of papers by lantern light. We sat on wooden chairs beside him.

"Hullo, you two," he said. "How was your walk?"

"Fine," said Tom.

"What are you doing, Inspector Wallace," I asked him, "out here alone?"

"The other gentlemen both decided to retire early," Inspector Wallace explained. "I wasn't tired, and the evening was fine, so I thought I'd come sift through my notes once again and review those names the hotel proprietress gave me."

"May I see them?" I asked.

"My notes?"

I shook my head. "The list of names."

He handed them over to me. "I wouldn't expect you to know

any of them, but who knows? Perhaps you'll see something you recognize."

I held the pages up to the light and swatted away an inquisitive mosquito. The paper was divided into four columns, headed: "Checked in late last night," "Checked out today," "In residence all day," and "Checked in today."

I scanned the list. Mr. Lester Pinkney. Mr. and Mrs. Colson White. Miss Abigail Yates and niece. Mr. William Dale. And so it went, scrolling on through twenty-five or thirty names, all as unfamiliar to me as if they'd been Portuguese. Not a single shred of a clue.

But surely, one of them was the guilty party, wasn't it? In order to know which rooms the Poindexters and Bromleys occupied, the thieves would have to stay at the hotel, too, wouldn't they? The thieves couldn't be on the staff there. That would be far too great a coincidence. Could the thieves have bribed a staff person? Possibly, but that would have been an awfully quick bit of work and a risky move on their part.

"See anything?" asked the inspector.

You're missing something. My mind tormented me. But what? What was I missing? I couldn't think what. So I handed him back the papers. "Nothing at all."

"Chin up," he said briskly. "All that means is that there's more information to find. We'll find it."

"Not if my dad's right," said Tom, "and the thieves are long gone."

Inspector Wallace eyed us thoughtfully. "I've been doing this long enough," he said, "to learn patience. Some crooks do get away, it's true, but you'd be surprised how often the clue you've needed just lands in your laps, if you wait for it."

We sat in the cool quiet of the night, listening to a blackbird's song, and the chirp of a pair of crickets. In an instant, all became quiet and still.

"What—?"

Before Inspector Wallace could ask his question, something large and heavy slammed into the ground in the dark, at our feet.

I won't say whether Tom jumped and screeched, provided he never says whether I did, either, and neither of us will repeat the curse word the detective unleashed as he leaped to his feet. We recovered our senses after a few seconds, when the dark shapes proved not to be trained assassins—or corpses. We knelt down to examine the mystery.

A familiar woven roughness greeted my fingers. Leather-covered slats and handles. Metal rivets. Wiggling, squirming glee.

"Maeve," Tom whispered. "It's the carpetbags!"

CHAPTER 24

J ehoshaphat," murmured Inspector Wallace. He reached for his lantern and swung it around, examining the bags, our surroundings, and even the roof, searching for, I supposed, footsteps or someone who might have tossed the carpetbags down.

"However did they find us here?" I gasped.

"How did they escape?" added Tom. "The burglars stole them from us yesterday, in London!"

I scanned the horizon to see if anyone had seen them fly in. The last thing we needed was another eyewitness to magic. We had too many of those already.

"Tell me, you two," the inspector said, "on your honor. Is this some sort of stunt you pulled?"

I stopped where I stood. "Do you trust us that little, Inspector?"

He sighed. "No," he said at length. "I trust you. It's magic I don't trust."

"We had nothing to do with it, Inspector," Tom said, and that was the end of that.

I crouched down to greet the bags once more. "How could they have known where we'd be?" I couldn't leave the question alone. It made no sense.

"Well," Tom said slowly, "they do understand us, you know? When we talk to them?"

I nodded. "That's true," I said, "but—"

"Maybe," he said, "yesterday morning, they heard you say—"

I gasped. "We were *going to Cambridge*."

"I can't think of any other way they would have found us," said Tom.

"But it's not as if they've got a map!" I cried. "Cambridge isn't small. There are thousands of people here. And the landscape of Cambridgeshire doesn't have 'CAMBRIDGESHIRE' painted across it in giant letters."

"That would be jolly useful," said Tom, "if birds could read. Or if people could fly."

"Which we now can." I paused, considering. "What if the thieves brought them along to Cambridge when they followed us here?" I ventured. "Then the bags wouldn't have had such a terrible job finding us."

"That's true," said Tom. "I hadn't thought of that." He knelt down and gave his carpetbags each a hearty rub, for all the world like a boy greeting his beloved dogs and scratching them behind the ears. "I never thought I'd see you two again." He laughed. "This puts a spring in my step, and that's the truth. I could almost hope—" His voice trailed off. "Well, anyway, you're here. And think what good times we'll have."

My conscience give me a nice, swift kick in the shins. What he'd been about to say was he could almost hope that *Mermeros might somehow return*. I had the power to turn that hope into reality. Yet, even now, I didn't dare do it. I couldn't be sure we were safe. Where were our mysterious thieves?

Inspector Wallace brought his lantern down to the ground near the carpetbags. "May I examine them?" he asked. "Perhaps they carry some clue."

We stood back and let him study the bags all around and open them to look inside.

"Those are my socks," cried Tom. "And my spare clothes. But some things seem missing, and they're all mussed up."

"No doubt the thieves rummaged through them, searching for the sardine tin," Inspector Wallace said. "When they didn't find what they wanted, they abandoned the search. Ouch!"

We leaned in closer. "What's the matter?" I asked.

Inspector Wallace held up his finger, and Tom shone the

lantern's light upon it. A bead of blood had formed on the pad of his fingertip. The detective reached into his pocket and pulled out a handkerchief, which he used to dab the blood. With his other hand, he pinched at his wounded finger and plucked out something tiny.

"A shard of glass," he said. "I wonder..."

"Maybe," said Tom, "the bags had to crash through a window to escape their hiding place."

"Very possibly." The inspector rose to his feet. "Well, it doesn't seem that there's anything more that the bags can tell us."

Anything more the bags can tell us.

Their hiding place.

Was it possible?

I knelt down beside the bags.

"Carpetbags," I whispered, "however did you find us? Who are the smartest carpetbags the world has ever seen, eh? Who? You are, that's who!"

This wasn't flattery, but an absolute statement of fact. I defy anyone to produce more intelligent carpetbags. This pair wriggled and bounced up and down, delighted by the compliment.

"You must be tired," I said. "You must've been flying nonstop, trying to find us."

They hopped and cavorted like lambs, kicking up their heels, or whatever might be the heels of pieces of luggage. *We're not tired! Not in the least!*

"Would you look at that," whispered the inspector. "Frolicking like little goats."

"We're so sorry those bad men took you away from us," I told them. "We missed you dreadfully."

In reply, they nuzzled up to me in what practically amounted to a hug.

"Wouldn't it be fun," I whispered, "if you could show us where those bad men took you? After they stole you away? Could we do that? Could you take Tommy and me there?"

They leaped up in the air and did little loop-de-loops. Just like the Topsy-Turvy Railway had done only a few weeks ago at the Crystal Palace. *Of course we can take you there,* the carpetbags were more or less saying. *Hop on. Just like old times.*

"Maeve, that's brilliant," Tom said. "Shall we go for a spin?"

"See here, now," protested Inspector Wallace. "I can't just let you fly off alone to the criminals' lair." He raked a hand through his hair. "You're young. Who knows what danger might await you?"

"Why don't you come along, then?" I suggested.

He gaped at us. "*Me?*"

Who else? Adults could be surprisingly dense at times.

"You want *me* to fly with you on a *carpetbag?*"

"Suit yourself," I said. "It seemed like you wanted to come along. No one's making you. If you're afraid to fly, don't worry about it."

Tom threw a leg over his carpetbag. "We'll give you a full report when we return."

The inspector took a halting step forward. "They'll have my badge, back at the Yard," he muttered, "if I do, or if I don't. I can't go flying about on bags, and I can't let you two do it without me. How will I ever write this into a report?" He reached the carpetbags. "How do I, er, drive this thing?"

Tom and I exchanged grins.

"Tom and I had better share a carpetbag," I told him, "which will leave one for you."

He nodded uneasily. "Do you, er, just tell it where you want it to go?"

Oh, dear. This was going to take some work. "It's not like that," I explained. "Carpetbags aren't automobiles, or horses who've been trained to obey. They will only carry you somewhere if they feel you're a friend."

He backed away. "I–I don't know about this," he stammered. "I've only got one neck, and I'd rather not break it tonight, if the bag decides I'm not friendly enough."

"Do you have any children, Inspector Wallace?" Tom asked.

He stiffened. "I'm a bachelor."

"Any nieces or nephews?"

The inspector admitted that he did. "Two nephews. Around five and six years old."

"Perfect," said Tom. "Talk to your carpetbag just as you would to them."

The inspector made a baffled face.

"Be cheery," he explained. "Be nice. Be fun."

I leaned closer to whisper in the inspector's ear. "It always works best," I said, "if you let them think something is their idea."

He stared at me with a stricken look. It quite took me by surprise, seeing the inspector, who always seemed so bold and resolute, quailing at the sight of a flying magic carpetbag.

I strode over to where Tom stood and straddled the carpetbag in front of him.

"Come on," I told him. "Let's show him how it's done." We settled ourselves atop the bag, which was always a rather crouched and uncomfortable business until we were aloft. I seized the carpetbag's handles between my knees, which involved some hoisting up of my skirts, and left Tom without handles of his own. "Better hold onto my waist, Tom," I said. "Care to do the honors?"

Tom, after a moment's awkward pause, wrapped his arms around my waist and held on tight. "Carpetbag," he called, "wouldn't it be fun to go see the place where those bad men took you? The place you escaped from? Could you show us where it was?"

Our carpetbag shot straight up into the air as if borne by a geyser. I felt that familiar lurch in my stomach and that rushing of wind, blowing wisps of hair into my face and sending my petticoats flapping about my legs.

When we reached a certain height, the bag slowed and hovered, circling in the air. Down at our feet we saw Inspector Wallace's face, gazing up at us from far below, the twin carpetbag hopping and skittering about at his feet.

"Do you think he's coming?" Tom asked.

"Come on, Inspector Wallace," I called softly. "You'll be fine!"

He gazed up at us a moment more, then crouched down beside the carpetbag. He almost seemed like one in prayer, perhaps commending his soul to the Almighty, just in case. Then, with an awkward side step, he straddled his carpetbag, spoke some words to it that we couldn't hear, and rose into the air.

I wouldn't have guessed that the distinguished Inspector Andrew Wallace of Scotland Yard was capable of a shrill, high-pitched giggle, but that just proves that one never knows.

"I'm flying," he squealed. "By Jove, by gum, and by billy-o, I'm flying!"

"And a good job of it, too," said Tom. "Shall we be off?"

I saw the inspector's Adam's apple bob up and down. "Right then," he said. "Would you two like to, erm, navigate?"

I patted the side of our carpetbag. "Show us the place, will you, carpetbags?"

And we were off.

The carpetbags wove in and out, braiding their paths together like trailing ribbons. Inspector Wallace kept on laughing, which might have been putting a brave face on terror, or it might have been the frenzied laughter of the doomed. Below us, Girton College faded into the distance, and the twinkling lights of the city of Cambridge came into view.

By night, the grandeur of Cambridge University, with its many colleges, each with their stately halls and Gothic churches, and with starlight reflected in the glassy surface of the slow-moving River Cam, was even more wondrous than it had been on our daylight bicycle ride. Stained-glass windows, lit from within, glittered like gemstones. Towers reached so high that we had to dart to weave around them. From this high, it somehow felt both staggeringly vast and adorably miniature, both at once.

Tom pointed down toward a wide-spreading building in a narrow lane. "Isn't that the Cavendish Laboratory?"

"Let's go see," I said. "Oh, Carpetbags, would you mind taking us down there for a look in the windows at that big building? The Cavendish Laboratory?"

They swooped us down as the wind snatched Inspector Wallace's "Whyyyyy? What are weeee doooooing?" out of his mouth.

The building was mostly dark, but a trio of dimly lit windows in an upper floor suggested someone working late.

"Over there," I called softly, and the bags obligingly slowed to a hovering stop outside the first of the windows.

It was the laboratory we'd visited, or one just like it, lit only by a pair of wall sconces by a far door. A tall figure worked at a table closer to us, but we couldn't see his face until the tube he was fiddling with lit up with a green, unearthly glow.

I gasped at the sight of it. Bands of green light pulsated in the darkened room. By daylight, we hadn't realized fully what a ghostly luminescence it was. Now it cast its wavering beams over the broad features and mustached face of Ernest Rutherford.

"Cathode rays," whispered Tom. "Golly!"

Ern seemed to work feverishly, fiddling with something that made the green arc of light move up and down slightly. He took measurements of some sort—the angle, perhaps, of the beam—and scribbled them into his notebook, one after another. He took another measurement and frowned, fiddling once more with his apparatus with a look of desperation.

"Maeve," Tom whispered in my ear. "Look. Behind him. In the doorway."

Behind Ern Rutherford, in the open door to the corridor, stood a shadowy figure, peering around the doorjamb.

"Who's that?" I whispered. "Ern doesn't know he's there."

"The Cavendish thief?" said Tom.

"We've got too many thieves," I muttered.

"Who is this chap?" demanded Inspector Wallace, much too loudly, "and why are we stopping to gawp at him? Is this the thief?"

At the sound of Mr. Wallace's voice, Ern Rutherford looked up sharply toward the window.

"Do we bolt?" whispered Tom.

"Wait," I whispered back. "He probably can't see us." We weren't too terribly close to the glass. Surely the night's darkness swallowed us up.

Rutherford set down his pencil and notebook, and came out from behind the table, striding toward the window purposefully.

"Uh-oh," I said. "*Now* we bolt. Carpetbags, would you mind whisking us away?"

They didn't mind. We were off like shots from the barrel of a gun, but not so fast that we couldn't hear the scrape of a window frame sliding upward, and Ern Rutherford's booming voice calling after us: "Maeve? Tom? What in thunder?"

So much for remaining unseen. Perhaps he would scratch his head and decide his eyes were playing tricks on him after too much gazing into the light of his spectral tube. I wished he would turn around and catch whoever was lurking in that door.

We soared in a loop over the Cavendish Laboratory, past the town hall. Inspector Wallace didn't appreciate the sudden acceleration from hovering to rocketing about above the rooftops and chimney pots of Cambridge.

"That's the Lion Hotel, I'll wager," he said, finding the courage to release one hand from its death grip on the handles long enough to point downward. "Are they taking us there?"

But the carpetbags didn't stop. They kept on traveling over a city block or three until they settled down, gently, on the flat rooftop of a row of connected buildings. We landed and rose to our feet, Inspector Wallace seeming more than a bit thankful to stand on solid ground or, rather, roof.

"I say," he declared. "That was a marvelous thing. Flying over the rooftops like a blooming pigeon! Imagine what would happen if I told the chaps at the bureau—"

"Don't," I said. "Please don't tell them. We have enough problems as it is."

It was dark up here, but enough light from nearby windows and streetlamps illuminated our surroundings that we could see where we were. I took off to investigate. The air smelled of coal smoke, and of frying fish and chips, probably coming from the pub on the corner. Bits of conversations and laughter from pedestrians on the street wafted up to where we stood.

"Step gently," cautioned Inspector Wallace. "They'll hear you clear as crystal in the rooms below."

We crept around the rooftop, looking for any clue as to what the carpetbags intended us to see.

Inspector Wallace peered over the front roof and down to the street. "Looks like some sort of boardinghouse," he said. "Rooms to rent for lodgers. Makes sense. Our thieves would have arrived last night, or this morning, and looked for some inconspicuous place to stay."

We roamed around the roof but could find no way into the house.

"Carpetbags," I called softly, "you say this is where you've been waiting? Up here on this roof?"

In reply, the carpetbag closest to me nudged and prodded itself against the heels of my shoes.

"I think he means for you to go this way," said Tom. We tiptoed across the building until we reached the back of it, away from the street, where a ladder was mounted to the exterior wall. It reached all the way to the ground, so I swung myself around and started my descent.

"Maeve!" hissed Inspector Wallace. "Come back here! Let me go down first!"

I pretended I hadn't heard him and kept on climbing down.

The first story I passed looked quite normal. Silhouettes in the lit windows on either side of me seemed to suggest people moving about their rooms. One story down, however, I saw, to one side, a darkened room with a shattered windowpane.

"This is it," I called up softly. "This room, on my left. Climb down to the street, and go up the stairs. I'll be there to let you in."

"Do *not* enter that apartment, Maeve," the inspector called. "Wait there on the ladder. I absolutely forbid it! It isn't safe. I'll be down. Under no circumstances—!"

I didn't hear the rest. I'd already swung myself onto the window ledge, kicked out the remaining jagged glass shards with my shoe, and hopped on in.

I couldn't see a thing. The air smelled of burnt coffee grounds and cigarette smoke. My feet crunched against shards of glass. I felt around and located the electric lights and switched them on.

The dim bulb's glow revealed an untidy room that looked as though nobody had given it a proper washing in years. Cots in one corner seemed unused, but they had some clothing items draped over their surfaces. Newspapers and half-empty coffee cups cluttered the only table. The washbasin in one corner seemed to be all that was provided for hygiene.

The room made the Lion Hotel feel like Buckingham Palace. Its floor was strewn with suitcases, trunks, and hatboxes.

Our luggage.

I heard the crunch of Tom's feet landing on the glass-ridden floor beneath the window.

"Oh." I remembered my plan. "I'll go unlock the door for Inspector Wallace."

"No need," said the man himself, with a grunt, as he hoisted himself through the window. "Miss Merritt, if you were in the employ of Scotland Yard, you'd be fired on the spot. We're breaking half a dozen laws as we speak."

"But you *are* the law," I told him.

Inspector Wallace snorted. "Hardly. I'm breaking and entering, searching without a warrant, based on evidence provided by a magic carpetbag." He shook his head. "I should resign my post in disgrace."

"But look," I cried, pointing around me to the cluttered mess. "It's our luggage! All of it!"

"Ours too," cried Tom. He seized my arm. "Maeve," he said, his eyes wide, "do you think it's possible that Mermeros is here? In this very room?"

Once again, my hand slid to my traveling bag, where I felt the rounded rectangle of the djinni's sardine tin.

"I suppose it's possible," I managed to say.

Tommy reached for the nearest trunk and began rifling through it.

"Here, now," said the inspector. "Leave off! You can't just go prowling through people's things!"

"But they're *our* things," I protested.

"Not this suitcase," said Tommy cheerfully. "Mistook it for one of ours." He held up a clump of clothing. "This must belong to the burglar." He sniffed. "Smells like cigar smoke."

"Better search another bag," I told him.

He did so, and I knelt down and began perusing the bag of the burglars' things that Tommy had just abandoned. Maybe something would have their name on it.

Inspector Wallace pressed his fingertips into his temples. "How I let myself get talked into this..."

"Maeve," cried Tom, "this bag must be yours. Look!" He held up a shoe of mine. I hurried over to reassure myself. It *was* mine. And there, tucked into one corner, was my diary! I snatched it up and held it close to my heart. My scrap of magical map! It was mine once more. Scotland and its magical secrets—well, a small square of Scotland's magical secrets—were still mine to discover.

Inspector Wallace seemed to rouse himself. "Now, see here," he said. "We can't do this. We shouldn't be here. We may well be tampering with the investigation, coming here without a warrant and sneaking in through broken windows like common burglars. Besides," he said, warming up for a second round in the boxing ring, "for all we know, those burglars may come barging through this door at any moment."

I shook my head. "I think not," I told him. "I'm quite certain that they're staked out somewhere at Girton College, watching for us. They probably saw us fly away just now."

I'd done it again. Said too much. Me and my mouth!

Tom turned to study me. "Why do you say that, Maeve?"

"Well," I said, choosing my words carefully, "they've tracked us pretty thoroughly this far, so it stands to reason that they would follow us to Girton College tonight. But also…" I threw caution to the wind. I'd already passed the point of no return. "Also, I invited them."

"Great Scott." The inspector clapped a hand over his forehead. "You ought to be kept on a leash."

"Why would you invite them to come to Girton College tonight?" insisted Tom. "What were you thinking?"

"I'm sick of waiting for them to strike," I said, still pawing through the suitcase, "with no idea who they are, or where. I thought if we could draw them out into the open, we… Yuck!"

I'd felt something hairy in the midst of the clothes. A rat! Holding it up, however, I discovered it was a pair of wigs, gray and disheveled. I looked through the suitcase more and found the uniform and cap of a railway porter, and underneath everything, a large wooden chess set.

"There it is," I whispered. "Eureka."

They both came over to investigate.

"There *what* is?" demanded Tom.

"Did you find a name?" Inspector Wallace's curiosity got the better of him.

"No," I said slowly. "But I know who the burglar is."

They stared at me.

"Are you going to make us ask you who?" demanded Inspector Wallace.

I held up the railway porter's uniform. "He took our luggage at Victoria Street Station," I said. I caught sight of another button-studded jacket in the suitcase and lifted it up beside its twin. "Pardon me. Not *he*. They."

"Or perhaps they're simply porters," Inspector Wallace pointed out.

I set the uniforms aside and picked up the itchy, greasy, gray wigs, wishing I wasn't. "They were the two old men playing chess across the street from the Bromleys' home, in the park," I said.

"Rather a stretch, don't you think?" Inspector Wallace said.

In reply, I pulled the chessboard from the suitcase.

Tom whistled. "That's how they knew when Dad and I drove off in the taxicab."

"They followed your cab," I said, "probably in a carriage or automobile..."

"And robbed us not too far from Grosvenor Square," Tom said breathlessly.

"They would've had to hightail it back from there," I said, "leaving the luggage in their vehicle and changing clothes..."

"Then following you and the rest of the family to Victoria Street Station," supplied Tom.

"Where they impersonated luggage porters," I said, "and made off with all of our luggage."

Tom snapped his fingers. "They probably had a wagon or carriage filled with all that luggage, and they searched it for Mermeros," he said. "When they didn't find him—"

"They burgled the Bromleys' home," said Inspector Wallace, "while Mr. Bromley dined for luncheon at his club on his way home from the train station."

Tom and I turned to stare at the inspector.

"You see it, don't you?" I crowed. "We must be right!"

Inspector Wallace huffed through his mustache. "It's a theory," he admitted, "worth investigating further."

"But why would they bring everything here?" Tom asked. "Why go to that trouble? What would be the point of it?"

"Hiding the evidence?" suggested Tom. "Keeping it away from their home in London? If they're even from London, that is."

Inspector Wallace didn't seem convinced. "I suppose, though I could think of easier ways to hide it than this."

I frowned at the mess, trying to think of a reason. It did seem like a waste of effort.

Inspector Wallace pushed aside a pair of shoes blocking his path. "They've been busy, these thieves of ours."

"That's why," I said, as realization dawned. "They brought everything along, because—"

"—Because they had to hurry to chase us," Tom said, sensing my train of thought. "When they didn't find Mermeros after the first day of robbing the luggage, and the house, they decided we must still have him."

"Which you did," the inspector said. "But they couldn't be sure that the sardine tin wasn't hidden in one of the suitcases. Not without conducting a proper, thorough search. They needed more time to look, to make sure. So they chased you to Cambridge, and brought everything with them."

"The last thing they'd want to do," said Tom, "is to accidentally leave him behind. To actually have Mermeros, and let him slip through their fingers."

As he'd just done. Tom's face fell.

"It must have driven them wild," I said, going with the first thought to pop into my head, "to keep on thinking they must have captured the djinni, only to be wrong once more."

"I don't see what's so funny," Tom said crossly. "Don't forget, they got him in the end."

I mashed my lips together tightly to keep from smiling and giving it all away.

"Right," I said. "Anyway, you did it, Tom!" I patted him on the back. "You solved the mystery of the luggage. Now we've got them all figured out."

Inspector Wallace chuckled to himself. "I wouldn't go that far."

"We still don't know their names," said Tom.

"Nor what they look like," I said. "Though we've seen them several times."

"It's a horrible feeling," said Tom. "Being hunted by invisible thieves. Like being bitten by bugs one can't see."

We both looked at him strangely.

"There were bedbugs," he said sheepishly, "at the orphanage."

We looked around us at the mountains of mess. All our things, scattered about. I thought about poor Mrs. Harding and her aunt's cameo brooch. I wished I could fit all our belongings in the carpet-bags and bring them safely home.

"For now," the inspector said, "the most useful thing we can do is find out who has rented this room. Wait here."

He tried the door, which opened easily, and stepped cautiously out into the hall. He poked his head back inside the room and fixed me with a look. "Maeve. Don't do *anything*."

"Honestly, Inspector!"

"I mean it," he said sternly. "Don't move a muscle. Don't so much as breathe."

He left. We heard his footsteps fade.

"You're breathing," observed Tommy.

"Don't tell on me." I sat down on the untidy cot. "Imagine, those chess players, spying on us all the time!"

He shuddered. "It makes me feel sick."

"They looked like harmless old men," I continued, "but all the time, they were watching, waiting for their chance to pounce."

"Not old at all," added Tom. "You're less likely to suspect old people."

"But who *are* they?" I scuffed my feet across the floor. "And how did they learn about Mermeros?"

We sat in silence, waiting and wondering.

"We've figured out so much," said Tom, "yet it still feels like we know nothing at all."

I leaned back on the bed, propping myself up with my elbows. "I keep on feeling like there's something I'm missing."

"That's obvious, isn't it?" said Tom. "We're missing the answers. We're missing the names of our thieves." He kicked at a suitcase lying nearby. "We're missing my djinni."

I took a deep breath and spoke before my annoying conscience could get a word in. "That's not what I mean," I said. "I mean, with what information we do have, I feel like there's something we're missing. Something I ought to have figured out, but I haven't. The puzzle piece is right in front of me, yet I still don't see it."

We heard footsteps approach the door. Inspector Wallace entered.

"Whose room is it?" I asked, jumping up off the cot.

"By Jove," he said. "You actually didn't get into any mischief while I was away."

"Very funny," I said. "What did you learn?"

"Come on," he said, leaning out the window. "We've got to get back up to the carpetbags on the roof and get back to Girton College." He offered me a hand to climb out after him. "Nobody answered the office door, and I couldn't locate a landlord. But I placed a telephone call to Scotland Yard at the pub next door, and someone will follow up as soon as possible and send me word."

CHAPTER
26

We flew back to Girton College in silence. The wondrous little city scrolled past us below, but I barely saw it. I kept turning over the mystery of our determined burglars in my mind. Had they found my note? Would they come tonight? If they did come, would I know what to do? And would I have the courage to do it?

And what was the missing piece of the puzzle? The detail right in front of us, that I still couldn't see?

Girton College loomed out from the wooded darkness near the village of Girton. I saw its dark, glassy pond, and the thick blackness of the trees surrounding the Woodland Walk. Would the burglars come tonight? Might they be there, even now?

I swallowed down a rising tide of dread. The time was drawing near. Time for some quick thinking and some very hard decisions.

The carpetbags slowed us to a lazy, spiraling landing on the lawns near the school.

"That takes some getting used to," said Inspector Wallace as his feet touched the ground. "Can't say I'm sorry to be back on good old terra firma."

We looked around to see if anyone had seen us land. We were all alone, more silhouettes and shadows than people. We could see just enough by moonlight and some distant light spilling from windows. From somewhere in the Girton College building, a choir of girls' voices sang an evening hymn. The strains, echoing faintly across the dark grounds, sounded angelic, yet melancholy. Mournful angels. Young women whose academic hopes might soon be granted—or dashed. Dashed by all those rude, tomato-throwing undergraduates, and even the graduates, returning in droves on trains, going to such pains to keep us females in our places.

Returning to Cambridge on trains.

Returning on trains, and staying in hotels.

Robbers in hotels.

Oh.

"Inspector Wallace," I said, "I've thought of something."

"Oh?" said he, rather warily, I thought. "Let's have it, then."

I took a step closer as if perhaps the ducks in the pond might overhear us.

"I met a gentleman at lunch today in the hotel," I said. "We exchanged a few pleasantries."

The inspector nodded. "And?"

"Well," I said, "I suppose it would be more accurate to say I wasn't very pleasant to him."

Tom snickered.

"Astonishing," said Inspector Wallace drily. "Go on."

"Later on," I said, "I saw him in the stairwell at the Lion Hotel, heading up. Presumably going to his own hotel room."

"Hotels have many guests," the inspector pointed out. "Guests who eat downstairs and go back upstairs to their rooms."

"No, but listen," I said. "When I saw him in the stairs, I felt bad for having been a bit rude at lunch. So I apologized to him. He looked at me rather strangely for it, I must say."

Inspector Wallace exhaled loudly. "Scotland Yard," he said, "doesn't investigate cases of poor manners."

I ignored it. This evening must have rattled him.

"That's not the point," I said. "The point is, I told him my name, and he told me his. Sam Haley."

Whatever the inspector was about to say, he changed his mind. "Sam Haley?"

"Is that someone you know?" inquired Tom.

"No," I said. "And that's the point. His name is not on the list of hotel guests. I would have spotted it immediately. It wasn't there. Funny thing, though," I went on. "When we spoke on the stairs, it almost seemed as if..."

I began to second-guess myself, but Inspector Wallace pressed the point. "Almost seemed as if what?"

"It almost seemed," I said, "as if he didn't remember talking with me, just an hour, or maybe less, before."

Inspector Wallace chuckled. "Maybe you're easy to forget."

"Not Maeve." I'd have to decide later whether Tom was being loyal or cheeky.

"Right you are," agreed Inspector Wallace.

"What I mean is," I said, "there seem to have been two people who looked very much alike. So much so that I thought they were the same person. But they weren't. And the one gave a name that doesn't appear on your list."

Inspector Wallace nodded. "Listen, you two," he said. "I need to go inside for a few minutes. I want to make a few telephone calls."

"I thought you made some at the pub," I said.

"I didn't know about your Sam Haley then, did I?" He threw up his hands. "I'm explaining my methods to a thirteen-year-old girl."

"With flying carpetbags," I added, just to be helpful.

He waved a go-on-with-you hand at me and headed back inside the school. Then he stopped and turned around.

"Where and when," he said pointedly, "did you tell the crooks to meet you?"

I pointed toward the darkness of the trees. "In the Woodland Walk," I said. "Tonight. After dark. I didn't specify a time."

He peered, unseeing, into the distance. "So they could be there now?"

"If they saw my note," I said. "Maybe they never did."

"Or maybe," said Tom, "they came and then left."

"All right," he said. "See here, you two. I'll be as quick as I can. Don't get any ideas. You're both to stay here, is that understood?"

"Clear as crystal," I told him. "We'll stay on that bench over there."

"See that you do," he said sternly, "and try not to start some sort of international criminal incident from that bench."

"Who, me?"

"I wouldn't put it past you." He hurried inside.

Tom and I carried the carpetbags across the dewy grass and parked them beside us on the bench. I thought about our evening's adventures.

"Did we learn anything?" I wondered aloud. "Was this flight, tonight, a waste of time?"

"Of course we did." Tom plucked a blade of grass from the lawn and chewed on it. "It was fun, anyway," he said. "Flying is never a waste. And it was too dark for lawn croquet."

Good old Tom. Even now, making me laugh.

Good old Tom. My conscience, which had been rattling against my bones all day, now began to dance the tarantella. I'd been wrong. Wrong to steal the djinni from Tom. Wrong to tell myself I could fix what he wouldn't be willing to fix. Wrong to appoint myself the judge of all magical matters. I'd robbed and defrauded my best friend in the whole world, next to Alice. He trusted me. He'd stood loyally by me. And I'd betrayed him and stolen his djinni.

I looked up to see him watching me in the thin glow of moonlight. Studying my face. Concerned.

"What's the matter, Maeve?" he said. "Are you all right?"

"Tom," I said. "We need to talk."

CHAPTER
27

Few things are more miserable than confessing to someone you care about that you've done them a dirty deed. But if there is anything worse, it's this: the friend doesn't get angry at you, but you see the disappointment, the hurt, the confusion, the sadness in his eyes. He pulls back. He starts to doubt you or, worse, doubts himself. Doubts his judgment for believing you were his friend. Doubts his intelligence for not knowing he was being duped.

But he wasn't being duped. I was trying to help.

Why should he believe that, either? I wasn't sure I believed it myself.

I told him everything, and I handed him the sardine tin. He took it reluctantly. He wouldn't meet my gaze.

"I'm sorry, Tom," I said. "A hundred times sorry. It was wrong of me."

He spun the tin slowly between his finger and thumb. "What happens now?"

His lifeless tone broke my heart.

"That's up to you," I said.

"You must have had something in mind," he said, "when you invited our thieves to come tonight." Then realization dawned. "You knew," he said. "You knew the burglars would still be on the hunt because you knew they didn't yet have Mermeros. He was the prize they were after."

I nodded.

"Dad thought they got Mermeros from his hotel room," Tom said, "and I thought they got it from my jacket, but...but you knew."

I nodded. "That's right."

"I suppose I should thank you," he said with a hollow laugh. "You saved Mermeros for me." He set the tin down on the bench. "I almost don't want him now."

I turned to look at him. "Yes, you do."

"All right," he admitted. "It's true. I do. But so what? I can't make wishes now and admit to my dad that I stole Mermeros from him."

"He'll forgive you," I said.

"Just as I've forgiven you?" he said bitterly. "I'm not so sure."

I waited. For a long time, I heard nothing but the sound of crickets chirping in the grasses.

"This will never end, will it?" Tom said at length. "When I first saw Mermeros, that day you found him back at school, I thought it was better than Father Christmas, better than anything. The thought that there was real magic in the world—a real wish-granting djinni..." His voice trailed away. He gazed off at the distant dark. "It filled me with hope. With possibilities. For the first time, I thought, maybe my life might have something to look forward to. Something more than working myself to death in those cotton mills."

"And now you have something more," I said. "Much more."

He hung his head. "But I'm the lucky one. My mates back at the Mission Home don't even have that."

It was true. I thought of those poor orphaned lads, playing cricket out in their schoolyard, with their grubby faces and their shabbily-dressed, underfed bodies.

"So what did I do?" Tom went on. "I made a plan to *steal it from you.*"

"But you didn't steal it," I pointed out. "You became my friend."

"But don't you see?" he persisted. "That's been the pattern ever since. Where there's magic, there will always be someone wanting to steal it." He held up the sardine tin. "I once thought I'd give me front teeth to get my hands on this thing. Now?" He set it back down. "Now I barely even want to look at it."

Don't take it personally, Mermeros, I thought.

"I could almost just give the villains the sardine tin," said Tom. "Just hand it over and be done with it."

I sat up straight. "Tom," I said, "you can't! You mustn't!"

He held up a hand. "I know," he said. "I know. If Professor Fustian had gotten to keep Mermeros—"

"Or Mr. Alfred P. Treazleton," I said, remembering that corrupt businessman, the first villain to try to extort the djinni from me.

"Right," said Tom. "If either of them had gotten hold of Mermeros, the things they would have done would've have set off a chain reaction of greed, and stealing, and people getting hurt."

I ran a finger around the edge of the sardine tin. "Wars could be fought over this."

"So what was your plan?" Tom repeated.

I tried to think what to say. "Catch the burglars, I suppose," I said. "I hadn't really planned it all out. I guess I thought I'd...improvise."

He almost smiled. "The Maeve Merritt way." His face grew serious. "Whom could they be, Maeve?" He looked out toward the wooded area. "Our mysterious chess-playing railway porters. Who are they?"

"And are they out there?" I joined him in looking out at the darkness of the trees. "I think I made rather a bloomer of all this. Inviting them here has to have been my most foolish move to date."

"In a long career," said Tom, "of foolish moves."

"Thanks a lot."

He rose to his feet. "I've made up my mind," he said. "I'm going into the woods."

I gasped.

"You don't have to come," he said. "I don't want anything to happen to—"

"Of course I'm coming!" I said. "But shouldn't we wait for Inspector Wallace?"

Tom shook his head. "He'll tell us we ought not to go. He'll tell us to leave it to the authorities. But we can't entrust the authorities with Mermeros."

I agreed. "Not in a million years."

"If police come," added Tom, "the thieves will make a run for it. So no matter what, there won't really be an end to things. Even if they arrest these burglars, others will come after them. Nothing will change."

He took off toward the Woodland Walk.

"But, then," I said, jogging to catch up to him, "what will you do?"

"Just what you were going to do," he said. "I'll improvise."

It hit me then. "You're giving up your wishes," I said, "aren't you?"

He said nothing but thrust out his chin and kept on walking.

"But, Tom," I protested. "The orphans you were going to help!"

He stiffened. "It was always a foolish dream," he said. "There have always been kids in need, and there always will be. It was grandiose and foolish of me to think I could make a difference."

My eyes stung.

"I thought it was wonderful of you," I said.

He paused, then pressed on toward the woods.

I learned then that there is something worse than disappointing a friend. It's watching them abandon their dreams.

I reached into my traveling bag and pulled out one of the magic mirrors. I placed it facedown on the bench, just in case, then hurried after Tom.

By day, the Woodland Walk had been a charming, leafy bower, making me think of gnomes, elves, and fairies, and leading out to cricket fields where teams of girls played. A practical paradise. By night, it made me think of demons, goblins, and bogey-men, leading to gangs of thieves, defeat, and despair.

Here the moon's light hid behind a canopy of swaying leaves. Ferns and fronds of foliage clung to us with probing fingers as we passed by. Every tree's shadow seemed to suggest some lurking fiend who might leap out and grab us. I'm not the fearful type, but after this long day, these two long days of being hounded and harried by cunning thieves, I was more than a little bit on edge.

You invited them here yourself, Maeve, I told myself. *There's no one to blame but you.*

"If they have come," whispered Tom, "where will they be?"

"Anywhere," I said. "This *is* the Woodland Walk. We're on it now."

He stopped. "Then let's wait here."

"All right."

We stood and listened.

I don't have a great deal of experience with forests at night. The sounds of the suburbs, in Luton, where I grew up, or in London, where I went to school, or in its stately neighborhood of Grosvenor Square, where I lived with the Bromleys—with any of these, I could rest easy. They were comfortingly noisy, a steady rumble of carriage wheels and voices and the sounds of people living their lives—the ordinary chaos that lulled one to sleep at night.

But the silence, the suffocating stillness of rural woods was something I had no reference for. It tricks you into thinking it's silent, but as you really listen, you realize it's not quiet in the least, but positively slithering with rustling leaves, and rattling branches, and wind in treetops; with the chirpings and munchings of unseen millions of insects, quite possibly munching each other, or you; and the scuffle and scratch of claw-footed things that lurk and scuttle and swoosh about by night. Right about then, I'd have felt safer in the midst of a drunken brawl at a rowdy West End London pub.

Stop it, Maeve, I told myself firmly. *You're feeling skittish about unseen burglars, not mice and bats and squirrels.*

I backed up into Tom and jumped, then seized his hand. The

better to know where he was, and where he wasn't. Otherwise, I might mistake him for an intruder and sock him in the teeth.

"Of all the places I've followed you, Maeve," Tom whispered, "this might be most bizarre yet."

"If you'll recall, it was you who charged into these woods," I shot back, "and I had to chase after you."

"But only because you invited a pair—maybe a gang—of criminals to come meet us here."

I harrumphed. "Nobody seemed to have any better ideas."

A crack, perhaps the snap of a twig, sounded in the distance.

"What was that?" I whispered.

Another, and then another. Footsteps.

"Someone's coming," said Tom.

I tugged hard at his hand. "Off the path. Come on!"

We scurried into the underbrush. Contrary to what happens in stories, the underbrush put up a good fight, with stout branches and gnarled roots we couldn't see in the dark tripping us up. When Tom stumbled, I pulled him upright, and he returned the favor. At last we dared stop and look around.

But what could we see in the dark? My heartbeat thrummed in my veins. At least, before, the path showed us where we were, to a point. Now we were simply lost in suffocating blackness.

"Look."

The word was barely more than a breath in my ear. I felt, more than saw, Tom point back toward the path we'd just left.

A small gleam of light appeared. It grew wider. It was some kind of lamp, and someone was holding it, but I couldn't see who. All the light shot forward in a beam from the device.

"The djinni and the lamp," I whispered. It had sounded more amusing in my mind than out loud.

"It's a dark lantern," Tommy whispered. "Police use them."

"A dark *what*?" I whispered. "The police are here?"

"Shh," he whispered. "I don't think so."

Additional footsteps sounded. The holder of the lamp swung it around and pointed it toward the newcomer.

It was a man, dressed in dark clothes, with a black mask over his eyes and a scarf over his mouth and nose. He opened the beam of a dark lantern of his own and shone it toward the other man, who, I could now see, in reflected light, was dressed and masked much the same. Both men looked sturdy and strong.

"That's them," whispered Tom. "The blokes who held up our taxicab. I'd swear it. They were masked then, too."

"You go that way," one of the men was saying, gesturing toward the right, "and I'll go this way." Gesturing toward us.

Tom gave my hand a squeeze and let go. "Stay here, Maeve," he whispered. "Please."

"No, Tom!"

Two lantern beams swung our way. They'd heard me! I felt sick. I thought I'd whispered softly. Not softly enough.

Muttering at me under his breath, Tom stepped forward into the light. "So," he said loudly, "you've come."

It was very brave of him. Possibly also idiotic, but brave all the same.

In all the desperate times we'd faced since Mermeros had brought us together, all the hairy tangles we'd had with villains and fiends, supernatural and otherwise, nothing before had ever felt like this. Alone, in a dark wood, with two large, faceless men blinding us with their lanterns, prepared to do devil-knows-what to us, and nobody to see it happen, nor hear our cry of help.

I was glad Alice wasn't here.

One of the men made a lunge toward us, but the other held him back.

"Wait," the second man said. To us he called, "Who's with you?"

I hesitated. If we said "Nobody," what would they do to us? If we said we were surrounded by a ring of armed policemen, then what desperate move might they make? There was no good answer.

"Show yourselves," I called. "Who are you?"

A low chuckle came from the second man, the one doing the talking. "It's the little girl."

"The brassy one," the first one said. "Get her."

"Hold it," the second man growled. To us, he said, "Why did you leave that note at the hotel?"

Tom turned and looked at me, his eyebrows raised, silently asking, *What should we do?*

"It's rather tiresome," I called out, "getting robbed every other minute."

"Give us the djinni," barked the first man, "and we'll leave you alone."

I reached into my bag and pulled out my mirror. Maybe, I thought, Inspector Wallace had found it. Maybe, if he could see us now, help would soon be here.

But the mirror's glass was black as pitch.

"Well?" demanded the first man, taking a step forward.

"Why should we just give it to you?" I called out. Every minute they were talking to us, they weren't murdering us. And that was something.

"Because," said the first man, "you might not enjoy the way we take it from you, if you don't cooperate."

"Shut it," snarled the second man.

"They have the same voice," observed Tom.

"They must be brothers," I whispered. "Probably twins. Remember Sam Haley?" Then I decided not to whisper. I bellowed to our pursuers: "Are you brothers?"

They stiffened a moment.

"It's our voices," said the first man.

"I told you to let me do the talking," said the second. A muffled argument erupted between them.

"Definitely brothers," said Tom. "Keep them talking, Maeve."

"So," I said, "which one of you is Sam Haley?"

They both stopped and turned toward me once more.

"Who's Sam Haley?" demanded the first man.

"Never mind," said the second.

"Did you tell someone your name was Sam Haley?" the first man said.

"Never *mind*," said the second.

"Why would you use that name?" said the first.

"Shut your *mouth*," bawled the second.

"You're an idiot," said the first. "That's enough talking. I'm getting the kids." He began wading through the grasses and under-brush toward us.

My heart pounded. Each footfall through the brush seemed to crash upon my ears.

"We don't have the djinni," I cried out.

"Fine," the first man said. "I'll hold you hostage until somebody brings him to us."

"Lou!" said the second man. "You're going to land us in Newgate!"

"Listen to your brother, Lou," I panted. "Prison's no fun."

Lou, the first man, and our pursuer, paused once more. "Here. How'd you know he's my brother?"

"He's not just your brother," I told him. "He's your twin."

After a pause, I heard one of them mutter to the other, "How can she tell, in our masks?"

"So help me," groaned the second man, not Lou. "Can you keep your mouth *shut*?"

"We know all about you," cried Tom.

"That's right," I added, "and so does Inspector Wallace. Of Scotland Yard."

Well. That got their attention.

Inspector Wallace must have been a good deal more famous than I had realized. The mention of his name froze them both in their tracks. Lou turned back for an emergency huddled conference in tense whispers.

Tom and I held one of our own.

"Maeve," he said, "you should run and get help."

"I'm not leaving you," I said. "If I ran, they'd just tackle and chase us both." I reached into my bag and checked my mirror one more time. Still nothing.

"All right, then," Tom said. "I'll fall back just a few paces and summon Mermeros to deal with them. If they notice anything funny, try to distract them, all right?"

"Are you sure?" I asked. The brothers were still engaged in their urgent argument. "Summoning Mermeros seems so risky."

"What other hope do we have?" he said. "We can't outrun them, nor could we best them in a fight. They could carry us away as easily as two pounds of sausages."

Everything in me prickled. We should *not* summon Mermeros. The spectacle of him would be more temptation than this pair of fiends could resist. They'd have him at any price, even if that price was Tom's and my heads on a platter.

But I'd told Tom that the decision was up to him. For once, I needed to mean what I said. Especially to Tom.

"Go ahead," I said. "I'll distract them till they wish they'd never tangled with me."

Tom grinned. "I know you will, Maeve."

Tom slipped away, ducking behind a tree.

I sidled over toward the miscreants, tacking off to one side in the woodland forest so their gazes, and their torch-lights, would be less likely to find Tom.

Their debate was still in full force, but at the sight of me, they closed ranks and set their differences aside.

"Where's your little friend?" asked one of them, whom I was pretty sure was Lou, though honestly, if they'd switched places, I could be wrong. "Your little beau?"

"Don't be revolting," I snapped. "He's nothing of the kind."

"Well, where is he?"

"Pardon me," I said, "but it's very confusing dealing with the two of you. You're a pair of matching spoons. Are you Lou?"

"Nah, I'm Lou. He's Jim," said the other, and he received a cuff on the ear from Jim for his pains.

"Why don't you just tell her our address, while you're at it?" said Jim.

"Ah, you live together," I said. "I hope you don't argue all the time at home, too, but I imagine it does save on rent and the grocer's bill. Does your mother still do your cooking and washing?"

"Make her stop talking," pleaded Lou, "before I do something I'll regret."

A whiff of breeze brought the scent of sulfur. Tom had gotten Mermeros open.

"Avoiding regret is a wise policy, Lou," I told him. "Stay strong."

"Who *is* this brazen little wretch?" cried Lou.

"And what's that smell?" Jim scented the air like a bloodhound.

"Something unmentionable, I imagine," I said. "Possibly Lou's dinner did not agree with him."

"It ain't me!" cried Lou.

"I beg your pardon," I said. "It must be your brother. So. You gentlemen have had a busy week. You burgled a taxicab, a home, a hotel room, and several sets of luggage from a railway station, and you still couldn't find a djinni, eh?"

Now it was Jim's turn to lose his temper.

"Where've you hidden it?" he demanded. "Do you wear it around your neck? Hide it in your boots?"

Over the rustle of the wind through the trees, I heard a distant tone of voice that could only belong to Mermeros. Probably sneering and making snide remarks at Tom.

"How do you even know," I cried, hoping to drown it out, "there's a djinni?"

"We know," Jim said.

"Ah," I said, "but *do* you?"

I could see it. I'd found his little chink of doubt, and now I wedged a brick inside it.

"I have no djinni," I said, "but I do have a magic mirror. Look into it. What do you see?"

He'd see nothing, I knew. Perhaps I could make him doubt everything. Make him think all of this was nonsense. It was the best strategy I could come up with on short notice.

Jim took the mirror and stared into it. His brother peered over his shoulder.

"There's nothing there," said Lou.

"Are you sure?" I cried. Inwardly, I fretted. What could be taking Tom so long? Why hadn't Mermeros handily nabbed these burglars and trussed them up like a pair of fresh-caught trout?

"Wait a minute," Lou said slowly. "There *is* something there."

I gulped. There was?

"Someone," he corrected. "Whose face is that?"

He held it toward his brother, Jim. Jim frowned at the image, then flung the mirror from him into the bushes. "It's Wallace!"

My heart leaped. Inspector Wallace had found the mirror! He wasn't far away. He must be looking for us.

And *Jim recognized his face?*

Never mind that now.

"We've got to hurry," Jim cried.

Lou pointed off into the distance. "What's that?"

He was pointing straight toward Tom. There, peeking out between limbs and tree trunks, was a green and ghostly glow. Like Ern Rutherford's cathode ray tubes. Like the magical aura of Mermeros.

"Probably a fairy," I panted. "Or an elf. Or a gnome. They're rumored to infest these woods."

But the brothers were tired of me. They plunged past me toward the light.

I've never played rugby, but I imagine I should like it immensely if I did. In that spirit, I plowed into Lou, the one closest to me, and, though I couldn't quite tackle him, I did my utmost to trip him up.

Unfortunately, I'm on the skinnier side, and this man had a good seven stone on me in weight. I only succeeded in ripping the mask off his face, infuriating him and slowing him down, but I couldn't stop him. He swore a streak of curse words and pushed me away with a hard shove that sent me toppling down onto my tailbone. The pain knocked the wind out of me for a moment, and my eyes swam. Before I knew it, strong arms had pinioned my arms to my sides and hoisted me up in the air.

"Little Miss Sass can come along with us and keep her mouth shut," said Lou's voice right in my ear.

I kicked and kicked with all my might, landing several good cracks with the heel of my boot on his shins, till he howled in pain.

"Grab her legs, Jim," he yelled.

"Never mind that," said Jim in a dazed voice. "Look."

For a second, we all looked.

There he was. Mermeros the Mighty. Bigger than ever. Gigantic. Translucent. Bobbing among the branches and leaves like a massive balloon. Like a glowing moon of green cheese.

It hit me all at once. What a wondrous thing, a djinni.

I saw him as if for the first time. As if none of our exploits together had ever happened. A miracle, a marvel, spilling out from a common sardine tin. The sight filled my eyes with tears. Our Mermeros. Our djinni. Our curmudgeonly scalawag. Our arrogant, insulting, ensorcelled ancient prince.

I loved the old rascal, and we were about to lose him. These villains would steal him, and this would be our last goodbye.

Mermeros's green, fishy eyes swiveled from their gaze at Tom to take in the sight of Jim and Lou, still imprisoning me. His eyes narrowed.

"Who are you?" Mermeros sneered at the brothers, as cold as ever. As proud as an emperor.

"Gorblimey," breathed Lou, right in my ear (a very unpleasant sensation).

"What are your intentions," said Mermeros in a voice that could make one's flesh crawl, "toward the mortal girl hatchling?"

Oh, Mermeros! After all this time, had you finally begun to care?

"Because," Mermeros told the two brutes, "she owes me three books."

Thanks a lot. In spite of myself, I laughed.

Tom turned to see me imprisoned in Lou's grip. "You let her go!" he cried. "Mermeros, make—"

"No!" I screamed. "No, Tom, don't!"

He hesitated. That was all the time Jim needed. He lunged through the air, landing with his hands clapped over the sardine tin on the ground. Tom tried to fight him off, but he was no match, either, for the man's bulk. He did manage, though, to claw the mask off Jim's face. He was a mirror image of his brother.

Jim rose to his feet, bringing Mermeros with him. The great djinni spun on the tether connecting him to his tin like a kite on a string. Tom rushed in, seizing Jim's hands and fighting him for the djinni. Lou, my odious captor, relaxed his grip on me for a second as though he would go after Tom, but I stomped on his feet, elbowed his ribs, shoved the crown of my head up into his jaw, and kicked his shins with all my might.

"You rotten little minx!" Lou roared in my ear.

"He's mine!" Jim screamed at Tom. To his brother he yelled, "Can't you manage a little girl?"

"Give him back!" Tom cried.

"She's no girl," cried Lou. "She's a rabid weasel!"

"Desist!" bellowed Mermeros, in a voice that shook the ground.

Everyone did pause, then, just for a second.

Jim held the sardine tin up, high in the air. "I have him," he cried. "He's mine."

Mermeros, high among the treetops, met my gaze. He shook his head once, only slightly.

"Do it, Tom," I called. "Do it now."

"But—"

"Now!"

"Leave the kids, Lou," Jim said, "and let's go before Wallace gets here."

"Mermeros," Tom said, in a loud voice. "Hear my wish."

All heads turned to Tom.

"I wish you mortal," he said, "and human. I wish you a comfortable life, lasting long enough life to read all the books you want, and then, I wish you a peaceful death."

Oh, Tom.

Mermeros let himself deflate in size. He swam down to where Tom stood, held at bay by Jim's long arm, and peered at him through his monocle. "You would do that?"

Jim, still holding the sardine tin like a trophy, started laughing.

"You're too late," he cried. "Your wish didn't work, kid. I got to him first."

Mermeros kept on gazing at Tom, as if he'd never seen anything like him in all his long years. "But what about your own ambitions?" he asked.

"Those are my three wishes," said Tom.

"Too late, kid," Jim said. "You imbecile children don't see what a djinni's power is good for." To his brother, he said, "We've got what we came for. Let's go."

Through the trees, I saw a light bob, swaying this way and that. Hope sprang up inside my chest. Maybe, there was still a way. If I could just keep them here a moment longer.

"If you're so much better at wishing, Jim," I said, "what would you wish for?"

"She's just playing you, Jim," Lou hissed in my ear. "She's trying to hold us here until the police show up."

"I'm not afraid of police." Jim laughed. "I've got a djinni!"

"*We've* got one, you mean," said Lou. He released his hold on me all of a sudden, and I stumbled free. Tom reached out and steadied me. I felt, then, the bruises I'd acquired from my tussle with Lou.

"You wouldn't have even heard of the djinni," Jim said, "if it weren't for me."

Another snarl began in Lou's throat, but before words could follow it, a bolt of lightning split the darkness, painting everything in blinding, terrifying white.

A crash of thunder followed in the wake of the lightning and
left us all doubled over, clutching at our ears.

"Maeve," said Tom, close by, "are you all right?"

"I think I'm alive," I gasped. "Are you?"

"Let me get back to you on that," he groaned.

"Lou," shouted Jim in desperation, "where's the sardine tin? Did
you take it?"

"What do you mean?" his brother called back. "You were holding
it in your hand."

"One minute I'm holding it," called Jim, "and the next, I'm
holding a handful of dirt, or dust, or something."

The two men fumbled with their dark lanterns, aiming their
beams wildly this way and that among the trees and shrubs. They
pawed at the ground, looking for Mermeros's sardine tin.

"Ahem," said a voice. "Are you looking for me?"

We all turned. The brothers swiveled their lanterns toward the sound.

A tall man stood leaning against a tree. "Tall" doesn't begin to do him justice. He wore a suit of large plaid checks and a colossal bowler hat. Curly whiskers sprouted from his cheeks and chin, and a fine silk cravat sat neatly tied over a ruffled blouse. Though dressed like a dandy, he was built like a prizefighter or, possibly, two prizefighters, one standing on the other's shoulders. He didn't seem possible. Goliath from my Sunday school storybook would have nothing on him.

They pointed their beams directly at his face. Set within a familiar face, now a ruddy brown, glittered a pair of green eyes, meeting my gaze with a knowing look. A golden hoop earring glinted in one ear. Around his neck, over his silk and lace, hung a shark's-tooth necklace.

"Gor," whispered Tom, "blimey."

"You're the djinni?" cried Jim.

"I am Mermeros," said the man.

My heart swelled. "You did it, Tom," I whispered. "You did it."

Tom couldn't speak. He reached and took my hand.

Jim seized Mermeros by the wrist and tugged at him. He might as well have tugged at Mount Everest.

"Well, come on, then, djinni," cried Jim. "Hop back into your tin. We're going."

Mermeros flicked Jim off his wrist as if banishing a fly from his cuff.

"I *said*," ordered Jim, "we're going. If you prefer to stay this size, have it your way, but it'll make travel a nuisance."

"I don't propose to travel anywhere," said Mermeros coolly. "Not at present."

"Now, see here," cried Jim. "I'm your master, and you're to do as I command!"

"Oh?" said Mermeros.

"What do you mean, *you're* his master?" demanded Lou. "We agreed *we'd* command the djinni. Together."

"Why don't you try it?" I suggested. "Make a wish. Either of you."

"Oh, no," said Jim. "You won't get the better of me with your trickery, little miss."

"I'll try it," said Lou. "Djinni! Make me a lord, with a castle, and farms, and lands, and pots and pots of money."

Mermeros crossed his gigantic arms across his chest. "You would have been amusing," he observed. "I would have enjoyed watching you glut yourselves on greed and folly, and fall to pieces." He looked from side to side at the twins. "Probably after murdering each other."

"Aren't you going to do it?" demanded Lou. "Twiddle your fingers, or whatever it is... *Poof*, and I'm a lord?"

"Not today," said Mermeros, "nor ever again." He nodded in our direction. "Didn't you hear? My last master wished me mortal."

"Jim," cried Lou, "you said you'd nabbed the sardine tin away from the kid!"

"I did," cried Jim. "I had him fair and square!"

Mermeros shrugged. "It was the young man who had summoned me from my dwelling. I was still his to command."

"He's fibbing," Lou told his brother. "I'll bet he's lying."

"Look at him," groaned Lou. "Does he look magical now? He looks like a prison guard in fancy togs."

Just then, a wonderfully familiar voice reached us through the trees, followed by the light of another lantern.

"You're under arrest," it said. "Stop where you are. Well, I'll be... *Jim Brennan*? Is that you?"

The brothers jumped where they stood. "Run," cried Lou, while Jim cried, "Get him!"

Inspector Wallace came into view. "Both of you," he ordered, "are under arrest. Cooperate, and it will go well for you."

"And if we don't?" cried Jim. "What about it, Boss?"

Boss?

"You can't catch us both," jeered Lou.

"We'll beat you to a jelly," said Jim.

They took off, crashing through the woods in opposite directions, and were gone.

Inspector Wallace appeared at our side and rested a hand on my shoulder. "You two all right?"

"We will be," I told him. "Aren't you going to go catch the burglars, sir?"

Inspector Wallace made a strangled noise. "I can't," he groaned. "There's two of them, and one of me. I haven't got any weapon, and I can't run the risk of one of them circling back and hurting you or taking one of you hostage."

I stared at him. "You'd let them go," I said, "to protect us?"

He muttered to himself. "I'm protecting myself, too," he said. "But yes. Of course I would."

"Inspector Wallace," I asked him, "how did you know those villains?"

"Know them?" he echoed bitterly. "That's Jim Brennan, my former secretary, who just quit." He shook his head "A man I hired and trained myself. He quit the day after he typed up my report about Professor Fustian kidnapping your father, Tom."

Tom let out a slow breath. "So that's how he knew about a djinni."

"He wasn't even a good typist," muttered Wallace. "Believe me, if I'd had any idea..." A new thought struck him. "Did they get the djinni from you, then? Was I too late?"

"See for yourself." I pointed toward where Mermeros stood.

There was no one there. No sign that anyone had ever been here.

"Tom," I said slowly, "where did Mermeros go?"

Tom turned left and right. "He's gone," he said. "No sign of him."

Inspector Wallace's eyes narrowed. "What's going on here?" he asked. "Is there something you're not telling me?"

Tom began to laugh. "You might say that."

Inspector Wallace took us each by the arm. "Come on, you two. Let's get back to the college building."

"Excuse me."

Inspector Wallace flashed the beam of his torch toward the voice. It wasn't a person, but a group of people, picking their way toward us. The detective quickly placed himself in front of us, which was jolly decent of him.

Mermeros appeared, carrying the brothers, one in each hand, by their jacket collars. The other men punched the air about as effectively as kittens protesting being carried about by their napes by their mama cats.

"You are the gendarme?" asked Mermeros. "The captain of the guard—I mean, the member of the constabulary who was in pursuit of these two wicked fellows?"

"Unlawful arrest," cried one of the captured brothers. "Put us down!"

"I am he," said Inspector Wallace. "That was a stroke of luck, having you nearby just now, sir. I'm much obliged to you, Mister..."

"Mermeros," said he. "At your service."

"You're Mermeros," Inspector Wallace said flatly. "You're the djinni."

"Not anymore," he said. "Now I'm just Mermeros."

The detective threw up his hands. "Nothing makes sense anymore. But what do I care?" He cleared his throat. "I'm obliged to you, Mister, er, Mermeros. Could I trouble you to help me bring these men out to the college building? I believe a police wagon will be waiting for us by the time we get there."

They trudged off, the brothers' arms flailing uselessly, unable to even leave an impression on the colossus carrying them off.

Tom and I watched them exit through the trees. I bent and picked up a dark lantern one of the brothers had dropped. Miraculously, it was still lit. I panned its beam out across the grass and started sweeping it back and forth.

"What are you doing, Maeve?" asked Tom.

"Looking for my magic mirror," I told him. "They flung it somewhere."

Tom began looking around to help me. We browsed through the low bushes and leafy plants of the woodland floor, attempting to retrace our steps.

"Here it is." Tom held up my mirror and waved it at me. It caught the beam of my torch.

We headed back toward the Girton College building.

"I wonder what time it is," said Tom. "Feels like midnight."

We came out onto the grassy grounds. The moon shone full overhead, its reflection shimmering upon the pond. Low murmurs, and the occasional plop of a frog in the water, were the only sounds in the quiet night.

"Tom," I said, "you were magnificent."

He groaned. "I can't," he said. "Don't let's talk about it just now."

I understood. "All right."

We walked on.

"But I have to say," I said quickly, "that wishing him long enough life to read all the books he wants to read was a splendid stroke."

He let out something like a laugh.

"Though you may have saddled him with immortality all over again," I added. "One can never run out of books to read. People keep on writing more."

"You should write one," Tom said. "About all your magical adventures."

"*Our* magical adventures," I corrected him.

The lights of the college building drew near. We could begin to hear the official-sounding commands of policeman. I hoped they cinched their handcuffs around those horrible brothers' wrists good and tight.

"Mermeros, a mortal man," I mused. "I still can't believe it."

"What do you suppose he'll do?" asked Tom.

I laughed, picturing his towering size. "Anything he wants, I imagine."

Tom smiled. "I'll have to come clean," he said, "and tell my dad everything. But perhaps, once I do..."

"Your father could hire him at the Oddity Shop," I cried. "Nobody will know more about artifacts and antiquities than someone who is thousands of years old."

"Maybe." Tom smiled. "That could be fun. But I think he's taller than the ceilings in the shop."

We crossed the grassy cricket pitch. Oh, how I longed to play here someday as a Girton College student, leading a girls' cricket team! Could it ever be possible?

"At least we still have the carpetbags," Tom said.

I handed him my magic mirror. "Here," I said. "Why don't you keep this?"

"For me?" He took it in surprise. "They're a set, aren't they? One's no good without the other?"

"On the contrary," I said, "if you have yours, and Alice and I have ours, we can send messages to each other from all the way across the city."

He flinched.

"What's the matter?" I asked.

He chuckled. "It might take some getting used to, walking into my room and seeing your face peering out at me through the frame."

"In that case, never mind." I reached indignantly for the mirror.

He held it high out of my reach, laughing. "I'm just teasing you," he said. "I'd like to have it. This will be fun." He aimed the mirror at the moon, catching its radiance. "If I have a message, I can write a note, maybe, and hold it up so you can read it in the glass."

"That's right." A thought occurred to me. "I'll need to borrow it back tomorrow, though," I told him. "We've got some important work to do, and the mirrors are just what we need."

"Are you sure about this?"

Ern Rutherford drummed his fingers on a laboratory table.

"Positive," I assured him.

We stood, Alice, Tom, and me, with Ern around a heavy oak table in the upstairs laboratory at the Cavendish, bright and early the next morning. The table was littered with batteries and wires and unused cathode ray tubes, but it served as a perfect cover for the magic mirror Alice held furtively underneath its rim. She glanced at it shyly from time to time, shaking her head ever so slightly.

Ern's brow furrowed. "I don't see how you could possibly know," he said, "that some rogue thief is trying to steal my papers, unless you're tied up in it somehow."

"Mr. Rutherford," I said sternly, "obviously, someone is stealing your papers. But I'm thirteen years old. Why would I steal them? I could no more understand them than I could understand"—I tried to think of good comparison—"Chinese poetry."

"Yes, well," he grumbled, "you were connected to Miss Northam, and she—" He caught himself.

"Had nothing to do," I said, "with the disappearance of your paper."

He rubbed his forehead distractedly. "I'm going to have a heap of explaining to do," he muttered. "Spreading word all about the department about a fictitious new paper that doesn't exist to try to draw out a thief? J. J. will have my head for this."

The door burst open, and a man entered, slim, dark-haired, with a high forehead, gold-rimmed spectacles, and a heavy mustache. He waved a magazine of some sort at Ern.

"Here it is, here it is, my boy," the newcomer cried. "My article on cathode rays! Appearing in *The Electrician*. Today's edition. My remarks from last month to the Royal Institution." He elbowed Ern cheerfully. "Our little corpuscles are about to take the world by storm, my lad." He seemed to notice us for the first time. "Hullo, who's this?"

"Young friends of mine," said Ern. He made our introductions, and we each shook hands with the gentleman. "This is Mr. J. J. Thomson," Ern explained, "head of the Cavendish Laboratory and my faculty mentor."

"Jolly good, jolly good," the older man said amiably. "And what are we doing this fine morning at the Cavendish Laboratory?"

"Catching a thief," I told him.

Mr. Thomson blinked in surprise. "You don't say." He turned to Rutherford. "Not stealing equipment, I hope?"

"No, sir," said Ern. "You remember I mentioned that a paper of mine went missing yesterday?"

"Ah, yes," said Mr. Thomson. "Bad typist. Most unfortunate."

Bad typist. We'd certainly met one of those, but Pip Northam wasn't one.

"That, sir," I said, as politely as I could, "is where I believe you are mistaken."

He peered at me closely. "Is that so?" He smiled. "Well, it won't be the first time. Everyone thinks I'm mistaken." He waved the paper at Ern once more. "Mr. George FitzGerald had to get his two cents in here, of course. Article just before mine." He peered through his spectacles at the text. "He says, if our corpuscular theory is correct, we'll be alchemists before long. Transforming lead into gold. What do you say to that?"

Before Ern Rutherford could answer—though I got the immediate sense he didn't like the mention of alchemists—Alice caught my gaze. Her eyes were wide and urgent, and she twitched her head in the direction of her hidden mirror.

"I say," I said, "that if you trot down, right now, to the typist's office where you left your paper, Mr. Rutherford—"

"Ern," he corrected.

"Ern," I said, "you'll see something quite interesting."

"First alchemists, and now fortune-tellers?" cried Mr. Thomson. "What sorcery is this, Rutherford, my boy?"

"Please," I begged. "Talk later. Investigate now."

"Just what I often say to my researchers," said Mr. Thomson approvingly. "Well, my boy, this could be a lark. Shall we go catch a thief?"

Ern and his mentor trotted out the door and down the hall.

"Shall we go, too?" inquired Alice.

"Let's just watch in the mirror," I said.

Someone was leafing through the papers left conspicuously on the desk. A young man, though I couldn't see his face. He surreptitiously slid the papers into a folder in a leather notebook he had tucked under one arm. Ern Rutherford and Mr. Thomson appeared in the doorway, and the young man froze. Some words followed, though I didn't know what, and the three left the room.

A moment later, they appeared in the doorway. Rutherford, Thomson, and the unpleasant young man who had interrogated Tom and me in the downstairs supply closet, where we'd stowed our bicycles. He looked somewhat sick to his stomach.

"LeFevre," said Ern, pointing to us, "do you know these young people?"

His lip curled. "Know them?" he said. "What do you think I am, a nursemaid?"

"So, no?" pressed Ern.

"No," LeFevre said. "I saw them about yesterday, but no, I don't know them."

Ern nodded.

"Why," I asked, "did you put a page of Mr. Rutherford's paper in the typist's bag yesterday?"

LeFevre blinked. "I...that is, I mean, I didn't...*she* put...I mean, she *took*—" He gulped. His face paled. "I don't even know what you're talking about."

"Would you be willing," I said, "to show Mr. Rutherford and Mr. Thomson what you just put in your leather folder?"

"This is an insult," he sputtered. "An outrage." He gestured indignantly toward the director of the Cavendish. "Mr. Thomson," he said, "why am I being questioned by mere children?"

"Now, Peter," said Mr. Thomson calmly, "I'm sure this is all a misunderstanding. But just to clear it all up, you wouldn't object to sharing with us the contents of your notebook, would you? Just to set the record straight?"

The young man's nostrils flared. He clutched his notebook tighter, but Ern Rutherford held out a large, expectant hand.

"You're trying to steal my research," cried LeFevre.

Ern's eyebrows rose. He held out the hand once more. "May I, Pete?" He nodded toward us. "Just to prove the kids wrong?"

Peter LeFevre deflated visibly. He cast a look of cold hatred in our direction, and then at Ern. He thrust the notebook at him.

Ern opened it up and leafed through the pages. There, in typed capital letters, were two papers, both with "Ernest Rutherford" listed as the author.

The three men were silent for a terrible moment. Then all three looked at Alice, Tom, and me. We tried to look like normal, innocent young people, curious about science, without another care in the world.

Mr. Thomson sighed. "Oh, Peter," he said. "This doesn't look well, does it? This is a bad, bad business. You'll need to come to my office so we can get to the bottom of this." They left, though who dreaded their impending conversation more, it was hard to say.

When the door closed behind them, Ern Rutherford fixed us all with a penetrating stare.

"All right, you three," he said, "I want to know what in thunder you're up to, and how on earth you could ever possibly know if someone's burgling the typist's office."

In all my scheming of how to pull off this bit of magically aided detective work this morning, I confess I hadn't thought far enough ahead to develop a convincing lie to hide the truth.

"I notice, Miss Alice," said Ern, "that you keep glancing at something under the table." He held out a hand. "May I see what it is?"

Alice gulped. Hesitantly, she held up the silver mirror.

"It's a mirror," she said, blushing hot. "I carry it around to, er, um, check my hair."

Tom developed a sudden coughing fit. We were corrupting Alice into quite the liar.

"Ah," said Ern. "I see."

I couldn't meet Alice's gaze. Though she was undeniably pretty, she was the last person on earth who would ever be so vain as to check, much less admire, her hair all day long. It must have mortified her half to death to say such a thing.

"Now then," I told Ern, "our agreement?"

Ern sat heavily in a chair. "Ah, yes," he said slowly. "Miss Northam." He placed a hand over his heart. "On my honor, I solemnly swear that I will write to her immediately, restore her to her post, and make sure J. J. knows fully that she was mistakenly and wrongly accused."

"J. J.," I said, "and the Girton College mistress, Miss Welsh."

"And the Girton College mistress, Miss Welsh," he parroted back.

"Immediately?" I repeated.

"Without a moment's delay."

"Realizing," I said, "that even now, the damage to her standing at her college could already be irreparable?"

"I shall deliver the note personally," Ern said, "galloping on a white charger."

"Don't talk rot."

He grinned. "All right. No white charger. But I'll send it by special courier."

"You swear it?"

"On my grandmother's grave," he said. "But you must tell me, Maeve, Tom, Alice."

We waited.

"Tell you what?" I prompted him when he didn't speak.

"You know jolly well what," he protested. "How you knew about Peter. How could you tell, from in here, what was going on in a room down the hall?"

"Ah, yes," I said, giving Alice a significant look. "*That room down the hall.*"

Ern Rutherford looked baffled. "Excuse me?"

"I beg your pardon," said Alice, heading for the door. "May I be excused to find the, er, water closet?"

"Of course," said Ern.

She left the room to carry out her secret mission—to fetch the other mirror back from its hiding place, wedged behind a potted plant in the windowsill of the typist's office.

Ern wagged a finger at me. "Don't think I haven't noticed," he said, "that you haven't answered my question. How did you know when a thief was burgling the typist's office, Miss Maeve? I must know."

He was a persistent one, this New Zealander man of science.

"Perhaps we have excellent hearing," I said.

He leaned closer. "And perhaps you have carpetbags," he said, "that can fly."

"Carpetbags?" I repeated. "That can *fly*?"

He watched my face just as I'd watched Peter LeFevre's. Waiting for a mask to fall, for a pretense to crack.

I put on my best and sweetest smile. "Sounds like rubbish to me," I said. "I thought you scientists preferred to stick to cold, hard facts."

He scowled, though not unkindly. "Facts are neither cold, nor hard," he said. "They're the most wondrous, liberating things. Progress marches along on trails blazed by facts, and not fancies."

"Such as flying carpets," I said. "I expect you've been overworking yourself, Ern. Wearing yourself out with nervous strain."

He laughed ruefully. "You wouldn't be the first to say so."

"Maybe," I told him, "you need to stop working so late at the laboratory and get some more rest at night."

Too late, I realized my mistake.

"How would I know," he said slowly, "that I work late at the lab?"

I gulped. "Well, you do, don't you?" I said. "They all say you're the golden boy of the department. So, naturally, one assumes, to maintain your edge, you would—"

Alice returned just in time to rescue me by holding out a hand. "It's been lovely meeting you, Mr. Rutherford," she told him.

"Ern," said he.

"Ern," she repeated. "Thank you for explaining the cathode rays and corpuscles to us."

"Goodbye, sir," said Tom. "I'll keep an eye out for your name in my dad's science journals."

"Cheer-o, Ern," I told him. "Get some rest. Don't believe everything you see. Unless, of course, you can repeat it in the laboratory and get the same results twice."

Y ou should've seen her," crowed Pip, passing us ice cream spoons in our crowded booth. "I'd just gone into her office, like Marie Antoinette, ready to face La Guillotine. Miss Welsh says," (her impersonation of the college mistress was quite impressive), "'Miss Northam, I can't express how deeply I regret this,' and I'm bracing myself for the blade, when *there's a knock at the door.*"

"Excuse me, young ladies, young gent," said a smiling, aproned serving man carrying four glass dishes of ice cream. "I have here rhubarb ice cream..."

"That's me," said Alice, accepting her dish.

"Marmalade," the server continued.

"Mine," said Tom.

"Tangerine?"

Pip reached for the dish. "Right here."

"And that leaves you, miss," he said, "with the cucumber." He presented it to me with a flourish, bowed, and left.

"Cucumber?" said Tom. "I still can't believe you'd choose cucumber."

"It's my favorite flavor," I protested. "Try a bite."

He wrinkled his nose. "No, thank you."

Friday morning was hot and sunny, and a celebratory ice cream fit the bill perfectly. Though it wasn't even yet lunchtime, Pip had brought us to one of her favorite little tea shops in Cambridge, one that also sold ice cream. My first pale-green dollop was already melting over my tongue when I remembered Pip's story.

"You left us," I said, waving my spoon at her, "with 'a knock at the door.'"

She licked a blob of tangerine ice cream off her own spoon. "Righto," she said. "There's a knock at the door. I'm seated in that stiff, uncomfortable chair in Miss Welsh's study, waiting for the curse to come upon me."

"The what?" asked Tom.

"The curse," explained Alice. "Meaning, getting expelled from school. She's quoting 'The Lady of Shalott.'"

Tom looked at her blankly. "Someone famous?"

"It's a poem." Alice smiled. "By Alfred, Lord Tennyson. You'd like it. "The curse has come upon me,' cried the Lady of Shalott.'"

Tom was clearly unconvinced, but he hid that behind a large bite of marmalade ice cream.

Pip had found this whole exchange quite entertaining. It also gave her a chance to catch up on her ice cream.

"Waiting for the curse to come upon you," I prompted her.

"Right." She swallowed a mouthful. "There I sit, waiting, when the knock sounds at the door. Miss Welsh says, 'Come in,' and in comes Gregson with a letter on a tray. Miss Welsh, to be honest, looks a bit miffed to have been interrupted for a mere letter, but she maintains her composure. 'Leave it on the table, Gregson,' she says, with more than a touch of her usual Queen Elizabeth manner, when he says, that dearie lamb of a butler, *he* says, 'Pardon me, madam, but the letter is marked 'Urgent' and was brought here by special courier.' And her eyebrows pop up like jacks-in-a-box, and out comes her little silver letter opener."

She paused her soliloquy for another bite of ice cream. My dish of cucumber was disappearing much faster as I, for once, wasn't doing much of the talking.

Fortified by several more bites, Pip resumed her story.

"I, of course, had no idea what was in that letter," she said, "so I remember wishing Gregson would have waited, so that the guillotine blade could fall and I could be put out of my misery, rather than waiting and silently watching as she read her letter. But what could I do? I watched her read, and I'm dashed if she didn't turn mauve about the face. I was just imagining that maybe Miss Welsh has a secret romance somewhere who sends her love letters marked 'Urgent' by special courier."

Tom snorted on a spoonful of marmalade ice cream.

"But then she turned to me," continued Pip, "and said, 'Miss Northam, I've just received a letter from Mr. Thomson, the head of the Cavendish, and one of his researchers, a Mr. Rutherford, who wish to express their *deep* remorse for mistakenly suspecting you of mishandling sensitive research documents.'"

She looked at each of us as if expecting a response she didn't get. I realized we weren't acting surprised enough. Naturally, we weren't; we knew all about the letter, but we didn't want Pip to know that.

We all three realized our mistake. I fear we overcompensated in reply.

"You don't say!" cried Tom.

"You're joking!" I cried. "That's fantastic!"

"How wonderful!" Alice gushed. "I knew the truth would come out."

Pip beamed. "There's more. She said, 'They wish to exonerate you completely, as they have found firm proof that another party was responsible for the thefts.'"

"That must have felt good," said Tom.

"An eleventh-hour pardon," declared Pip. "It felt like waking up from a terrible nightmare to find it was all a dream. Still, I wonder, how did they ever determine that it wasn't me?"

Tom, Alice, and I suddenly got very busy scraping the last drips of melted ice cream from the bottom of our dishes.

"Did the letter say anything about it?" I tried to sound casual.

"It said that one of the researchers, who has quietly been dismissed, has an uncle who is also a physicist at a university somewhere on the Continent," she said. "France? Germany? I can't remember. They suspect that he was somehow sent here to try to pilfer findings and siphon them off to his uncle's laboratory so the uncle could replicate the research and pass the findings off as his own."

Tom frowned. "I can't imagine how such a scheme would ever work," he said. "Wouldn't the Cavendish be able to prove that they did the research first?"

Pip shook her head. "It might not be as easy as you think," she said. "Getting published in the right journals first is the name of the game. Filing for patents first. Possibly, even, being the first to develop findings into new products to sell. There's already a surprising amount of wrangling and bickering over that in the science world, even without scientific *spies*, for pity's sake."

"Golly," I said. "I never knew science could have so many scandals." I smiled at the knowledge of our secret. I hoped she'd never know that we were the ones who had helped her get her job, and her sterling reputation, back.

"In any case, Pip," I told her, "congratulations. It's wonderful news."

She gave me a long look. "You were right," she said quietly, "when you told me not to give up hope."

I smiled in spite of myself. It's nice when circumstances prove you right. They could just have easily proven me wrong. But whatever might've come to pass, isn't hope still the better choice?

Pip seemed to need to look away, so she got to work finishing her ice cream. The rest of us were already done and looking out the window.

All at once, a commotion sounded from outside. A press of people went hurrying past the window to our little tea shop.

A look of concern crossed Pip's face. She rose from her seat.

"Come on, you three," she said. "Let's go see what's going on."

As we left the shop, we saw rush of people moving past like a river swelling its banks after spring rains. We took each other's hands, just in case, and stepped into the flow.

Coming around the corner, we came upon a city square that seemed to be the eye of the storm. A roar went up.

The square was swarming, absolutely crawling with students clad in straw boater hats to ward off the sun. Young men, mostly, it seemed, dressed in the black robes of undergraduate students, but some young women moved about the throng as well. The young men chanted, hooted, and shouted. Some stood on overturned crates, waving large signs reading DOWN WITH WOMEN and NO WOMEN.

Tom pointed silently, drawing my attention to a corner of the square, where two scarecrow-like figures hung, made of cloth and stuffing, wearing raggedy dresses, and strung up on poles that leaned askew at unnatural angles. Their painted mouths leered vacantly at the crowd. JEMIMA CLOUGH, read a sign on one of them. KATHARINE JEX-BLAKE, read another. With a pang, I realized this must mean Miss Jex-Blake, the friendly woman I had met the day before, who had invited me to a meeting in the Stanley Library about women earning their degrees.

Worst of all was a figure hanging over the crowd, seated on a bicycle. It took me a minute to realize that the lumpy, bloated, grotesque stuffed shape atop the bicycle was supposed to be a woman, dressed only in scanty underclothes and striped stockings.

"Oh!" Alice, standing beside me, had realized it, too. "How horrible! How vicious and cruel!"

"Defeated!" cried a nearby voice. "Uppity females shoved right back in their place!"

"Overruled!" cried another. "Seventeen hundred to six hundred!"

"God, sense, and science have prevailed!" boomed another man.

Someone set a torch to the skirts of the effigies of Miss Clough, whoever that was, and Miss Jex-Blake. In seconds, they went up in flames, to loud cheers. Other students grabbed at the effigy on the bicycle from a second-story window and tore her to bits, scattering pieces of yarn, cloth, and stuffing to the crowd below.

Pip stood, aghast, staring at the wild spectacle. Alice covered her mouth with her hand. My own eyes stung till I could hardly see clearly.

"The brutes," said Tom. "Don't look, Maeve."

But I couldn't look away. I wanted to cry. I wanted to scream. All my life, I'd heard boys and men—and mothers, and aunts, and schoolmistresses—telling me what a girl's place was, and how she should be content to stay in it; how she wasn't fit to compete or work or learn alongside men. This was nothing new to me. So it surprised me how deep was the well of grief and hurt now bubbling up inside me. How sharp was the sting of this malice hurled at me, and at every girl and woman, just because we *were* girls and women. The rage and venom our very existences produced in so many men... I couldn't understand it. All because some of us wanted to embark on a formal course of learning and receive the same certificate to prove it.

All my life, in the face of bullies, I've refused to back down. Maeve Merritt has always fought back. With words. With fists. With my cricket bat.

None of that would help here.

By heaven, I swore to myself, I would find a way to earn a university education. Even if it meant paying strict attention to Latin and Greek for the rest of my life.

Pip searched the crowd, her face stricken. Finally, she saw a familiar face. She waved her friend over.

"Megs," she cried, when the girl was close at hand. "Megs."

Megs' face, it was plain, had already done some crying today. "Oh, Pip," she sobbed, "how could we have lost?" She embraced Pip tightly. "The Senate vote is done. They brought in all those alumni from all over Britain, and we lost. Almost three to one."

"Too right, you did," said a rude young man standing nearby. "We sent you girls packing."

"Jealousy stings, doesn't it?" cried Pip hotly to the repellent young man, disentangling herself from Megs. "Women start outscoring the men on tripos exams, and you can't handle it! You can vote us out. But score for score, *we can still beat you.*"

The young man jeered at her. "Jabber and cackle all you like," he taunted, "but it won't earn you a degree. Bluestockings, go home!"

"Pip," said Megs firmly. "Pip. Let's get back to Girton."

Pip's face was hot and flushed. She had so much more she wanted to say. I could see the words fighting to break free. I took her hand, and she looked down at me.

"This is no place for you three," she said at length. "Let's get you out of here."

It took some maneuvering to find a way out of the throng of bodies choking the square, but at last we were out of it. We made our way slowly through the streets of town, pausing only whenever Pip encountered a Girton friend. We stood silently by as, in each case, they wept upon each other's shoulders, then joined us in our mournful journey home.

CHAPTER
33

When we reached Girton College, we found Inspector Wallace standing out in front in conversation with Mr. Bromley and Mr. Poindexter. Standing in their midst was the titan, the behemoth, Mermeros, mortal and in the flesh.

Alice and I bid a fond adieu, for the moment, to Pip, who was borne along indoors by her throng of friends. It seemed they might prefer a moment to be alone with one another. We drifted, therefore, over to where the Scotland Yard detective stood talking with our family and friends.

"Good afternoon, young ladies, Tom," said Mr. Bromley, doffing his hat to us in turn, and offering Alice his arm.

Mr. Poindexter reached an arm around Tom and pulled him close. "Good morning, son."

Mermeros met my gaze. "Girl Hatchl—" He caught himself. "Er, good morning..."

"Maeve," I told him. "That's my actual name."

He looked affronted. "I knew that."

Inspector Wallace's eyes twinkled. "This fine gentleman," he said, indicating Mermeros, "was an invaluable help to us last night, bringing in that pair of rotters."

Mermeros, I saw, was still capable of inflating like an aeronaut's balloon with egoistic pride. Flesh and blood hadn't changed that.

"I'll wager the Yard will have a use for him," the inspector continued.

"How about it, Mermeros?" I asked. "Care to be a policeman?"

Mermeros shrugged nonchalantly. "I am considering my options."

I tried not to laugh.

"Meanwhile," Inspector Wallace said, "there's room for you at my flat in the city. Though possibly..." He chuckled. "I'm not sure I have the right, er, furniture for the job. But we'll manage."

I tried not to laugh, thinking of a typical bed or couch groaning under the weight of Mermeros's titanic frame, never mind his height. His feet might have to stick out the window.

Mrs. Bromley emerged from the front door of Girton College and hurried out to greet us. "Good afternoon! Oh, good. You're back, girls, and young Thomas. You're just in time. Come in, do. They're about to hold a meeting for the entire school, and I want you present for it."

Inspector Wallace tipped his hat to Mrs. Bromley and to the rest of us. "Good day, madam," he said, "sirs," and to Alice and me, "young ladies. I must get back to London. A pile of work awaits me and, I confess, an even larger pile of reports to type." He frowned. "I guess I'll be typing more of my own reports for a time. Perhaps if I'd typed the last one up, none of this trouble would have ensued."

I'd been thinking the same thing, ever since last night, but I kept that thought to myself.

"Mr. Mermeros," said Mrs. Bromley. Looking up at him forced her to squint her eyes against the noonday sun overhead because he was so tall. "I must say I'm glad to meet you in person, and not in a sardine tin."

"I am unworthy," Mermeros said with a gallant bow, "to aspire to an acquaintance with so regal a lady as yourself."

"Well!" Mrs. Bromley's eye bulged wide, then her cheeks blushed pink. "Maeve, you never told me your djinni was such a charmer."

I forced a cough rather than laugh out loud. "I suppose it slipped my mind."

"Mr. Mermeros," Mrs. Bromley said, "What will you do now?"

Mermeros hesitated before answering.

"He's going to stay with me for a few days," answered Inspector Wallace, "until he makes his longer-term plans."

"Then you must both come visit us for supper, some evening

very soon," declared Mrs. Bromley. "I confess I have quite a number of questions for you."

Mermeros bowed deeply. "I would be honored to eat bread and meat at your table, honored lady, may your days be long."

"Yes," said Inspector Wallace, laughing. "Um. We'll have time on the train for a bit of a talk about modern language and customs."

"I don't think he needs to change a thing," declared Mrs. Bromley. "Though we will," she added, touching Mermeros's sleeve, "also serve some vegetables, if that's all right with you."

"Goodbye, Mermeros." I shook his hand. Its ordinary flesh-and-blood touch still came to me, somehow, as a surprise. There was no more tingle or hum of magic about him, no sense of timeless fire. Just ordinary human skin. I must admit, it was a bit of a letdown. Does a person become less magical if they become...less magical?

Inspector Wallace and Mermeros climbed into the police wagon that had carried them here and made their departure. Mrs. Bromley hurried the rest of us inside.

She led us to the Stanley Library. Tables and easy chairs had been moved aside, and rows of folding chairs had been set up to accommodate, it seemed, the entire faculty and student body of Girton College. At the front of the room, on a wide table, stood a three-dimensional architect's model of a building. Almost like a grand dollhouse with exquisite detail. It was Girton College,

I could see, but so greatly expanded that I almost couldn't recognize it.

Mrs. Bromley took a seat toward the front near where Miss Welsh and other faculty sat. The rest of our party found seats in the back. I saw Pip, Trixie, Megs, Maud, Lizzie, and the rest of their cohort of friends among the throng. They seemed subdued, many of them leaning upon each other's shoulders. More than one girl showed signs of pink, puffy eyes. With so many hopes dashed, who could blame them today for crying?

Miss Welsh rose and addressed the room.

"My dear friends," she said. "Faculty, colleagues, students, and supporters of Girton College—thank you for being here. As you know, the results of the Senate's vote have been announced, and Cambridge University has voted, by a wide margin, to deny women students the opportunity to earn degrees on an equal footing with men."

A murmur of dismay rippled through the room. This was no surprise to anyone, yet there still seemed to be a need to mourn. Isolated sniffles and small sobs could be heard in the ensuing stillness.

"I know this news falls upon us painfully," she said, "and no words of mine can erase the disappointment we rightly feel at such a setback."

She rested her hands upon the table, and surveyed the room from side to side.

"However," she said, "please know this: when Girton College had its beginning, back before we were even in Girton, but in the village of Hitchin, back when we were only a small handful of students, and I, a new undergraduate, we already knew we would face a long, slow battle, marked with grave opposition, in order to attain the kind of education we yearned for—the chance to develop and stimulate our minds, and train them to some useful and beneficial purpose in the world."

"Our founding mothers knew then that the road would be long and the struggle difficult, but they did not allow that prospect to dampen their commitment to carve out a place, here at Cambridge, where women might learn and study and prove themselves equal to the opportunity to learn and achieve alongside young men. They did not shrink from that opposition; rather, their determination was fixed to meet that opposition."

All eyes in the room were upon her. I'd had little opportunity for hearing speeches before this, but I found myself hanging on her words. Was this how grown-up educated women spoke? Would I need to use such fancy words if I went to college?

"And here we are," she said. "Nearly one hundred students, when once our student body could be counted on one hand. This beautiful building, when once we had none. A roster of graduates, who, though they lack official Cambridge University degrees, hold Girton letters of completion, which earn them positions of respect in professions and teaching posts throughout the British Isles and beyond. And a growing list of donors and sponsors who are determined to further our mission."

Mrs. Bromley, I noticed, sat a bit taller in her chair.

Miss Welsh continued. "On this very day," she said, "when we must absorb such disappointing news as the Senate's vote, I beg you not to lose heart. I present to you these plans and models"—here she indicated the artist's three-dimensional rendering—"produced for us by our architects, showing our vision for how to grow Girton College into what it will soon become." She held up one end of the board on which the model sat, tipping it upward so those seated before her had a better view of its scope.

"I'm delighted to announce," she said, "that due to the generosity of these many friends and donors, we are about to commence a building program that will add to our campus a new and expanded dining hall, modern kitchen facilities, three new corridors of classrooms and residence facilities, a chapel with an organ, and a swimming pool."

Excited murmurs now skimmed about the room, especially at the words *organ* and *swimming pool*.

"Furthermore," added Miss Welsh, "additional scholarship funds will be made available, both for existing and future students, based on merit and need, so as to make a Girton education available to deserving young women, whom we will need in order to grow to fill out our new space. Construction will begin as soon as plans, permits, materials, and available labor will allow. So tell your sisters, and your ambitious friends—Girton College has a place for them."

A buzz of excited chatter now filled the room. Mrs. Bromley beamed. Pip Northam left off talking with her peers. She turned in her seat, found me, and winked.

Miss Welsh waited for the excitement to settle. A small smile played about her lips.

"Those who oppose higher education for women at Cambridge University," she said, once she'd regained the room's attention, "may feel today that they have dealt a fatal blow to our hopes, our aspirations. But in years and decades and centuries to come, Girton College shall mark this day, May 21st in the year of our Lord eighteen hundred and ninety-seven, not as a day of defeat, but as a day that fired us with resolve, with determination, and with courage to persevere, to build, and to overcome."

Pip leaped to her feet and began to clap. Her friends joined her, and soon the entire room was on its feet. I glanced up ahead to see Alice watching her grandmother and Miss Welsh with rapt attention, and Mr. Bromley gazing down at his granddaughter with love and pride.

Alice would come here to Girton, I knew. She had the brains, and she had the funds. But I had a few brains sloshing around in my skull, too, and by gum, I'd give those brains a workout for as long as it took so that I could earn a scholarship and come here with her. If Pip could do it, so could I. After all, Alice and I are roommates for life or, if not for life, for as long as I have anything to say about it.

Epilogue

Two weeks later, the dining room table at the Bromleys' home at Grosvenor Square glittered with crystal, china, and silver. Course after course had already come and gone, yet platters, dishes, and tureens filled with elaborate dainties still extended the length of the table.

Dinners at the Bromleys' weren't usually such elegant affairs, but perhaps the thought of entertaining a Persian prince had made Mrs. Bromley feel she must extend her hospitality beyond its normal bounds. Very likely, the exaggerated descriptions of legendary royal feasts, Roman banquets, and the like that Alice had read to her all week had gotten into her head and into her menu.

I can say this much: Mermeros didn't mind. He did justice to the table, and then some. It's possible that his mode of eating was a *bit* too enthusiastic for an elegant dinner party, his smacking his lips and swallowing a *bit* too loud, his calling imperiously to the serving staff, who struggled to keep straight faces, to bring more and more helpings a bit, shall we say, astonishing, but the Bromleys and everyone at their table viewed him only with affection and geniality.

"I like nothing better," declared Mr. Bromley, "then the chance to extend genuine pleasure to the guests at our table."

"Matilda has outdone herself tonight," observed Mrs. Bromley, speaking of Mrs. Tupp.

"You have acquired a most talented cooking woman," Mermeros told our hostess. "Keep her well supplied in good linen robes and ankle bracelets, so she long remains with you."

I snorted into my jellied chicken. The thought of cheerful Mrs. Tupp, the cook, making sticky toffee pudding in the kitchen to the tune of tinkling ankle bracelets was too hilarious.

Inspector Wallace raised a glass as if to make a toast.

"To Mermeros," he said, "and to a crime well solved, and to an end of magical crimes plaguing Scotland Yard."

"Also," added Mr. Abernathy, now back from his holiday in Scotland, "to Mermeros's memory of eras past." Our tutor, a classicist and scholar of the ancient world at heart, was simply beside himself at having someone who actually remembered the Persian and Roman Empires, and the Hellenistic Age, whom he could question to his heart's content.

"To Tom," I said, holding up my glass of fruit juice, "for showing more courage and presence of mind than most adults ever do."

"Hear, hear," said Mr. Poindexter, "and to him putting an end to our woes at the hands of magic-stealing criminals."

"To Master Thomas," said Mermeros, "for my new life."

We were all still a moment. I'm sure we were all thinking of the price Tom had paid to give Mermeros that gift.

"And to Miss Maeve and Miss Alice," added the former djinni, "for my new books."

I laughed. Alice and I had visited Hatchard's Booksellers and, pooling our allowances, had replaced his copies of *Jane Eyre* and *Great Expectations*, which, I supposed, were still floating somewhere in magical limbo, and had added many other titles to his collection as well.

"To Maeve," added Tom, "for being a thieving rascal, which turned out well, in this instance."

"To higher education for women," cried Mr. Abernathy, "and to Maeve's marked improvement in her Latin studies."

"To Mr. Poindexter," Alice said, "safe and whole and home for good."

"To our hosts, the Bromleys," I said, "for simply everything."

Mr. and Mrs. Bromley reached out and held each other's hands and beamed at us all. But only for a moment, for then the dessert course appeared. Or rather, the four dessert courses began to appear.

It was a long and glorious feast, well-befitting an ancient Persian prince, or a modern Victorian schoolgirl.

After supper, we all gathered in the drawing room. There was none of this business of ladies going one way and men another. We were all company at the Bromleys'. Alice was just fetching a box of playing cards and parlor games when the butler, Mr. Linzey, appeared.

"I beg your pardon," he said, "but there is a gentleman here, asking to see Master Thomas."

Mr. Poindexter sat up in his seat. A cloud of worry passed over his features. I could just imagine him thinking, *Now what?*

"Show him in," Mrs. Bromley replied.

"Mr. Geoffrey Bowers, Esquire, of Messieurs Pinson, Marquette, Bowers, and Lounsbry," announced Mr. Linzey, depositing the visitor in our presence. We all rose to greet him.

Mr. Bowers, apparently a lawyer, was a small man of older years, prone to sniffling. He clutched a leather-bound folder against his frail frame.

"Good evening, ladies and gentlemen," he said. "I do beg pardon for this interruption. Young man, are you Master Thomas Poindexter?"

Tom nodded. "I am." His face was pale.

Mr. Poindexter extended a hand. "I'm Tom's father, Siegfried Poindexter."

"A pleasure," sniffed Mr. Bowers. He turned to Tom. "I have been searching for you for two weeks," he said, "and only just managed to locate the business establishment above which you make your home—the Oddity Shop, is that right?—and I learned from a neighbor that you were spending the evening at this address." He blew his nose loudly on a handkerchief. "As I am leaving tomorrow for a summer holiday in the Lake District, I took the liberty of looking for you here tonight." He looked around apologetically. "Though I confess I did not expect to intrude upon a gathering such as this."

Tom gulped. "Is something wrong?"

"Well," said Mr. Bowers, "that depends. Does the name Edward Meekham mean anything to you?"

Tom's expression glazed over. He said nothing.

Mr. Poindexter put an arm around Tom's shoulders. Mr. Bowers busied himself with some papers in his leather case.

"My mother's maiden name," Tom said quietly, "was Meekham."

Tom's voice as he spoke of his mother—something I'd never before heard him do—gave me a pang.

Mr. Bowers nodded. "So I have been led to understand," he said. "As you heard, I am with the firm of Pinson, Marquette, Bowers, and Lounsbry, and we represent the estate of Mr. Edward Meekham, a gentleman of some property, now dead these past six months. He died without heir at a ripe old age this past winter. He was your mother's uncle."

Tom turned to his father, confused. "You mean," he said, looking stricken, "I've had living family? All this time that I was in the orphanage, I had a living relative?" He gulped down the quaver in his voice. "A gentleman of property?"

He sank down onto the sofa and buried his head in his hands.

The others in the room kindly looked away. Mrs. Bromley rang for Mrs. Harding and requested refreshments for our newcomer. Mr. Abernathy made small talk with Inspector Wallace. Only Mermeros kept his bright, glittering green eyes fixed firmly upon Tom. Well, only him and me.

How many years had Tom endured that wretched Mission Industrial School and Home for Working Boys? How many nights had he likely dreamed of an imaginary relative finding him and whisking him away to better things?

Mr. Poindexter gently stroked Tom's shoulders. The lawyer waited quietly for Tom to look up. When he did, the room again went still.

"My understanding," said Mr. Bowers gently, "is that there had been some estrangement between your mother and her family. It seems that when she married your father, she did so against her parents' wishes. Consequently, all communication was cut off between them. Your grandparents died, and your great-uncle, my former client, Mr. Edward Meekham, was unaware of your existence. The news that a child had been born to his niece and her husband had not reached him."

Alice found a way to place a handkerchief for Tom beside him on the couch without drawing any attention to the fact. If ever anyone embodied quiet kindness, it was Alice Bromley.

Tom wiped his eyes and composed his features. "Poor Mum."

Mr. Bowers again waited tactfully.

"I'm ready," Tom said quietly.

The lawyer blew his nose sympathetically. "Toward the end of his life," he said, "our client, Mr. Edward Meekham, commissioned our firm with the task of locating his niece, or, if she was no longer, determining whether she had left any issue."

Tom's brows furrowed. "Any what?"

"Issue," the lawyer repeated. "Children. Descendants."

Tom nodded.

"We located records of your parents' deaths," Mr. Bowers said gently, "and thus we learned that she had borne a son. But the process of finding you, in the orphan system, proved extremely challenging."

Mr. and Mrs. Bromley frowned. Ever since Tom had joined the family, so to speak, they had taken an active interest in charities relating to orphans and orphanages. The inadequacies of currently available resources and programs to serve orphans was something I'd often heard them discuss with real concern.

"About a fortnight ago," Mr. Bowers continued, "we finally heard from a woman on the Orphans' Committee that you had been placed with the Mission Industrial School and Home, and from there it was relatively straightforward to learn that you had recently been adopted and were now living at your new address on Mantlebury Way. And now, here we are."

Tom looked baffled. "Here we are...?"

Mr. Bowers eyed him in puzzlement. "Aren't we?"

Tom sighed. "It seems, sir," he said, "begging your pardon, as though you expect I should understand something. But I don't. You've told me that my, er, great-uncle was your client and is now dead." He looked to his father for encouragement. "I'm very sorry to hear it, of course, but as I never knew he'd existed, I–I fear it will take some, er, mental adjustment to mourn him properly."

Mr. Bowers cocked his head at him. He looked like an inquisitive bird. "I haven't come here to ask you to mourn for the loss of my client," he said. "I've come here to tell you that you are the heir to his estate and will inherit his property."

Tom sat still, as though he'd heard nothing.

To say that the occupants of the room were thunderstruck would be no exaggeration. The entire room erupted into cries of wonder, surprise, and congratulations for poor bewildered Tom. Myself included.

Except for Mermeros. He might have been carved in stone. All but for his glittering eyes.

Mr. Bowers blew his nose and shuffled his papers. "As to the details of the property," he said, "I imagine you will wish to sell it. His property, in Kent, features a very comfortable home, with barns, stables, outbuildings, and substantial acreage. Moreover, it features a set of buildings suitable for operating a school, a seminary, or some other facility, with classrooms and a large library, and with residential accommodations for up to fifty persons."

Tom looked perplexed. "It *does*?"

"Your uncle was a deeply charitable man," Mr. Bowers explained. "Years ago, he operated a religious school for poor boys."

Tom's gaze met mine. "A school," he echoed.

"For fifty persons." I couldn't stop grinning at him.

The lawyer handed Tom a sheaf of papers. "These documents describe the property in detail. Should you decide you wish to sell or lease the property, our firm can set about locating a suitable buyer or tenant."

Tom turned to his father. "Please, Dad," he said, "can I keep it?"

Mr. Poindexter scratched his scalp. He was at a loss for words. "This isn't a puppy, Tom," he said, laughing. "It's yours. Of course you can keep it. But it's not that simple."

"Why isn't it?" asked Tom.

Mr. Poindexter turned back to the lawyer. "We're indebted to you, Mr. Bowers," he said, "for your efforts to locate Tom and share with him this most unexpected news." He took the papers the lawyer had held out to Tom. "It's all quite a lot to take in." He looked once again at Tom's pleading face and smiled. "No decisions need to be made tonight, Tom," he said. "We'll visit the property and explore this more." His expression grew serious. "You must understand, though, my boy, that such properties cost a great deal to maintain and keep up. It can't just sit there empty, and the cost of keeping it running is, er, likely to be beyond my means."

Tom's face fell.

"As to that," said Mr. Bowers, "the investments and income associated with your great-uncle's estate, Master Thomas, are more than adequate to maintain the property."

Tom and his father looked at each other in astonishment. Mr. Poindexter was at a loss for words, but Tom wasn't.

"Dad," he pleaded. "This is my dream."

His father watched him.

"I want to run a home for orphans, Dad," Tom said. "Please."

Mr. Poindexter ruffled his son's hair. "Let's go see it, son," he said. "We'll figure all of this out." He smiled. "You are a bit young to run a school, my lad."

"So is Alice," I said, "but it's her dream as well."

Alice's eyes shone. Her grandparents, watching her, beamed at her.

"It would be our honor," said Mr. Bromley, "when the time is right, and if, Siegfried, it meets with your approval, to help Tom develop the kind of program he has in mind. Develop it and fund it."

Mr. Bowers sniffled and rose to his feet. "I'll leave you to think things over," he said. "There's no hurry. I'll reach out to you when I return from my holiday. In the meantime, one of my junior colleagues can take you for a visit when you're ready."

He rose and made his polite goodbyes, then left the room. Everyone began talking at once. Mr. Linzey and Mrs. Harding were soon summoned to bring glasses of lemon squash for more toasts all around. Amid the excitement, I slipped away from Tom and Alice, imagining their plans and dreams aloud, and made my way over to where Mermeros sat reading in an easy chair that bulged and wheezed under his weight.

"Hullo, Mermeros," I said.

His eyes narrowed. "Good evening, Fish Spawn."

I smiled. Some things never changed.

"May I ask you a question, Mermeros?"

"You may ask," he said, "and I am under no obligation to answer."

"Well, of course you're not—" I began. Then I saw his chest swell with pride. It meant the world to him to be free. To command his own life, taking no orders from a living soul.

A living soul.

"Are you truly glad to be mortal, Mermeros?" I asked him. "I do wonder about that. Haven't you given up an awful lot? Living means you'll..."

Too late, I saw how rude it was to say what I'd been about to say.

Mermeros set down his book and looked at me for a moment.

"Dying means," he said, "you once held onto life."

Just the kind of absurd sentimentality adults often peddle. "Does that bring any comfort," I asked, "when one's life ends?"

He took off his spectacles. "Have you ever held a butterfly?" he asked me. "Had one land upon your finger?"

Yes, I had. I remembered how those soft, paper-thin wings opened and shut, how sunlight played upon their vibrant, velvety colors. A little miracle settling down upon me.

"Life is a butterfly in your hands," he said. "Fragile and fleeting. Wondrous and beautiful."

"Golly, Mermeros," I told him. "That's pretty poetic. I think."

"Much you would know," he sneered, "about poetry."

I conceded the point. But I still wasn't sure I liked his answer. "And a butterfly is better," I asked, "then living forever?"

"If you can't keep a butterfly forever," he said, "is it better to never hold one at all?"

"Don't talk in butterflies and riddles, Mermeros," I said. "You could have lived *forever*."

"Existing," he said, "and living aren't the same thing." He cocked his head to one side and looked at me searchingly. "You longed for the riches I could have given you," he said. "No, don't try to deny it. I could always see right through you."

He wasn't wrong. "Why mention that now?"

He shook his head, as if I truly was a lost cause. Much as Mr. Abernathy often did when tutoring me, though since my return from Cambridge, things had gone a good deal better.

"You dreamed of money solving your problems," he said. "Money creating the future you long for. You still do. You have no idea how rich you already are."

My vision swam a bit before my eyes. Those weren't tears. Definitely not.

"Alive," he continued, "and young, and quick, with a loving family and caring friends."

I couldn't bring myself to look directly at him, so I let my gaze settle upon his shark's-tooth necklace.

"And a stubborn, relentless, willful sort of personality," he added in an altogether different tone, "which, though irritating, often proves useful in getting what one wants from life."

I laughed. So much for sentimentality. Good old Mermeros.

"What do you like best, Mermeros," I said, "about being alive now? In this place and time?"

He settled his spectacles back on his nose and resumed his reading. It wouldn't be the first time he'd ignored me completely. I wasn't offended. I turned back toward Alice and Tom.

"Hot water," said Mermeros from behind me. I turned back. "Right from the faucet, whenever one wishes."

Hot *water*? Of all the things to say! We needed to get Mermeros out and about a bit more. Take him to the Crystal Palace. Maybe the beach at Brighton this summer.

"Ice cream," he said. "A wondrous invention."

I smiled. "Ever tried cucumber?"

He turned a page in his novel. "Lending libraries," he added in a reverential tone of which I wouldn't have thought him capable. "All the books I can read in a year for one small fee."

"And how does it feel," I asked him, "to see the stars in the night sky?"

He snorted. "I hardly can, here in London," he grumbled. "Too much soot and smoke."

"But you saw them that very first night," I reminded him. "Out on the Woodland Walk at Girton College."

He was quiet for a time. His green eyes seemed to gaze off into space, picturing a very private memory.

"Have they changed?" I asked him.

He startled out of his reverie. "Hmm?"

"The stars," I reminded him. "Have they changed?"

"They always change," he told me. "And they always stay the same."

"People are that way, too, I think," I said. "And djinnis."

He rolled his eyes, the last bits of him that were still poison green.

I leaned in closer and jabbed a finger right at his big solar plexus. "Did you do this?"

His thick beetling eyebrows, now brown instead of white, waggled as he glowered at me. "I don't know what you're talking about."

"You *did* do it," I said. "I know you did. You gave Tom his wish, since he'd given his to you."

He scowled. "You heard the legal person speak," he protested. "The events leading up to this inheritance had nothing to do with me. The aged relation died months ago."

I wasn't fooled. "Yet something in the process shifted," I said, "or came unstuck, around *two weeks ago*. Quite a coincidence, don't you think?"

He shrugged. "I don't waste time in idle speculation. Neither should you."

"All the same," I said, "this sounds exactly like what someone who has just read *Jane Eyre* and *Great Expectations* would cook up. The mysterious inheritance, just in time to rescue the deserving orphan. The long-lost, unknown relative. Don't you think?"

"The pesky nuisance of a meddling female?" he retorted. "Don't think I didn't notice that you lied to me about the novel by Mr. Dickens, incidentally. *Great Expectations*, while enjoyable anyway, is positively *infested* with irritating females." He arched an eyebrow at me. "As am I."

I laughed aloud. "Mermeros," I told him, "I'm proud to know you."

He rolled his eyes once more. I left him in peace with his novel and headed over to the tray where Mrs. Harding was passing out lemon squashes.

I'm quite sure I wasn't meant to hear him, but I heard him all the same, muttering under his breath: "You too, Girl Hatchling. You too."

Author's Note

May 21, 1897, was a significant day at Cambridge University. It was the day the Senate voted down the university granting degrees to women. Women wouldn't be able to earn degrees from Cambridge University until 1948. The riot that followed the vote, complete with the burning effigies of Miss Jex-Blake and Miss Clough, both advocates for degrees for women, and the bizarre effigy of the scantily clad woman on the bicycle, suspended high above the square, happened exactly as described, although I have condensed the timeline of the riot's events slightly to fit them into one scene. Photographs of the strange spectacle can be found online.

May 21, 1897, was also the day that J. J. Thomson's article appeared in *The Electrician*, announcing his extraordinary discovery, or confirmation, of the existence of a subatomic particle smaller than a hydrogen atom (or in other words, smaller than a proton). What he and Ernest Rutherford called a *corpuscle* would soon be known as an electron. Thomson eventually proposed that the atom was made up of a cloud of electrons, in what came to be known as the plum pudding model of the atom, with electrons distributed throughout the cloud much as plums are distributed throughout a plum pudding, or, for a dessert analogy Americans might better understand, as blueberries are distributed throughout a blueberry muffin. The plum pudding model of the atom would not last long.

As head of the Cavendish Laboratory, then the world's foremost facility for physics research, J. J. Thomson spearheaded experiments leading to many significant scientific advancements, but possibly his greatest contribution to the world of science happened when he agreed to take on a young research student newly arrived in Britain from "the colonies," in this instance, New Zealand—Ernest Rutherford. We've met "Ern" here as a young researcher at around twenty-five years of age. His career would extend for another forty years of energetic brilliance and a tireless work ethic, leading to an astonishing pace of discoveries about radiation and radioactivity that would shape our modern understanding of the atom, its nucleus, its particles, and the forces that bind them together.

Rutherford's research with alpha particles helped us realize that the atom wasn't a plum pudding, so to speak, but electrons orbiting around a tiny, dense nucleus made up of protons and neutrons held together with a tremendously powerful force—a force which, if unleashed, might help supply the world with vast amounts of energy, or could lead to weapons of devastating power.

Rutherford would go on to become: the head of more than one university physics department, including, eventually, the head of the Cavendish itself; a Nobel Laureate in Chemistry (meaning, the winner of the Nobel Prize for Chemistry); the winner of scores of other scientific prizes and medals; the mentor to many other famous researchers and Nobel Laureates; the father of nuclear physics; and the greatest scientific researcher of his generation and possibly even the entire twentieth century. Many of the other titans of physics who emerged in the twentieth century could trace their academic roots back to Ernest Rutherford. He was knighted and made a baron for his achievements, and when he died, he was buried in Westminster Abbey near Sir Isaac Newton.

Ernest Rutherford was known for his big, boisterous voice and booming laugh, and for whistling the rousing tune to "Onward, Christian Soldiers" wherever he went. He did refer to ions (positively or negatively charged atoms) as "jolly little buggers." I couldn't resist using that detail. He was also known for saying, later on than the timeline of this story, that some fool in a laboratory might blow up the universe one day (if they misused atomic energy). Rutherford was well aware of the destructive potential of the forces binding nuclear particles together if it were to be used as a weapon, or if its power were to be placed in the hands of anyone unwise or untrustworthy. After Rutherford's death, his work, and that of the researchers he taught and trained, led directly to the development of the Manhattan Project that built the first atomic bomb, though many of the researchers he had trained shared his grave concern about the danger of atomic weapons and warned repeatedly against their use.

One especially admirable quality of Rutherford's was his championing of women in science. He welcomed women as researchers in his faculty posts at several universities and encouraged their involvement at the Cavendish. Women earned degrees at the schools where he had studied in New Zealand prior to arriving in Britain, and he could never understand the prejudices against their contributions to science that he encountered there.

In one scene in the story, as Ern Rutherford explains cathode rays to Maeve and her friends, I had Alice comment that lights moving through the air with no wires were similar to the northern lights in the upper latitudes. She was more right than she realized (or more right than I realized when I thought of having her say it). The northern lights, ghostly bands of sometimes greenish light that dance through the night sky around polar latitudes, in fact, are cathode ray tubes on a grand scale, though of course no tube is involved. Kristian Olaf Bernhard Birkeland, a Norwegian scientist, published this theory in 1908, eleven years after our story ends—that energetically charged electrons emitted from the sun are acted upon by the magnetic fields near the earth's poles, which produce lighted wave phenomena much like the lights that appear in cathode ray tubes. His theory was widely dismissed and mocked until the late 1960s, when the age of space exploration produced the kind of probes needed to detect the currents of electrons that proved his theory correct, many decades after his death.

I didn't know this as I wrote the scene. It seemed to me that our well-read Alice would mention the northern lights as a comparison to the mysterious free-floating arcs of light in Ernest Rutherford's tube. I wrote it, then paused a moment. Could that be true? Could they be similar phenomena? A bit of research—which, in my lifetime, only requires a bit of Googling—proved that indeed, they were. I loved the thought of Ern Rutherford chewing on Alice's idea. In reality, I don't know whether Mr. Rutherford would have ever considered the possibility. I do try to stick as closely to the truths of history as I can when I write about real people and events, but I do like to have a bit of fun now and then, so long as I confess it in these author's notes.

Returning to Girton College, one of the women's colleges at Cambridge University:

Miss Elizabeth Welsh was a real figure, and my portrayal of her is based on what limited information we do have about her. She had a large hand in the design of the pond, the grounds, the Woodland

Walk, and the substantial expansion of the campus that made Girton College look approximately as it does today. She was among the first group of undergraduate students at the college that formed in Hitchin and ultimately became Girton College, so its cause was always dear to her. She was known to be levelheaded, efficient, organized, practical, and kind, with a quiet sense of humor, though those handwritten notes summoning students to her office did strike fear in students' hearts.

One of the research titles I read, *Bluestockings* by Jane Robinson, paints a delightful portrait of what life was like for the young women undergraduates at all-women's colleges in the late Victorian era, including photographs of students at their cocoa parties. Competitive sports were just as I described. So, unfortunately, were classes, led by a mixed bag of male faculty who welcomed women learners and male faculty who treated women students with cold indifference or even active hostility. It took longer than we might wish for doors of equality to open to young women at venerable universities including Cambridge and Oxford. The disciplined, patient determination of generations of women students, and their generous and vocal supporters, helped pave the way.

One small bit of trivia: there really was a Lion Hotel on Petty Cury in Cambridge, near the Cavendish, and its landlady really was a widow by the name of Alison Moyes. Some previous owners also seemed to have the name Moyes, though not her immediate predecessors. I wasn't able to find out anything more about her than that, but I had fun playing with her character and personality.

To learn more about the topics explored in this story, I recommend *Bluestockings: The Remarkable Story of the First Women to Fight for An Education* by Jane Robinson; *A Sport-Loving Society: Victorian and Edwardian Middle-Class England at Play*, edited by J. A. Mangan; *A Force of Nature: The Frontier Genius of Ernest Rutherford* by Richard Reeves; *The History of the Electron: J. J. and G. P. Thomson* by Jaume Navarro, and for a deep dive into the electron's history, *Flash of the Cathode Rays: A History of J. J. Thomson's Electron* by Per F. Dahl.

It's been a joy to spend time with Maeve, Alice, and Tom, and the caring (if long-suffering) adults in their lives over the course of *Wishes and Wellingtons*, *Crime and Carpetbags*, and now *Burglars and Bluestockings*. I love them, and I will miss them, but I can smile imagining the marvelous things these three friends will do together, and the wonders and innovations they will witness in the rapidly changing world that awaits them. I also enjoy picturing Mermeros, that crusty old soul, curled up by a fireplace, perhaps with a cat on his lap, reading endlessly to his heart's content. (Mermeros, not the cat.) Perhaps he's doing it still, for, as Maeve observed, one can never run out of wonderful books to read.

~ Julie Berry

ACKNOWLEDGMENTS

Special thanks to my agent, Alyssa Eisner Henkin, for her support and advocacy for Maeve and her story, and to Heather Alexander, Molly Cusick, and Wendy McClure for helping bring Maeve's dreams and mine to life; to Susan Barnett and Chelsey Moler Ford for their insightful work on this manuscript; to Jayne Entwistle, for narrating the audiobook versions of these stories to absolute perfection; and above all, to Phil Berry, for his unfailing belief in me, and for so very many draft pages read through the years.

AUTHOR BIO

Julie Berry is the author of the *New York Times* Bestseller *Lovely War*, the Printz Honor and Los Angeles Times Book Prize shortlisted novel *The Passion of Dolssa*, and many other acclaimed young adult and middle grade novels, as well as picture books. She holds a BS from Rensselaer in communication and an MFA from Vermont College of the Fine Arts. She lives with her family in upstate New York, where she owns an independent bookstore called Author's Note.